'A brilliantly written psychological thriller, its twists and turns executed with devastating precision. Everyone *needs* to read this'
Janice Hallett, author of *The Twyford Code*

'An addictive, brutal read'
Woman's Own

'A slow-burn thriller which is both horrifying and touching but also manages touches of humour. Compelling'
Catherine Cooper, author of *The Chalet*

'By the last third of the book, I was scared to pick it up and scared to put it down. Brilliantly executed'
Eddie Mair

'This exquisitely dark, disturbing and explosive thriller gripped my throat and didn't let go until the final, searing sentence'
Caroline England, author of *My Husband's Lies*

'A pacy, heart-stopping, brutal yet humorous rollercoaster of a read'
J.M. Hewitt, author of *The Life She Wants*

'What I love most is the prodigious humanity Tina Baker manages to heap into her characters. She dares you to make judgements, delighting as you trip over your own assumptions. Every sentence is splinter-sharp'
Kate Simants, author of *A Ruined Girl*

'I couldn't put it down from the first page to the last ... a whirlwind of emotions. Compulsive and tense'
Louise Mullins, author of *I Know You*

nasty
little
cuts

TINA BAKER

VIPER

This paperback edition first published in 2022
First published in Great Britain in 2022 by
VIPER, part of Serpent's Tail,
an imprint of Profile Books Ltd
29 Cloth Fair
London
ECIA 7JQ
www.serpentstail.com

Copyright © Tina Baker, 2022

1 3 5 7 9 10 8 6 4 2

Printed and bound in Great Britain by
CPI Group (UK) Ltd, Croydon, CRO 4YY

The moral right of the author has been asserted.

A CIP catalogue record for this book is available from the British Library.

ISBN 9781788165273
eISBN 978 1 78283 704 6
Audio ISBN 978 1 78283 992 7

For my Bo

I

4.15 a.m., 24 December

Dolly is singing at the top of her voice, 'Deck the halls with bras of holly!', collapsing into giggles then singing it again. Pat-Pat catches the giggle, claps his hands and jumps up and down like a baby gibbon (*What are baby gibbons called?* Debs wonders) and Marc smiles at the kids and hugs her closer to him on the sofa.

Debs removes the candy cane from Pat-Pat's pudgy hand before he can ram it up the dog's nose and nestles back into Marc's arm. He kisses her head, picks up a large present immaculately wrapped in beautiful embossed white paper, and hands it to her.

'Wow! Thanks, love!'

It's heavy. He probably got the shop assistant to do the elaborate bow on the top. She strokes the shiny wrapping paper and starts to open her gift.

'Best Christmas ever,' he whispers into her hair.

It is. It's all they've ever wanted. It's everything she never really believed she could have.

She's about to kiss him when something stings her fingers. She looks down to see there's red stuff on her hands, on the box.

The pain starts.

She peels back the paper in slow motion to find – razor blades.

She tries to focus on her breathing. In, two, three. Out, two, three, four. Do not fight for air. It makes it worse. She can't let herself panic, although that icy sensation is already crawling up her spine, squeezing her chest tight.

She catches his sneer. Then the lights extinguish. Sudden darkness all around her. Inside her. Everything muffled, claustrophobic.

She can't see the kids. She strains to hear them.

Dolly! Pat-Pat! The words do not escape her mouth.

Dense fog, bruise-grey presses in. Like being wrapped in cotton wool. The leaden vapour seeps into her brain, clogs her lungs.

She's shivering. Tremors grip her in waves, shaking something loose inside. Her thoughts splinter.

Where are her children?

She stumbles forward. No idea where she is, no idea of direction. Faster and faster now, breaking into a run.

She has to find her kids. She senses they're close, but—

Something shatters. She jolts, spinning round too late.

Then it's on her. And she bucks and struggles, lashing out. She attempts to scream, but her mouth is filled with fog which stuffs words, pleas back in her throat. Gagging, gasping, she fights for air and tastes something metallic.

As nightmares go, it's not the worst.

2

4.15 a.m., 24 December

The clock glows four-fifteen. Around the time her mam died. Debs rubs her eyes to erase the dream. Shudders. She's kicked the duvet off the bed, and she's freezing.

Something's wrong.

For perhaps a couple of seconds her reptilian brain tells her the truth: run. Run *now*. But her conscious self takes over, layering theories on top of the fear, reasoning it smaller, making it more manageable.

She turns over.

The boy is in the corner. Not *her* boy; not her son.

No!

A shadow. There is no boy, never has been. Pat-Pat is asleep next door, not standing silent, watching her with hungry hollow eyes. But, just for a second... *Take a breath.* She's awake now.

She tries to talk herself down, reminds herself fear is only Fantasy and Expectations Appearing Real. She hates these night sweats, waking drenched and shaky.

Get a grip. Buy some bamboo pyjamas.

Breathe.

If only she could get back to sleep, she'd have a good couple of hours before she has to get up and see to the kids and see to the dog and see to everything else. But she won't sleep again. The flush of anxiety gathers, zinging through her bloodstream like a nasty drug.

Her jaw aches where she's been grinding her teeth in her sleep, despite the thing the dentist gave her which makes her look like a boxer.

She fidgets, restless, but when she reaches a foot across the bed, she finds nothing.

Marc's not in bed. Again. She doesn't even remember him coming in last night. When did he last sleep through? No. He's not one of the kids.

She props herself up, removes her tooth guard and grabs her inhaler. Her tongue finds a mouth ulcer.

So much to do. Christmas Eve already! How did that happen?

Her daytime brain's now completely off the starting blocks: she has to collect two parcels from the Post Office, which will be total carnage; she needs to pick up the Yule log from the baker's and the dog poo from the garden; wrap the last bits and bobs for the kids; email the last of the 'seasonal greetings'; drop off a client's present; prep the turkey, and possibly shove a stick of holly up her bum while she's at it. Merry Christmas, everyone!

Marc will have nothing to do with any of it; this year he can't seem to focus on anything, let alone Christmas preparations. He's been wandering around the house in a daze. It breaks her heart when the kids hug him and he seems to look right through them. It's not just his side of the bed that's cold and empty.

She's worried about him.

It's easier to tell herself that than to unpick the other feelings.

She listens. Can't hear him in the bathroom. He might be in his study, his headset on, so as not to disturb Dolly and Pat-Pat. Always considerate.

She probes her ulcer to check it still stings.

He'll be up working. She knows he's worrying about the latest reshuffle in the office although he's not said much. Never does. The unsaid looms worse, stress etched into the furrows on his forehead.

Will he go in today? On Christmas Eve? She shifts up the pillows, trying to gather herself before getting up.

But what's he got to worry about, really? She's always telling him that they can downsize. Give the Caribbean a miss. They'll survive. They don't need all this *stuff*. The kids have got so much more than she and her sister ever had growing up. Does it make them any happier? She doubts it. All kids want is attention.

And Marc used to be amazing. The best dad ever.

She takes a long pull of Ventolin through the device they gave her to stop her knocking it back like a tequila shot, then stretches out along the memory foam mattress, consciously clenching and relaxing her muscles as she counts her breaths, trying hard to stop the worries spiralling and knotting themselves around her chest.

But mindfulness just winds her up. And the lists won't leave her be, scritch-scratching at the back of her skull. Sweat gathers slick on her chest. She feels a tensing deep in her bowels. And she knows she'll have to get up and move on the adrenaline before it turns to acid in her gut.

Rattled, she sits and strips off the clammy nightgown, grabs the dressing gown from the chair, and wrestles herself into it as she shuffles to the loo. Dolly's Barbie has been thrust upside down in the toothbrush glass, so it looks like she's drowning, which tickles Debs. Her daughter has recently announced she's now 'too old for dolls'. Aged nine. Nine going on thirty-nine, that one.

She doesn't flush in case she wakes the kids.

She makes her way past Dolly and Pat-Pat's rooms yawning widely. Both of them have been banging on about Christmas for weeks. Pat-Pat's obsessed with Santa. Waking early. Rushing downstairs as soon as she's got him up, demanding, 'Has-he-been? Has-he-been? Has-he-been-yet?'

She doesn't switch on the hall light. She can see well enough thanks to the streetlights glaring outside, obliterating the stars. When did nights become so dazzling? Car headlights are impossible now.

Through the lounge door at the bottom of the stairs she notices the flashes of red, blue, green, white. Marc obviously forgot to switch off the Christmas tree lights when he finally came home last night – *if* he came home last night – so they might have all burned to death in their sleep.

That's not like him. Sloppy.

He has to get help. She'll try to talk to him; tell him he needs to address his ... what is it? Depression? The thought makes her feel slightly dizzy. She holds the bannister as she feels her way down.

Coffee will only ramp up her anxiety, so she considers making a cup of tea. Then perhaps she could lie on the sofa for ten minutes or so and—

The thought's interrupted by an urgent prickling at the back of her neck. She freezes a couple of steps from the bottom.

Someone's in the kitchen. There's a strange whispering.

It's not Marc.

Her heart batters. No! Of course it's Marc. The dog would go doolally if it were anyone else. Her mind rummages for explanations but her body remains in fight-or-flight mode, her senses on high alert.

She holds on to the wall to stop herself falling, a sensation of pitching forward drawing her into blackness. She blows air slowly out of her mouth, but she can't force herself to take another step.

She doesn't have to.

A quick movement to her left. A shape emerges from the kitchen. A man.

He's holding a knife.

3

4.17 a.m., 24 December

Lulu was chasing a rabbit, something she's never done in her life, but the old dreams are hard-wired.

She thinks her name is Get Down Lulu, but the man sometimes calls her For God's Sake. She doesn't know what to make of the man. She loves the woman. She loves the little girl. She hates the boy. Sometimes, she's so afraid of the screeching and chasing, her legs won't work fast enough, and she can't scrabble away under the chair or the table to escape the feet and she does a wee. Then, even the woman calls her Bad Girl.

She wishes the boy would go away.

The man woke her up. It's not food time, although she wagged her tail just in case. But he smells wrong. She squashes her bald, wobbly belly to the kitchen floor and tries to disappear by staying very still. But she can't keep her tail from wagging like a surrendering flag.

She hears footsteps on the stairs. Now the woman's here! It will all be okay!

She leans her flank against the dishwasher and closes her eyes.

4

4.23 a.m., 24 December

Of course it's him. Lulu didn't bark.

'Jesus, Marc! What the hell are you doing?'

He's silhouetted in the kitchen doorway against a lozenge of light from across the road. He doesn't move. The fact that he doesn't answer disturbs Debs. She backs away up one step, gripping the bannister. It's not a conscious decision.

She can't see his face.

Even though it's him, thank the lord, not some coked-up burglar come to murder her and the kids in their beds, the bad feeling doesn't ebb. If anything, it notches up a level.

In the lounge, the Christmas tree's perky glow of red and blue and green and white runs through its cycle, changing the shadow's colour, but not its menace.

There's something off in the way he's standing. He's holding the kitchen knife in front of him like a weapon.

She can't see his eyes.

'Love? What's happened?' Something bad, she just knows it's something bad.

Despite the premonition, she forces herself to move forward, slowly, holding out her hand like you might to a wild animal.

He doesn't reply. He doesn't seem to register her.

She grasps for some palatable explanation. He might have been defending them from some scrote on a bike messing with their car, or an intruder—

'Was someone trying to get in?'

She stands on the new wool rug (he liked the geometric print – beige, black and grey – not her sort of thing) but a chill starts at her feet and climbs the back of her knees, the sweat between her shoulder blades tickling and sickly. The hairs on her arms creep upwards. She tries to control her breathing.

He says nothing.

In those few seconds, she tells herself he's sleepwalking, a swift, calming thought, just as quickly dismissed. Her mind scrabbles for some other reason he might be acting like this but can find nothing close to comforting.

'Marc?' It comes out a cracked whisper.

The pit of her stomach knows before the rest of her realises. She's in danger. She and the kids are in danger.

She can't take her eyes off the knife.

5

Ten years ago

'Cut glass?'

'Yes. But understated. Classic.'

'Cut glass? Really?'

'Yes. It creates an impression.'

Debs can't get her head round the price. She's already terrified she might drop the goblet she's holding, let alone handle the set on a regular basis.

But the girl with the subtle lip fillers and rather less subtle stilettos concurs, tapping the order on to her iPad with manicured shell-pink nails. What must it be like teetering round on those shoes all day? She'll have back problems by the time she's thirty.

Marc's impressive shoulders, tennis player's shoulders, lead the salesgirl around the shop, discussing the merits of Welch and Wüsthof versus Zwilling chef's knives. Debs trails round behind them. She can't contribute. It's a foreign language. This is his domain. 'Entertaining' will be an important part of his 'career trajectory' apparently; his five-year plan, his SMART goals. And she has been invited into this rarefied world; she might be seated next to him at those dinner parties. A dinner party! Her!

He picks up a small 'paring' knife.

'That's not a knife,' she laughs, giving it her best Aussie accent. She grabs a huge blade from the counter, brandishing swashbuckling style. '*That's* a knife!'

He looks at her blankly. Turns out he's never watched *Crocodile Dundee*.

He laughs, though, after she explains it.

But three-hundred-odd quid for one bloody knife?

'You are only as good as your equipment.' One of his mantras.

She watches him stride around the shop. Assured, impressive. Belonging. Directing the assistant, who gazes up at him, expertly applied liner emphasising her dark, Bambi eyes. Expensive-looking red soles (fake) take the shoes from tarty to tantalising.

Debs yanks down her own skirt, which has ridden up, and a thought left-fields her – he'd be better off with the salesgirl.

No. Stuff that for a game of soldiers!

She forces down the threat of tears, catches up, inserts herself between the girl's caramel highlights and her man – *hers*, as of five weeks ago – sliding her hand into the back pocket of his chinos to give his lovely bum a squeeze and to hide her purple nail polish, which has started to chip round the edges. He blesses her with a grin, beaming dimples. An almost goofy, indulgent look. A benediction. And she can breathe again.

So what if he wants everything to match and his swanky new flat, his clothes, his favourite restaurants aren't really her style? It's his money.

So what if she's not *MasterChef* material, cut-glass material? He chose her. She can learn how to cook.

'And I think, a dozen ramekins,' he tells the girl.

Debs' heart sinks.

Debs told him she'd never been in that shop before. Not her neck of the woods. What she didn't tell him was that she'd never been into any shop remotely like it.

Those heady, early days. Everything new and different and shiny. An adventure. A promise that she was worthy of a lovely man and lovely things.

But as she smiled and smiled at the glossy shop assistant with the perfect blow-dry, she swallowed the taste of panic: she'd never fit in; she'd never be able to host a dinner party; she'd let him down; she'd always be found lacking. He'd dump her soon enough.

She talked him out of the most expensive knife, although those he chose were still extortionate. One for carving, another for boning, others for chopping and slicing. Serrated knives for sawing through God knows what. They all made her knees feel weird.

But then he took her for lunch at Bibendum. Beautiful! Like a film set. She ran her hands under the tap in the ladies and tried to dampen down her hair, which had gone from wild, winsome curls to full-on feral. She dabbed on more minty lip gloss – he'd kissed it off twice already – her dark, currant eyes bright with excitement.

She had oysters for the first time. They made her feel a bit sick.

She rang her sister that night to ask, 'What the fuck's a ramekin when it's at home?'

Marc likes nice things and he takes care of them. The knife is kept cleaned and honed. Ready for action. Proper Planning and Preparation Prevents Piss Poor Performance.

Yeah, she definitely missed some of the signs.

6

4.25 a.m., 24 December

He turns sharply and disappears into the kitchen. She follows on boneless legs.

'Marc, what's going on?' He's still wearing the suit he left for work in yesterday morning. 'What time did you get in? Have you slept?'

Lulu raises her head, like she might know.

He makes some weird noise, which sounds like he's swallowed a wasp and veers against the fridge. There's an uneasy pause. Then he slides down, crumpling, bringing Dolly and Pat-Pat's drawings with him, until he's sitting hunched on the granite floor tiles as if suddenly exhausted. It reminds her of a giraffe keeling over, or one of those giant chimneys buckling and imploding.

Perhaps she could do this in daylight, if she wasn't wrung out and shattered herself, but now she's reduced to, 'Is it work?'

There's a small movement in his shoulders, which might be a shrug.

Flailing around for suggestions, she tries, 'Did you crash

out on the sofa? Did you have a bad dream?' Like he's got the monopoly on those.

No response.

She puts her hand against the thrum of the fridge and ventures, 'Is your mother...?'

'No.' The word spat out.

'So, it can talk!' The attempt at a joke feels wrong in her mouth.

Nothing.

She comes a little nearer, takes a big breath, and squats down as near to him as she dares.

'Come on, love. Please. Tell me what's wrong.'

His face does something like it's melting. Jesus! Is he having a stroke? Then his head flops forward. She can't bear to see him like this.

'There's nothing, *nothing* that's as bad as it feels now. Whatever's happened, whatever it is, we can sort it out. Anything—'

A quiet part of her listens to this bold statement and wonders. Does she actually mean it?

What if he's seeing someone? Has a secret wife and family stashed away somewhere? Her mind runs riot in his silence.

'You're freaking me out.'

He finally looks up at her. She wishes he hadn't.

7

Two years ago

He tells their friends (his friends), rolling out the anecdote for clients they entertain in high-end restaurants and their own low-lit dining room, 'It was love at first sight.'

Perhaps. Lust, more likely; lovely, luscious lust.

He makes it sound like he did all the running. 'I saw. I conquered. She came.' One of his risqué jokes with 'the chaps' when he thinks she can't hear.

Tonight, they are entertaining potential clients, so he delivers the more romantic version.

'The hair, her smile. That figure!' he beams at her across the table, and she glows beneath his words.

One of their guests asks, 'How did you two meet?'

Debs can't remember the man's name. Flustered, she catches Marc's eye and says, 'You tell it, love.'

He straightens his shoulders and starts the well-worn schtick. 'Deborah Watson met Marc Johnson at a Pilates class. She said to him, "Nice core control." He said to her, "Do you come here often?" And the consequence was, years of wedded bliss, two beautiful children, and a six-pack each!'

She notices how he watches for his guests' reaction. She knows how important it is to him that the evening goes well. How many times has he gone on about it! This is the first dinner since his promotion; important clients. They see the charming confident host before them. She sees his nerves; all the effort he puts into preparing before they arrive. But she loves it when Marc cooks. A bloke cooking for her!

'He actually said, "Do you come here often?"' asks Marissa, who's married to the silver fox on her right, although Debs isn't sure if he's Swiss or Viennese; one of those dodgy bankers, in any case.

Taking her cue from Marc's glance, Debs presents her social smile and takes a sip of wine. 'He did. Although he later clarified that he'd meant it as a joke.'

The truth is, Marc doesn't really do jokes.

'And what about Marc caught your eye?' asks Marissa.

'I was dazzled by his juicy glutes. An arse to die for!'

The woman rewards them with a tinkling laugh. Marc looks pleased.

'And he bagged his very own personal trainer,' Marissa trills. 'No wonder you look in such fine fettle, Marc, darling. Dating your teacher. Naughty boy! Does she give you extra homework?'

Debs falters. The woman flirting with Marc is a slim, slick blonde, no stranger to the gym herself by the looks of her triceps as she reaches across to lightly touch Marc's chest through his shirt. Debs herself does not currently feel in fine fettle, despite the new keratin straightening treatment. You can't be a plump fitness instructor without a certain amount of self-flagellation and Debs is achingly self-conscious about the weight she's still not managed to drop since Pat-Pat was born. She sits upright and pulls in the softening layer now covering her abs, somehow managing to hold on to her smile as she reluctantly puts her glass down. Empty calories and all that.

Anyway, she wasn't Marc's teacher when they got together. There was no 'conflict of interest'. It wasn't even her gym – she'd never have been able to afford the fees at the Laboratory, Muswell Hill's flashy spa and health club, full of ladies who lunch, North London thespians and a few suits like Marc. At the time, Debs was participating in as many Pilates classes as she could (those her mates taught and could get her in for free) because her goal was to do a Pilates qualification. Or at least that's what she hoped. The courses cost a bloody fortune.

In the meantime, she was building up a batch of personal training clients and teaching everything from Zumba to circuit training anywhere they'd have her, to pay the rent on the Kentish Town Cupboard; the minuscule, mis-advertised 'studio living space' she'd taken when she just couldn't bear yet another messy flat share. And she really needed to get into Pilates before her body gave up on her; rolling around on a mat for an hour being an easier option than leaping up and down wiggling her bum for a living. Plus, better rates.

Marc was taking the class because his osteopath had recommended it for his back, even though it was miles away from his home and office. Being tall, being stressed, sitting at a desk all day and sometimes long into the night took their toll. Once a week he made the pilgrimage to the gym at Alexandra Palace, meeting a specialist trainer qualified in back rehab, followed by Restorative Pilates with a highly regarded instructor.

After their class, Debs and Marc got chatting over Green Machine Super Smoothies (extra spirulina for him, added royal jelly for her; she didn't exactly believe in royal jelly, a placebo with a good PR in her opinion, but he was paying).

She advised him on exercises for the Power Plate and showed him how to use it. He invited her for another drink after the next class as a thank you. They spotted two Bafta winners nibbling radicchio alongside them as she necked a cappuccino and he sipped a bulletproof coffee. A couple of hours after that and the deal was sealed with a making-out session in the private car park that lasted a good deal longer than any stretching they'd managed. He was a good kisser. He was very enthusiastic about her 'gorgeous lips'. She felt herself melting, although he didn't lay a hand on anything but her hair. Yet when he invited her back to his, she said no, even before she discovered how far away it was.

They held fire almost another month before the deed was done – the longest, she assumed, either of them had ever waited – because she wanted to make it special. She'd put the brakes on.

She was more confident back then.

She jumps as Marissa's husband drops his fork on his plate.

Debs doesn't mind Marc's version of events. It takes the sting out of some of the things that have happened since. It's also quite sweet that he casts himself as the great seducer.

It was all her.

Her body reacted the moment he walked into the class. She wouldn't have gone after him if it wasn't for that.

Debs describes herself as 'five foot plus VAT'. Her gym calls her 'the Pint-sized Punisher' on the timetable, on account of her hardcore HIIT sessions. But while she's no lanky super-model, she does like tall men, and she admired his dedication to bettering his posture. Plus, she's a sucker for dimples and dark wavy hair and she's always loved Marc's expressive hands and his beautiful long fingers.

But – being really honest – was that why she set her sights on him? Or was it when she watched him drive off in his BMW after the class?

She'd made sure he saw her the next week, wearing the Shock Absorber bra that gave her a boost rather than just battening down the hatches, and her brightest Sweaty Betty mesh leggings, positioning herself so he got a good view of her nethers in the roll-downs. She'd serum-ed her curls so they looked 'invitingly wayward' rather than 'woman being electrocuted'. And she'd applied a light fake tan and enough foundation to look 'dewy' as opposed to 'sweating like a pig'.

She engineered it. Praising his core, when in fact it wasn't up to much, his shoulders drawn back to over-compensate for tight hip flexors as far as she could make out. She advised him on his back problem. She flirted, while presenting a profes-sional front.

And didn't he just take the bait.

Then he pulled her right under with him.

*

Debs is proper soft-focus by the end of the night. She's well chuffed when Marissa suggests she might come along to one of her classes and *perhaps they could go for a coffee together afterwards.*

She grins at Marc. Result! She's relieved. And he can relax a bit now. He's been so wound up since his promotion.

But when Marc air-kisses Marissa goodbye in the hall, banker-wanker puts his hand on Debs' bum. Not just a pat but a full-on grope. She tries to laugh it off and push him away, but he grips harder, digging in his fingers.

Shocked sober again, with some wriggling and standing on his foot in a way that might be accidental, she manages to escape. She doesn't want to spoil things, so her face betrays nothing until she closes the door behind the guests, following Marc into the kitchen, spluttering her outrage.

'Oh, that's just Klaus,' says Marc, scraping the small portion of food he always leaves on his plate into the recycling bin. 'We need to keep him onside, darling. He's integral to the deal. That's the new role.'

'Really!'

'He was a little tipsy. I'm sure he didn't mean it.'

'Fucking *really*?'

Marc won't look at her. He switches on the kettle. 'You know how long it's taken to get this promotion, Deborah. Leave it, please. Mint tea?' His voice is cold.

She's dismissed. He doesn't even look up to see how not okay she is. He continues loading the dishwasher.

This is the man who said he'd protect her.

She wants to provoke a reaction. 'At least I stamped on the bastard's foot!'

He swings round.

'What?'

She has no idea what she's unleashed but she notices the energy change in the room. A plummet in pressure. A vacuum. An absence before a tsunami.

That was two years ago – the start of the slippery slope downhill in a bloody bobsleigh – and she still hasn't had the dent in the side of the washing machine fixed.

8

4.27 a.m., 24 December

It takes her a few seconds to steel herself before she manages to say, 'I'm going to make us both a cup of tea and then we'll talk about it.'

She doubts that entire sentence. Marc would eat his own liver rather than talk about anything challenging and she's hardly up for it, knackered as she is, firing on only two cylinders.

Despite the gnawing anxiety in her belly, she reaches across the floor to gather the kids' drawings, picks up the dinosaur and penguin fridge magnets that held them, and makes herself walk over to the cupboards. She looks round, telling herself it's to check if he's okay, but really it's because she doesn't like standing with her back to him. She wishes she'd put the light on. Too tired to think straight.

Lulu wobbles over to nuzzle her leg, so she reaches down and strokes her knobbly head. A whisper of a smile crosses her face as the animal executes a perfect downward dog.

'Do you want chamomile, or—'

Her other hand stalls halfway to the kettle switch.

Along the counter she notices a tumbler and the Grey Goose vodka. The bottle's more than half empty; it was full when she went to bed.

Next to it, the open bottle of Marc's prescription sleeping pills, also half empty.

9

Ten years ago

When they first started 'courting', as Marc quaintly put it, Debs would wind him up. Couldn't help herself. He was easy to tease and ridiculously easy to shock.

After a night of passion at his 'Sumptuous Chelsea Shag Pad' as she labelled it, she'd blithely announce, 'Right, back home for a shit, shower and shave!' just to see his reaction, and he'd almost shriek, 'Deborah!' Bless him.

But he liked her being crude, she could tell. Especially in bed. She had the upper hand there.

When, in all seriousness, after an intense session that started on his wing chair and ended in his super king-size, he murmured endearments into her hair before blurting out, 'I don't want to hurt you,' she laughed right in his face and said, 'Then don't!' and they'd both grinned. As if it were a joke.

Remembering that later, she feels queasy.

It didn't seem to matter that she and Marc had so little in common. It tickled her, like visiting a new country where some things are miles better and mind-blowing and other bits, well, you almost pity them.

On their second proper date – Oxo Tower, his treat – he asks what it is about 'that singer' she likes so much.

Debs is perplexed. 'What singer?'

'That rapper. The "I Believe I Can Fly" chap. You quote him all the time.'

'That nonce? No, I don't.' She takes another sip of her Espresso Martini, giddy on the alcohol and the view. 'Anyway, he's more R and B than rap.'

'But you do. All the time! "R. Kelly said this, R. Kelly said that"—'

She actually snorts cocktail out of her nostrils.

'No!' she laughs, choking as he thrusts a napkin towards her, a little embarrassed, and she dabs, gasping, '*Our* Kelly! Not R. Kelly. My sister! Kelly, my sister.'

Back at the Shag Pad she'd make fun of his oxblood-red leather chairs, the dark wood furniture, the tasteful prints of horses on the wall, the books on the shelves (management tomes, *The Art of War*, *The Seven Habits of Highly Effective People*) pretending to whisper like she was in a library. Apart from his sports clothes (Under Armour, good stuff) pretty much his entire wardrobe made her smile. Everything was so grown-up and old-fashioned. Good suits and smart casual. Preppy. Nothing like her style: cut-price versions of sports luxe, Sweaty Betty from the sales (plus her discount as a trainer), and a riot of Fonthill Road Zumba queen kit. Rita from her Thursday morning dance class reckons she looks like 'an explosion in a neon factory'. Given the number of synthetic fibres she wears, one spark and Debs risks spontaneous combustion.

Her mantra, cheap and cheerful: 'A bargain in the hand is worth two on the rail.' His: 'Some people aren't used to an environment where excellence is expected,' although how that translates into chinos, she's no idea.

With Marc she felt like she'd infiltrated a different world and even though he was the same age as her (in fact, she's three months older), a different era.

Everything neat. His desk, amazing. Fountain pens, not biros, lined up with the blotter. No clutter anywhere in the flat, a *feng shui* wet dream.

It occurred to her, as she put on clothes she thought of as tasteful – her best kit, subdued colours, tops which weren't so low cut as to suggest full-on slut-mode – that she was in camouflage. Don't ask her why, but she was careful to wear things that covered her tattoos for a few weeks.

When he eventually saw them, the first time they went to bed, he traced the outlines of the butterfly on her hip, the swallows on her lower back, hearts and stars sprinkled around the birds, and claimed to love them.

She also moderated her language when they were together, in the same way she did when she was teaching.

Marc still doesn't like her swearing. He feels it shows a 'paucity of vocabulary'. She doesn't agree. Nothing can convey her feelings towards most politicians as succinctly as 'fuckwits, bastards and epic twats'.

Her sister teases her because she worries about things like that: politics, recession, inflation, the world economy crumbling, queuing for water, not being able to feed her kids—

'You can always shave Lulu and sell her for bush meat,' mocks Kelly.

How else should Debs reply to that, except, 'Go fuck yourself'?

She and Marc go for a run together. She keeps up with him easily enough, despite his ridiculously long legs, and she enjoys the attempt at shower sex after, although, with the height difference, that was never going to happen.

He dries her with his towel, praising her 'magnificent breasts' as he leads her to his bed. Afterwards, he lies there gazing at her and she is mesmerised by his eyes; cool grey eyes, which she thinks of as kind. No one has looked right at her like that before. She bloody loves it.

She doesn't mention how much she also loves the fact that he can just buy stuff whenever he fancies, rather than doing without, or scrimping and saving for it. Good-quality stuff.

In the end, she lets him buy her stuff too.

10

4.30 a.m., 24 December

'What's this?'

She stands over him as he slumps on the floor gazing towards her bare ankles, his back against the sleek Smeg fridge. Debs campaigned to get it in pink, knowing Dolly would be thrilled. At that time, Marc would do anything for 'his girls', and he gave in gracefully. Dolly ran to hug it when it arrived, making the delivery guys laugh, bless her. It still tickles her, *Smeg*.

'Marc! What the fuck is this?'

He glances at the pill bottle in her hand like he's never seen it before.

A car door slams somewhere, and her muscles jerk so hard she almost drops it.

His focus slides across the floor tiles with a thousand-yard stare that doesn't register her or anything else.

'What were you thinking!'

He remains silent.

The realisation hits her like a punch in the gut. 'You're on it again, aren't you?' Back on the bloody coke and sleeping pills merry-go-round.

He doesn't deny it.

'You told me you'd knocked it on the head. You *promised*. At Whitley Bay, you swore it'd all stop.' Her voice is shrill. 'You've got to get help. Marc, are you listening to me? If you don't sort this, that's it! Me and the kids... I can't go on like this. I mean it!'

She doesn't know what she means. She's not even sure if she should stand there, or if she'd be best getting out as fast as she can.

She tries again, makes her voice softer, 'Love, what is it? What's wrong?'

He sighs and says, without inflection. 'Too late.'

'What?'

'Everything.'

'Work again?'

There's a mirthless laugh.

'Look, you can get something else. It's not worth it if it makes you feel like this. We can—'

He shakes his head, muttering, 'Because that's so easy, getting another job, isn't it? In case you haven't noticed, *darling*, it's a dog-eat-dog world out there.'

Lulu looks appalled.

He sighs. 'You have no idea.' And he folds in on himself, hugging his knees to his chest like Pat-Pat. His eyes look desperate. Part of her wants to hold him and rock him and tell him everything will be okay. But she can't.

'Will you please put that down?'

He looks at the knife, as if he's surprised to see it in his hand. He looks back at her. He doesn't put it down.

Strident now: 'Put the fucking knife down!'

She knows it's the wrong way to say it, the wrong tone to take.

He starts to get to his feet, and her chest tightens. Debs moves away to squash against the uncomfortable handle of the cutlery drawer. She knows these signs. She knows how this starts. She knows how it ends.

'No. No. No.' Quietly then louder, 'No. No. No. No. No.' As he forces out each word, he jabs the front of his thigh with the point of the knife. He doesn't seem to feel it.

Jesus.

She's wondering if she can make a grab for something to defend herself with as he stumbles towards her, when a stab of white light floods the kitchen and they both freeze.

Her rational mind computes that it must be half-four and Dennis next door is leaving for his early shift, tripping the security fixture on his garage. Dennis and Sylvia, the neighbours. Sylvia's nice enough. She watches the kids sometimes and she dotes on Dolly. It's just a light, that's all.

But the angle of the bulb makes it an accusation. A helicopter searchlight. Debs' limbs refuse to obey her.

'Marc?'

Red is seeping through the grey of his suit trousers.

Something in Debs' tone makes Lulu's ears prick up. It might be food time.

11

Three years ago

She found Lulu through her 'online dog dating habit', as her sister called it. Whenever she phoned, Kelly teased, 'You been on Growler again?'

Debs would never buy a pet when so many needed good homes, but she'd naturally assumed they'd get a puppy. It was only when she saw Lulu's grizzled, hopeful face on the website that she ever considered an older animal. There was just something about her. The forlorn expression, bat-like ears, the sticky-out teeth—

She'd not been sure Marc would say yes to a dog, what with the mess and disruption one would bring. But they'd coped with the chaos of the kids, or she had. And Lulu was already house-trained. And it would be good for the kids to learn about responsibility. And an older animal wouldn't require endless walking.

Marc gave a wan smile of acquiescence. Distracted by work even then and that was well before the promotion sent him over the edge.

When Dolly saw the picture of Lulu online, she said, 'But Mummy, why do you want an ugly dog?'

Her daughter had campaigned for a teacup ball of fluff like those she'd seen in pop stars' handbags. In Dolly's coterie of girly girls, these purebred accessories are highly regarded. Owning a pony (or more improbably, a llama, lemur or sloth) is the only thing to top it. When Dolly climbs alongside her on the sofa for a 'squish' she sometimes winds her fingers into Debs' curls and says, 'I would looooove to be a sloth, Mummy, then I could cling to your fur all day long!' It makes Debs smile. She answers, 'But if Mummy was a sloth, who'd make your tea?'

The moment they set eyes on each other in the rescue centre, Debs knew Lulu was indeed the One, although it churned her up something rotten leaving behind the discarded Staffie-cross with scars on her chest. The bald patches looked suspiciously like cigarette burns.

When she'd told Kelly, her sister said, 'My money was on you rescuing a bloody poodle with three legs.' So, it could have been worse.

When she first brought her home, Lulu was beyond thrilled and also more nervous than she'd seemed in the centre. But then, they'd saved her from God knows what. You never know what a rescue dog has been through.

She and Kelly had always wanted a dog, but it had never happened, despite their mam's 'one day' promises. Well, they'd had Shit Shep for a bit. Szymon the builder had moved in after he'd refurbished the snug, bringing with him some sort of collie-corgi cross.

'Why's he called Shit Shep?' asked Kelly.

'Because I wanted to call him Shep, but my boss goes, "What? Like on *Blue Peter*? That's a shit name for a dog!" and it sort of stuck,' explained Szymon, moving his bag of tools into the cellar space and the dog bed into the kitchen.

Shit Shep – stumpy legs, glossy coat – was far too bright for his own good. Their mam was not thrilled to find him chewing on the sofa legs, but he was bored off his tits, stuck in the flat on his own while the girls were at school and their mam and Szymon were at work.

Debs and Kelly were gutted when Szymon left, on account of the landlord not allowing animals in the flat, and also on account of Szymon messing about with a waitress over at the Maid Marian on the side, even though the girls there had to wear sludge-coloured forest-green polyester uniforms.

Debs is still a little over-protective of Lulu. For the first year, she spent a lot of time trying to stop Pat-Pat from toddling towards the animal like a wind-up robot, desperate to yank her ears or sit on her head, and telling both kids to be quiet and gentle with her until she settled in.

At first, Marc seemed to get a real kick out of watching the children with the new arrival. He'd take Lulu for walks, throw a ball for her, tickle her tummy and then tickle Dolly's, making her squeal.

Nowadays he doesn't get involved. Observation from a safe distance, his new MO.

Dolly immediately caved, won over by the animal's peculiar

charm. She campaigned to call her Beyoncé, although it was obvious the dog could never live up to that. Lulu, the name she'd been given in the kennels, suited her better. Debs liked its resonance of a superannuated trouper whose diva days were over. Unlike her daughter's.

Egged on by Dolly, the animal would yowl along to pop songs and stretch her back along the floor exposing her freckled tummy for more fuss. But over the last few months she's become more introverted. She follows Debs around the house for constant reassurance like, well, a dog. She's jumpy, occasionally wetting herself when Pat-Pat explodes into a room where she's sleeping. Debs wonders if it's a form of post-traumatic stress, because Lulu hates sudden loud noises. Something they have in common.

As Lulu has become increasingly nervy, Marc's become more irritated with her. He'd had a dog as a child, Victor, a Doberman, named after Victor Mature, an old Hollywood star, apparently. His father bought him for Marc before he left. Debs understood why this would make Marc's bond deeper, having lost his father at such a young age, but the way her husband would wax lyrical, as if the animal had been some amazing canine prodigy, needled her. A proud, intelligent creature, Victor. Marc would take him on long yomps where Victor would retrieve sticks from rivers. Victor was also a well-trained guard dog who could balance a biscuit on his nose and had the discipline not to move until given the command. A man's dog. Not a sad excuse for a pet like Lulu – a creature who wheezes if she runs for more than a few seconds and repeatedly fails to catch any ball, even if thrown with Marc's unswerving accuracy.

Victor might also have rescued orphans from burning buildings for all she knew. Debs loves dogs, but she could do without the amazing adventures of bloody Victor.

Yet knowing Marc's mother, a cold fish who is most definitely not a dog person, nor indeed much of a people person, Debs reluctantly conceded that the creature must have possessed some preternatural charm to be tolerated and allowed to stay on after his dad left them.

Lulu could never compete with Victor. Not in the same league.

12

4.35 a.m., 24 December

As the car draws out of their neighbours' drive, the light next door clicks off, leaving a more profound blackness behind. Debs tries to focus. Thoughts scurry in an unhelpful loop.

The dog's nose makes her jump as Lulu pushes at her hand.

Marc makes some noise which she takes as a sour laugh.

'What?'

She's ignored.

She hates being ignored. It makes her feel ... useless. The kids pretending not to hear her when she tells them to be careful crossing the road; the older ladies in class doing squat exercises the wrong way, no matter how many times she tells them they can hurt their knees doing it like that.

'What is it? Love!' The word comes out angrily.

He looks through her.

She feels forced to fill his silence. 'Are you not well?' A ridiculous question.

For weeks, months now, he's been slipping in and out of some sort of fugue state, leaving Debs to fly solo. She initially missed his sullenness, the kids' natural buoyancy and incredible decibel level distracting her from his grim soundless presence.

By the time she did notice, he'd started sucking her down with him. And she's at a low ebb herself.

The other day she had to fight her way round the big Waitrose on Holloway Road for the Feeding of the Five Thousand Christmas shop (including his kombucha and some overpriced ham, because he insists on all their meat being organic and free range and having died naturally in its sleep on the way to his plate) and she hates shopping at this time of year. She's got enough on without that to deal with.

She had to apologise for being in the wrong queue. Woe betide any poor sod who mixes up the self-service and cashier queues snaking back down the aisles because, like her, they may have been looking at their phones.

Then there was the equivalent of a bust-up over the lack of kimchi, with the man in a duffle coat in front of her bleating, 'Well, this is just not acceptable.' And the last she heard kimchi does not feature heavily in celebrations for the birth of the baby Jesus. Then there was the incident in the car park. She had trouble pulling away because there were two cars fighting to get into her space, effectively blocked her in.

When she finally got home, it took her so long to put everything away she hadn't time to grab something to eat before she had to go back to work. And that class was exhausting and the next client demanding. And, and, and—

She tried to tell Marc about her day when he came home, but her words seemed to slide off him. He'd really listened when they'd got back from Whitley Bay. He'd made an effort. But since Dolly's birthday, since her mam died, it's like he's not here again. All she wanted was some sort of acknowledgement for how hard she's working to make a nice Christmas for them all, the kids, *his* family.

She realises that she's taken her eye off him for just a moment. Now she notices the hand that's not gripping the knife is curling and uncurling into a fist. A strange half-smile twists his lips. There's tension in his shoulders. His grey eyes look mean. They fix on hers.

She moves back. There's a strange sound behind her. She looks round to find Lulu, legs set, staring at Marc, growling low in her throat. She's never heard her do that before.

All Debs' sphincters tighten.

Suddenly all she sees is a man that she and the dog no longer recognise.

13

Ten years ago

She learned a new language over those first months together – comforting words said in his remarkable accent: 'Cashmere', the softness of it becoming a reality; 'Hush', said gently, as he put a protective arm around her and she snuggled into his chest, a traitor to the sisterhood. She became acquainted with words she never thought would apply to her: 'Bollinger'; 'Champneys'; 'a Hollywood'. Words redolent of an old-fashioned glamour; quality words promising comfort and security.

When the engine on her clapped-out Nissan Fugly finally gave up the ghost, he bought her a car, so she didn't have to go on public transport. A car! And, be honest, who the hell wants to do buses and tubes?

Some words she forgot, like 'independence', 'caution', 'moderation'. They were sucked under the intoxicating wave of their mutual obsession.

Some words she refused to dwell on, such as 'Where?' As in,

'Where's all this coming from?' And 'What?' As in, 'What's the true cost?'

But it seemed a small price, a fair deal at the time.

For her birthday he bought her a cookery lesson at Divertimenti. She'd have preferred new trainers, but she knew home entertaining was going to be an important part of his career. *Consultancy*.

She could almost hear her mam cackling, 'What sort of job's that when it's at home then?' As far as she could tell, Marc's high-powered role involved him getting paid shedloads to streamline businesses; his brief, to 'chop off dead wood'. Still, better than putting his life at risk with the 'security solutions' in foreign countries that he used to do before they met. When he told her about that – no details, broad brushstrokes – she wondered if it was a polite job description for a mercenary.

When she told him that she felt sorry for the people who lose their jobs, he countered, 'It comes with the territory, Deborah. It's a risk all employees accept when they sign their contracts.' Zero hours contracts, some of them, not worth the paper they were written on. Debs knew all about that world. No chance of a mortgage; hard enough to scrape together a deposit to rent some shoddy shoebox-sized rip-off conversion. No sick pay, no redundancy. She was always a twisted ankle away from going under financially.

'No one likes to do it,' he reasoned, 'but it's my job. It pays for *this*,' he gestured around his flat. 'It's for our future. I'm sorry, Deborah, but the brutal truth is that it's better them than me.'

At the time, all she heard was 'our future'.

On the next cookery course – she pretended she liked the first, so, inevitably, he bought her another one immediately – she was surrounded by women blessed with the sort of healthy sheen that a surfeit of money and leisure can buy. Groomed, confident ladies, cashmere cardies draped classroom-style across their seat backs. Girls with pearl earrings.

Debs watched them like an anthropologist.

There were two older women like Marc's 'Ma', a brittle creature who gave her the creeps. At the time, Debs had only encountered the 'mothership' for half an hour, and that was at least forty minutes too long.

Marc seemed cowed by his mother.

More warning signs.

One of Debs' classmates was also taking a flower-arranging session at Jane Packer. Another announced she 'dabbled in oils'. One highly recommended the Baking for the Winter Solstice session, which she'd already booked, despite it being months away because, 'It's *so* popular.'

It wasn't that these women weren't awfully kind to her, but they might as well have come from a different planet. Their hobbies, gossipy lunches and shopping trips went far beyond anything experienced by her clients, most of whom juggled children and careers. Being able to afford a personal trainer once a week was the limit of their self-care.

She tried to explain what they were like to her sister when she phoned.

'I bet they all have jade love eggs and Botox their fannies!'

sniped Kelly.

'They're *nice*, Kel.'

'Sugar and fucking spice,' was the final judgement from Nottingham.

The other thing the women on the course had in common were their diamond rings. She was more or less sure that Annabelle's story about her nephew's ex was not aimed at her, a mere girlfriend, because Annabelle and her hairband didn't appear to have that much nous.

The woman in the tale had spent four years with Annabelle's nephew only to be dumped for a younger, racier model (an actual model, naturally) leaving her without a flat or a car or any nice things. At thirty-one! What a time to have to start again!

The woman was younger than Debs.

'And she'd wanted children with him. And he'd promised they would, one day. But now—'

As Annabelle smiled a well-meaning smile, Debs' hand was slightly unsteady as she stirred the Hollandaise and she was furious with herself for reacting. As bad as a bloody footballer's wife.

But she'd lost two clients that month. They'd not died or anything, just moved out of London, which pretty much amounted to the same thing as far as she was concerned. The gym had put up the rent they charged personal trainers. Again. Her old knee problem grumbled each time she demonstrated plyometric moves in her hard core classes. She was the oldest Zumba teacher she knew and still getting nowhere fast trying to save up for the Pilates course.

Her sister, only two and a bit years older than Debs', was gearing up for her first round of IVF. No kids. Too many miscarriages. Plus, their mam went through the change really young. The doctor told her that meant her girls might have an early menopause too.

It all weighed on Debs. She started doubting herself and her future. It was the moment she knew she needed to 'shit or get off the pot', as her mam would say, one of Shirley's heart-warming mottos, delivered with the obligatory puff of Silk Cut.

The smell of their mam's cigarettes used to knock Debs sick. Now she found herself slowing to breathe it in when she passed gaggles of smokers outside bars.

Depending on your point of view, you could say Debs was unlucky or blessed when she fell pregnant with Dolly.

The truth was she might have been a little sloppy when it came to contraception in the weeks following that cookery course. She had a lot on. She was distracted. You couldn't really blame her for nature taking its course. At her age, with her genetics, it was never a given.

But he said he loved her. He definitely said that he wanted to be a father. Something like that, she was pretty sure. So maybe that's why she took a risk. Left it up to the gods.

And perhaps it had something to do with all the sex. At it all hours.

'God, you're insatiable!' he'd exclaim, sweating, spent.

But she was sated. She'd fall asleep a few seconds after, like a bloke.

'You silly, silly twat,' says Kelly when Debs tells her she's pregnant. 'Is he going to stick by you?'

'Dunno.'

'Make him pay for it,' counsels Kelly. 'Whatever happens, he owes you that.'

'Yeah,' sighs Debs. 'Feminist of the fucking year, me.'

Kelly is a bit jealous that her sister, like so many, has got pregnant without even trying, perhaps more than a bit jealous. But mainly she's scared for Debs. She's always been afraid for her little sister. Bad things happen to good people. And Debs has no safety net. No Plan B.

But then, a miracle!

When Debs tells Marc she's pregnant, he proposes straight off! Kelly tries hard not to be jealous of that as well.

Marc's not stupid. Some part of him knows.

He felt ambushed at the time. As his mother pointed out, an 'accident' was the oldest trick in the book. Although he hadn't exactly asked Deborah about contraception. He'd assumed. As a manager, one must never assume.

He adores his children, of course. Lives for them. Would die for them. They're the best things that ever happened to him.

Perhaps some residual resentment might bubble away, corroding the cool exterior from within. But that's not the worst thing inside Marc. The bad things deep, deep beneath the surface are far more dangerous.

14

Fifteen years ago

Gunfire explodes across the ridge and it all kicks off. Zings and shouts. Rocks shatter, splintering mica fragments. Screams and curses. Pressing himself flat against hot earth. Trying to work it out. An ambush? Here? Reduced to an animal crawling on its belly, scrambling, shitting itself, desperate to survive.

Then sand erupts and he can't tell which way the world is, and he's thrown into a quiet so profound he thinks it's finished – he's finished.

The pain comes. It insists he opens his eyes. The sun's an assault.

Terry is lying across him. Parts of Terry are metres away.

Automatic pilot. Pressure on the wound. He shouts words no one can hear: 'Hold on! Hold on!' and forces down vomit.

Then someone grabs his shoulders and hauls him backwards into a whirlwind. He tries to resist. Can't. A jab. And he starts to feel nothing. He's being dragged away. But that's his mate, or what's left of his mate, and he tries to hold on, to tell them. But he can't.

His one thought: leave no man behind. His single, remaining feeling: cold.

And his eyes are full of smoke and blood and then he can't see either.

But he can smell it. Scorched flesh.

The burning is worse inside. Scalding shame. Even when you wake, you never leave that behind.

15

1.27 a.m., 24 December

One twenty-seven in the morning when he quietly opens the front door. An animal crawling back to its hole to die. A night of terrible actions. Pumped with chemicals, a final bump in the taxi. How long has it been since he slept? He's been trying to cut down. Too many nose bleeds. His heart battering as he struggles in a race he's already lost.

Recently, when he wakes in the uncertain hours, he can't bear to lie next to her. The way she grinds her jaw in her sleep like a vicious, ruminating cow, the mouthguard pushing her top lip out in a petulant manner, inviting him to punch it. He will swing his legs out of bed the instant his eyes are shocked open by dreams of violence, otherwise he might make them a reality.

Sometimes when he wakes and comes back to himself, he's disappointed. Sometimes he wishes everything was over, done, finished; that he was finished.

He often needs something to 'chill out', as Deborah says.

Something mindless and repetitive. He will turn on the Xbox and play for so long his eyes waver and his hands start cramping and he has to splay his fingers to stretch them. Some nights they itch to shut her stupid mouth. On and on, moaning some nonsense about the treatment of female characters in his games. She can't even allow him this brief escape, a respite from the incessant demands. And it's not like he's fucking whores then smashing in their skulls in *Grand Theft Auto*; he's not seventeen any more.

Sometimes he turns to the online poker games, which are soothing. They keep part of his mind occupied, so he doesn't have to deal with the darkness. He learns the tells without the aid of twitches and smirks. Predicts patterns. It can be settling to watch the numbers accumulate. He sips his vodka: sometimes just the one, albeit a generous measure, in freshly squeezed orange juice, thus qualifying as one of his five a day; more often, too many.

He doesn't get a huge buzz from winning. Small wins usually. And he knows he'll play on until he loses; he has that much self-awareness. After a while, the losses cease to mean anything. On and on. Then, somehow, he's ambushed. The numbers spawn more and more numbers, a weight of numbers which start pressing in on him.

His mounting debts prove something he already knows: there will be consequences.

He just needs a few hours alone, quietness, a space to feel absolutely nothing. His plan, although not clear – nothing's clear any more – is to tire himself sufficiently, to numb as much as possible, so that a dreamless sleep might be achieved.

But she'll be on at him as soon as she wakes. Demanding this, demanding that, as bad as the children clamouring at him, on and on, like the incessant emails from work.

They all require something from him.

He pours himself a vodka. A pill. Another line. Another vodka. Too much is never enough. Shame washes over him. And he could weep.

He can't do this any more.

He has done terrible things.

16

4.37 a.m., 24 December

He's back in the room. The horror still on him. He tastes it.

Last night ... only a few hours ago, but a different life ...

If only—

What he wouldn't give for one more night where shame and loss and failure were the worst things he has to face.

There will be consequences.

He is a killer.

He's in the kitchen, sitting on the floor. Christmas Eve. They will not celebrate this year.

She's jabbing at him. 'Just get yourself together, Marc! You need to get yourself cleaned up. What if the kids see you, scrabbling on the floor like this? It'll frighten Dolly.'

Then the wrong words spill out of her mouth. 'Get a grip. Come on. This is bloody pathetic—'

He interrupts, his voice clipped, quiet. 'You're as bad as her.'

Debs doesn't need telling who 'her' is. Jeanne – her name's Jean, but she insists on the French-ified *Jeanne* – his ever-loving fucking mother.

17

11.22 p.m., 23 December

Jeanne is in her uniform. How lovely that was. The golden age, when air travel was for the select few who appreciated it, and she, the model hostess. Envied, feted, admired.

Her husband, Dudley, had such an unfortunate name, but he refused to answer to her suggested amendment, the more romantic *Leigh*. He was supportive of her career.

She flies high above the clouds, her hair and make-up just so, not a single speck of lint on her skirt. She has a tray for the bourbon. Her balance is exceptional. She walks tall, sashaying down the aisle. Her waist is a miracle. Was. The child would put paid to that.

Captain Browning said she could be a Playboy Bunny, as if that tempted her. 'You'd make more in tips in a week than you earn in a month doing this, pussycat,' he smiled as he casually stroked her bottom. A neat bottom, a shapely leg. She was on her feet so often. She would not slump as the other girls did after service, she preferred to sit up straight, to remain 'on call'. Posture conveys so much.

The sun sinks below cloud level, splashing the sky with its gaudy oranges and tangerines, like one of those ridiculous 'paintings' where models writhe around naked on the canvas. The so-called artist, some friend of a friend, had suggested that to her at the party in Mayfair last week, disguising his goatish lust with the word 'muse'.

She is the only one awake in the galley, her private moment, high above the squalor beneath.

Then it sours, as it does every time. The demands start. A passenger who wants another drink, although he's already had so many. Harsh words if she's too slow dispensing it. The captain – which one is this? – sliding his hand up her thigh as she delivers a sandwich. Always married, the captains.

And the hands; always the hands.

Dudley never pawed her. Their 'arrangement'. How ironic that it was his hands she yearned for. How she hungered for a little affection from her husband, scraps of love from her son.

Her boss laughing in her face when she mentions those maulings while on duty, a short sharp laugh, like a sealion. The other girls smirking, warning her about the man with the blue tie in 24B, but not minding. Not really.

'They know which side their bread is buttered. You'd do better to play along, missy.' Advice from her mother. A little star-struck by the glamorous professions, her mother.

But now the hands are everywhere, and she slaps at them and pushes them away, but they grip and grasp and bruise and there are too many, pulling her down. Yanking her down beneath the clouds.

Always the hands.

She wakes, heart pounding. Someone is banging on her door.

18

Ten years ago

Every word is enunciated, clipped. 'And I know there will be an outcry of pots admonishing me for calling the kettle black,' she allows herself a small smile. 'A plethora of pots mocking me for my noirish inclinations.'

What is Jeanne going on about? Debs presses her knuckles into her knees and listens hard in case she's missing something.

'But Tilly's tree is beyond the pale. *De trop. Répugnant.*'

'Why, Ma?' asks Marc, surprisingly solicitous in his mother's company. Almost fawning.

'It's pink, for goodness' sake!'

Oh, do shut up, thinks Debs.

Jeanne sits across from them, poised, her legs folded at the acceptable royal angle, thighs demurely together, lavender lambswool sweater artfully slung across her slim shoulders. She sips her second Bombay and tonic. The smokescreen suggestion, 'Shall we have Earl Grey?' was never pursued. Debs alone has a cup.

His mother wears a dusky lilac polo neck beneath the sweater and an A-line skirt in similar muted heather hues. Her artfully waved hair is a softly enhanced silver, like the delicate ornaments on the festive tree in the corner.

'Pink!' says Jeanne, in the same tone she might say 'open sores'. Her precisely arched eyebrows rocket skywards.

But Marc's all, 'Pink is a very on-trend colour, Ma.'

Jeanne rolls her eyes as she does each time her son calls her Ma.

Debs clocks that the pastel shades of both the outfit and the room belie the woman's gunmetal heart.

'Marcus, *chéri*, pink is only acceptable if you are twelve years old or younger. When this one's born,' the mother-in-law-to-be nods towards Debs' bump, poorly masked by her fifties-style ensemble, 'she shall be allowed a pink Christmas tree.'

Debs, in the new bright green frock, purple cardi and fuchsia shoes, which – yes – are indeed a shade of pink, so she clocks the dig at her, shoots Marc a furious look. They'd agreed not to disclose the sex of the baby. He's hopeless under interrogation from his mother.

But that's not the *coup de grâce*. After a painful political discussion, fuelled by gin number three, all the while recoiling whenever Debs opens her mouth or if the younger woman's bright red curls and perky primary colours cross her eye-line, Jeanne blithely announces, apropos of fuck-all, 'Of course, Marcus's father was one of *those*.'

'One of what?' asks Debs, who'd just been extolling the virtues of Graham Norton in a desperate attempt to lighten the 'Irish issue'.

'A fag,' pronounces Jeanne.

'A what?' asks Debs, unused to the intonation. For a milli-second, she genuinely wonders if she's being offered a cigarette.

'His father – a poof,' Jeanne clarifies.

As Debs splutters into her cup, it's Marc's turn to wince and shoot his mother an outraged look, before turning to his fian-cée with an apologetic smile.

That was only the second time she'd properly met mummy dearest. On the first occasion they went to her immaculate flat 'for afternoon tea', Marc asked Debs to take off her engagement ring before they arrived. He needed to 'break the news' at a later date; 'prepare her', for Jeanne had recently been under the weather.

Debs was hurt. She intuited, quite rightly, that her intro-duction to Jeanne as the 'intended' might not be greeted with unbridled delight.

Marc's 'later date' was one where his fiancée wouldn't have to see the look on his mother's alabaster face. Disappointment hardly covered it. Jeanne had hoped Marc would marry Hetty; she adored his ex. She'd thought she'd have both a daughter-in-law and a friend. Instead, she got *Deborah* – a girl with hard, knowing eyes.

On the silent journey home, a chill in the car already shadowing their first Christmas together, Marc's lovely long fingers gripping the BMW's steering wheel as if to forge through a Force 9 gale, Debs realised that his mother had never once said anything directly to her, or asked her anything about herself, at either of their meetings. Their *audiences*. On subsequent visits, which she would only attend on a three-line whip, Jeanne did address her:

'Those slacks, very brave, *chérie*.'

'And clients pay you to tell them how to lose weight, do they?'

'Your hair is so *joli*! I expect children love it. Like Ronald McDonald!'

Awful bloody woman.

And even though Debs had dropped most of the baby weight since Pat-Pat came along, just half a stone to go, there was that classic quip last Christmas, 'More good news, Deborah?' with a pointed glance to her stomach.

A-grade hag.

When she'd tried to talk to Marc about his dad on the way home from those first, less-than-jolly Christmas drinks with Jeanne, he'd blocked her with a curt, 'Don't.' And he refused point-blank to discuss anything of note regarding either of his parents from then on.

He often clammed up when she attempted to draw him out emotionally. He'd deflect her questions or answer in platitudes. But later, perhaps the next night when he got home from work, or the next day, he might apologise and be extra affectionate or buy her a present.

Initially, during rare pauses in the intense lovemaking sessions – a Smorgasbord of sticky sex – his reticence in the emotional arena had disturbed her. There was something more than a little shut down about him.

But then, with all the preparations for the baby and fighting off morning sickness and getting her classes covered and her clients allocated to other trainers, then all the chaos that ensued with Dolly's arrival, she didn't have a lot of time to pursue it. She put it to the back of her mind.

19

4.40 a.m., 24 December

'I'm nothing like your bloody mother!'

Lulu retreats to her basket.

'What's wrong with you?'

Debs could scream when he won't reply. She would scream if the kids weren't upstairs asleep.

She mutters, 'For fuck's sake!'

She knows he doesn't like her swearing. Nor does his mother. But then, that fake, snooty cow thinks Mary Berry's 'somewhat vulgar' based on absolutely bugger all. And when the kids aren't around, and they usually aren't on the rare visits to Jeanne's unwelcoming show home which has never featured a single photo of her grandchildren – not even one of her own *son* – Debs now makes a point of swearing to rile her.

Debs decides to make a cup of tea, trying for some sort of normality while she puzzles out what to say next, what to try next. Too tired to think straight. She fumbles for a spoon, hands unsteady, and as she closes the drawer, the handle catches her dressing gown tie, tugs the front, leaving it gaping.

Marc doesn't say anything, but he shifts his weight, comes to his knee and slowly gets to his feet, each move deliberate, as if he's wading through treacle.

He draws himself up to stand like he's on parade. The need radiates off him.

'Come here.'

Those two words are all it takes, and her fear convolutes into a different, primitive response.

20

Ten years ago

Some of her friends never liked him.

Tracy from the hairdresser's said, 'He's a bit Benedict Cumberbatch,' like that was a bad thing! Kirstie, a fellow teacher at her favourite gym, the Factory on Hornsey Road, accused him of looking down his nose at her when she met them in the Shaftesbury straight from Legs, Bums and Tums, whiffing a bit, with sweat smudging her mascara. The most common complaint was that he came over a bit stand-offish and a lot posh. Not the worst things, by a long shot.

'It's not like I'm shagging Boris Johnson,' she complained to Kelly.

'One of the few who hasn't, then!' snorted her sister.

Debs guessed her mates were a little intimidated. Still, most of them still fancied him.

Kelly got it straight off. 'Oh, *very* fuckable,' she'd enthused when she came down to stay with Debs for a shopping and theatre weekend. They'd seen *Les Mis*. With a numb bum and a will to live that had left the building at half time, Debs felt living through the actual revolution might have been an easier option, but the 'light supper' with Marc – steak, frites and a bottle of champagne – had cheered them right up.

'Better than old Needle Dick, what's-his-name?' said Kel.

'Les?'

'Yeah.'

Les was a brief fling, a barista, which meant Debs had to pay for pretty much everything, although she did get free flat whites. She regrets showing Kelly the photos he sent her.

Her mam got it too. When Debs posted the engagement picture on Facebook and Insta, after they'd finally told Jeanne, Shirley messaged, 'I'd do him!!!'

She was pretty sure her mam was joking.

A mixed reaction from the guys at the gym: Cai claimed neutral territory; Ali opted for visceral loathing; JJ declared Marc a 'total lust-bucket', fanning himself as he added, 'I'd climb over a Hemsworth for him, doll. He's *everything*!'

Kelly's partner, Boz, still can't stand Marc. He wouldn't go on the stag do – skiing in Chamonix. Obviously, it was the cost, but Debs reckons mainly because Boz is a short arse. Not many blokes like another man towering over them, not even the Hoxton metrosexuals. And Boz is from Donnington.

Debs argued his case with her mates, explained that Marc became flustered in company. She didn't tell them that he was fine surrounded by his old PPE chums (she'd initially confused the course with the equipment), Oxbridge types who made topical jokes that were so sharp she'd sometimes only catch on after they'd buggered off. A night out with them was like being blasted by a scattergun of spiteful tweets. She didn't mind his work friends, but his military buddies gave her the chills. Arrogant, most of them. Plus, they never gave anything away. Nothing real; nothing emotional.

His army pals didn't know what to make of *her* either. Most comments were aimed at her *décolletage*.

'Killer curves,' said James, Marc's former CO. 'Devastating! A proper bombshell, aren't you just? What a real woman *should* look like.'

It embarrassed her.

While most eyed her up in the usual way, several talked across her, and a couple looked at her like she was something they'd stepped in. One of her mam's homely little sayings came to mind: 'They wouldn't piss on you if you were on fire, that lot.'

'Yeah, he's got a nice arse and all, but you don't buy the Lord Snooty act?' said Kirstie on her third Porn Star martini in Kiss the Sky, the nice little bar in Crouch End where they went to celebrate JJ's birthday. 'And yeah, nice dimples on the rare occasion we see them.'

'Oh, shut it,' said JJ. 'He's all broody, like Jamie Dornan. Lush!'

Kirstie was having none of that. 'Just cos he's *brooding* don't mean he's nice. And if a woman looked that sulky all the bloody time, some bugger would soon say, "Smile, darling, it might never happen."'

Debs silently agreed. Marc did look good, a macho melancholy vibe – glowering if he encountered her mates – but she was becoming immune to that dubious brand of charm. It was exhausting. Mr Darcy and the entire brigade of mardy-arsed men could knob off into the sunset as far as she was concerned.

But she surprised herself by saying, 'I know. But I love him,' because that was news to her. She added hastily, 'Plus he's dynamite in bed.' And thanks to Debs sharing many delicious titbits from those early exuberant sessions, Kirstie stopped having a go.

The sex was very, very good. The best. He looked the part. A nice amount of muscle, but not so much that Debs couldn't breathe out on occasion. She put in the graft too. Blowjobs on tap, talking dirty, all the tricks.

After a couple of months together he'd sort of blossomed. He'd never been shy, exactly, but he started to come into his own, so to speak. He took control in a way she doubted some of the insipid snowflakes she trained and worked with would understand, with their shaved, plucked, neutered boyfriends asking permission for this, apologising for that. Too pretty. Too prissy. Pussyfooting around.

'Where's he put his foot?' whooped Kelly when they discussed it.

Marc was rugged and retro. Broad-shouldered. Military bearing. Strong. He became a little dangerous in bed. And his bloody voice! Deep with authority. Not ordering her, as such, but instructing her, as he might tell his men where to go on a battlefield, what to do, who to kill.

The things he suggested, manoeuvring her into position, not rough, but suddenly confident, insistent, twisting her this way and that, opening her up. And the words – ordinary words, which in other rooms, in other circumstances, weighed little – but his voice, thick with desire, filling them with a dark charge, a command:

'Show me— Swallow— Come—'

And she'd bloody loved it. Throbbed to it, given in to it like she was made for it. A deep, illicit shudder running all the way through her.

That stuff, she never talked about with her mates.

'Get on your knees—'

And, oh fucking yes, she did.

21

4.42 a.m., 24 December

'I said, come here.'

There are two Debs in the kitchen. One who wants to get as far away from him as she possibly can. He's dangerous in this mood. The other who's drawn to him for the same reason. Part of her still wants him. He's the man she loves. Loved. He's the one she hates, would like to hurt. More than that, there's the gravity of what they've become, what they've created together: something twisted. The undertow is strong.

'I won't ask again.'

It's her own stupid fault. She's as much to blame. She should have stopped it when she had the chance. She should have walked out the first time it happened. How old was Dolly then? Eleven months?

She was writing up a programme for a new client (slim, healthy, twenty; Debs joked that she hated her already) and she'd been interrupted twice by punters who wanted to know if they did off-peak membership (*look on the website*) and which studio the new Aerial Hoop class was in (*is there a hoop hanging in the studio? There's your clue*).

'Do you want to come for a drink with us after my shift?' asked JJ.

She gave him the look.

'Jesus O'Reilly, don't bite my head off.'

'Who's "we"?'

'Me and Frank.' Frank was JJ's new boyfriend.

'No ta. I'm knackered.'

'You're always too tired these days. Come on. You're no fun any more.'

Debs was aware. It came with the territory. She was a new mum, therefore always exhausted. Her work mates were a laugh, but they were all so much younger. She could grumble about the boss with them, or discuss kinesiology tape, but she couldn't share anything really *personal*. Nothing like her and Kelly. Sometimes she thought her sister was the only proper friend she had.

But she did go for a drink with the lads because she didn't want to admit defeat. And, out of practice, she got mortalled, traipsing home late and messy.

He was on her as soon as she got in. Hard kisses. Grabbing her hair, pulling her to him. A session that started passionate, turned rough and went on – her head banging against the wall, his hands round her throat – and on and on until it felt like punishment.

They didn't see her at the gym for two weeks until the bruises went down.

And she stayed with him despite that. She can't even remember the excuse she gave herself that time, but she stayed.

She always stays.

She's ashamed that the urge to go to him presses on her now. She wants to give in, but she doesn't.

He takes three swift steps towards her and she flinches. His face comes close to her ear and she feels his breath against her neck as he whispers, 'Did you hear me?'

To stop herself, to stop the compulsion to let him do what he wants – even now she might let him; even now there's an answering thrum, the echo of desire – she pushes him away.

She tenses a beat. He's still holding the knife like it's welded to his hand. There's a stink coming off him, stale sweat and booze; the coppery tang of the blood on his leg. His eyes are hard and piggy. It's all wrong.

His body has its own agenda. He grabs her hair.

22

Thirty years ago

'What are you going to do about it, Johnson?'

Ed pushes his knee down harder. His face mashed against the nasty brown dorm carpet, Marc wonders how much pressure it might take for his spine to snap.

'I'm sorry.'

'*He's sorry*,' mocks Graham.

'The little pig-fuck's sorry,' Ed cackles, so the others join in. Pavlov's pricks.

'Sorry won't cut it,' adds Stephen B., a lad who'd once been his friend, three terms and half a lifetime ago.

'Spastic Johnson's not sorry enough,' says Ed.

'Spastic!' went the echoing chorus.

Spastic Marc's schooldays passed like this: one humiliation after another; small drops of acid in a series of small incisions. He was never entirely sure what he should be sorry about.

Offer him a million pounds and he couldn't tell you what catalysed that time, as opposed to any of the other times. The only reason he remembers is when his back plays up.

He once confided in Mr O'Callaghan – 'Call me Mike' – Head of Pastoral Care, who took a very long time to explain to him, in a totally circuitous, overly-matey manner, that unfortunately this was the way of the world, you know, and that Marc must basically (although much of this was not said, simply implied) man up, swallow it, give as good as he got, and more essentially stop whingeing as no one likes a snitch. All done and dusted with a hearty slap on the back and an invitation to return at any time for a chat and chocolate digestives if things, you know, didn't look up.

Marc exited Mr O'Callaghan's office mumbling apologies.

In the holidays, he continued apologising to his mother, whom he never called 'Mother' – or, for a good while, anything else – after he was instructed to stop calling her Mummy. It was to be 'Jeanne' from now on, the pronunciation like the actress Jeanne Moreau, rather than her given name, Jean. Very modern. Very chic. He couldn't make himself say it.

When he forgot, if a 'Mummy' popped out, she'd give him a look that made him want to cry. He fought to swallow the urge.

He was admonished for tears, or if he showed an abundance of any emotion, because it reminded her of his long-lost father. If he ever became distraught or tried to tell her about the tortures inflicted by his peer group, she'd snap, 'Oh Marcus, do stop doing a Dudley,' and she'd stalk away.

He had to imagine how Dudley himself might have 'done a Dudley'. He was banned from seeing his dad and by the time he was old enough to realise she couldn't actually stop him, Dudley was dead.

He has blanked out most of the funeral.

When he challenged her about it, years later, in polite strangulated tones – 'Why didn't you let me see him?' – she waved her hand as she might a dismissive handkerchief and said, 'It was for your own good, *chéri*.'

He was left with a neat trust fund and a messy, impressionistic collage of memories from the time before his dad left the two of them, when Marc was five and a half. Not really enough to piece together a cohesive idea of a person.

When he eventually discovered the truth about his father, he realised how his mother had intended the comparisons of him being like Dudley as barbs. Up until then, he'd naturally assumed his dad had left because his mother was a total C-word. Although a small, guilty part of his heart always wondered, perhaps still does: if he'd been a better boy, might his father have stayed?

When, amazingly, Marc made it through to his teens, he once called his mother 'Ma' – a moniker used by some of the other pupils with their own mothers – and the startled look on her beautifully made-up face was so priceless, the perfectly plucked eyebrows shooting skywards, he continued to do so. One small act of rebellion. A tiny, sharp point inserted dozens of times from then on. Each a marvellous triumph.

Only his marrying Deborah rankled her more.

Coffee and a line or two of coke in the morning. Alcohol and sleeping pills at night. Different pills – anti-anxiety, anti-depressants – on and off and on and off, for months. A cocktail of despair. Dark months.

Nothing helps.

Gambling. Bigger risks. Trying to feel something; trying to feel nothing.

Work, work, work; grinding on.

Gaming. Hours on the Xbox. Deadening the constant worry with boredom and exhaustion.

Porn. Although he can hardly be bothered these days no matter how extreme. It's like someone has reached an icy dead hand inside his groin and twisted. Viagra doesn't help much.

He needs something to help him switch off his mind. Stop the images. If only he could talk to her, talk to someone, but probably her – who else is there? – try to communicate some of his internal chaos.

But he wasn't trained for that.

23

4.43 a.m., 24 December

The fridge is silent. There's something odd in the rhythm of his breaths.

'I don't want to, Marc.'

He pulls her hair tighter and whispers in her ear, 'You know you do.'

'No.'

The last time they played this out she gave in, her body gave in, so some might say she was asking for it.

More loudly, but not so loud as to wake the kids, she tries, 'Stop it. I'm not in the mood.'

But they both know that sometimes she gives mixed messages. It's a sick game they play.

'Come on, baby—' His expression changes to one she recognises, a look signalling cruelty, a shadow of a smile mocking her.

She pushes him and snaps, 'No! Get out my face!'

Lulu woofles.

Marc growls, 'Stupid bitch.'

He could mean either of them.

She can't blame him. She has said no and meant it as a challenge. Or perhaps she would really mean no but then be persuaded. And she's furious with herself for all that.

He leans across her to lay the knife on the counter. Finally! But he starts pulling on the dressing gown cord and draws her head back to bite her neck. She tries to turn away from him. He rams his knee between her legs.

'Stop!' It comes out like a squawk.

The dog trots across from her basket, responding to the note of urgency in the woman's voice, and as the man pulls the dressing gown one way and the woman pulls the other, she jumps up at Marc.

Tug-of-war! The Best Game!

He gives the dog a swift, unthinking kick, which catches her haunch and makes her yelp.

Lulu swiftly retreats to her basket. She doesn't understand. Earlier the man fed her ham from the fridge. Earlier he patted her on the tickly bit on the inside of her leg, the Best Bit, and his voice had been soft when he said, 'What's to become of us, hey girl?'

She'd licked his fingers where the ham had been.

Then he'd wiped his nose on his hand and wiped his hand down her side.

Debs clutches the dressing gown to her chest, demanding, 'What sort of person hurts a defenceless animal?' although she knows the answer. 'You bastard!'

He pushes her away so hard she's winded.

24

Ten years ago

He rarely lost his temper when he first started seeing Deborah. He'd learned to control his emotions. Mostly.

The closest his mother came to displaying anger was a sharp, brief, '*Assez!*' If he ever shouted or cried in front of Jeanne, she'd simply walk out of the room. Sometimes she locked herself in her bedroom and turned up the record player, leaving him alone until he calmed down. She preferred jazz to pop or classical, another affectation along with her stupid name. Sometimes he thought he heard her crying in there, but assumed he was mistaken.

Deborah was a different species to his mother. Something about being with her uncorked him and it was bloody fantastic.

She made him laugh – a proper belly laugh. She provoked him into fury. He felt unleashed. Light-headed.

And after the arguments, the heavy pull back towards her, the frenzied 'make-up sex' (her phrase) – the intensity of those times! The insanity.

During their first rows he was startled by the language, the tirade she launched at him. He was shocked yet thrilled. She read the excitement in his face and smiled. And then she fucked him.

That filthy mouth. In bed, she'd play up to it. That mouth sucked him dry.

Before Dolly.

Now she kisses his children with that mouth.

At the start, he once came home to find her on her hands and knees cleaning the oven – or, as he discovered, pretending to – dressed in stockings and little else.

'Want a piece of this, geezer?' she laughed, deep and throaty and lusty.

Later, 'Like that, like that, yeah, harder—'

The things that came out of her mouth! A wild joy in her eyes, like her words were a brilliant joke, but also deadly serious.

The talk. The clothes. The toys. It made him harder. She liked the games. Gave him a good seeing to. He could hardly last, it turned him on so much.

Stiff upper lip is all he can manage now.

Not only didn't she mind his rare flights of fury (because, very occasionally, if provoked, if stressed, tired, chemically challenged, he might momentarily erupt), she'd shout back and punch his arm, his chest, and engage. It was one of the things he admired about her.

Not that he ever really lost control. He might shout, but physical force ... that was confined to barracks, as it were. Only in the bedroom.

He couldn't get enough of that kind of sex. Angry. Raw. So much sex in the early days. She freed something in him. The pleasure, the wickedness in her face. Words spilling out of her beautiful lips.

He had never liked to look at himself naked before Deborah came along. The posing pricks in the gym changing rooms made him want to puke. Despite intermittent fasting, protein shakes, spin classes, squash and runs if his back allowed him, he'd never liked what he saw if he caught sight of himself.

But with her! He likes to watch himself with her. She's shaped like a carved fertility goddess. He once could lay his head on her thigh or belly and feel a comfort so profound it makes him blush to remember.

But they never made love; they fucked. His passion with her so different from the almost courtly love he felt for Hetty – the girl, the rose, the prize; the grand passion before Deborah – his *coup de foudre*.

His wife is nothing like Hetty. But her robust, earthy lust unlocks his own. She's amazing. She makes him amazing.

Used to.

25

Twenty-eight years ago

He did once snap at school.

'You do know it's American for penis, don't you, *Johnson*?' Ed had started it. Exhaustingly predictable.

Spastic Johnson. His clumsiness on the sports field had put him in their sights as 'the Spaz'. As if that wasn't enough, he was now also 'the Penis'.

He'd march out of the school grounds and down to the mini-supermarket and buy sweets, so many sweets, and by the time he got back, walking slowly, ever slower as he approached the school entrance, there weren't any left. He ate and ate and didn't even enjoy them after the first few. Gorging himself. Stuffing it all down.

Then he was Spazzy Pig-fuck. Fatboy. Jabba the Penis.

And it was one of those delightful names they were chanting, or all of them, when he cracked, lost control just for a moment, and grabbed the blackboard rubber, the old-fashioned varnished wooden kind, satisfyingly heavy in his hand, and hurled it with all his strength right at the smug face of bastard Ed.

The edge connected with the side of the boy's temple, which gushed blood. So much blood, it startled them all.

'He might have lost an eye,' tutted the nurse.

No one spoke to him after. They laid off, for a time at least. But no one dobbed him in, the taboo against snitching outweighing the delight they'd have taken in seeing him punished. Marc was grateful and relieved but, mainly, bitterly disappointed. If he'd been expelled, he might have been somewhere else, away from that shithole, away from them.

A different kind of mother might have labelled it 'puppy fat'. He might have been teased as plump, or encouraged to take up rowing, or eat more vegetables.

When he came home for the Easter holidays, Jeanne's eyes widened.

'Marcus! That!' she poked hard. 'Dis-gust-ing! *Quelle horreur!*'

Needless to say, Easter eggs were banned.

Later, she tried to talk to him, which was mortifying, telling him about her own 'battle with the bulge', a shocking revelation that made him retreat to his room. It was impossible to imagine Jeanne as anything but slim, and the time for confidences had long passed.

When the rolls of softness around his chin and belly had not dematerialised by the summer holidays, his 'light suppers' became very light indeed.

Throughout that August he'd take himself to the nearest McDonald's, risking hard shoves and elbows, nasty laughs and sneers from the streetwise boys and the hard-faced girls, the hoi polloi who frequented such establishments. And in an orgy of grease and sugar and salt and trans fats, he would stuff down the desire to do his mother, *Jeanne*, harm.

That small sad fearful person – Spastic Johnson, Blubber Boy – still exists. Beneath the Paul Smith suit, Brooks Brothers shirt and gold cufflinks, secreted away behind the reassuringly expensive Senior Manager business cards in the monogrammed calfskin wallet, is a hollow space where Spazzy Pig-fuck hides.

For a long time now a syrupy blackness has seeped back into this vacuum inside him. He didn't resist much. It filled him up. It seemed familiar.

Ever since the promotion two years ago – that poisoned chalice – he has fought it. After the shock of Deborah leaving with the children last November (to *Whitley Bay*, for God's sake), he has waged an internal war. He made advances. He was better. For a short period.

Now it is a losing battle.

So many domestic flashpoints: his mother-in-law dying; his daughter's birthday; Deborah's betrayal.

And work is carnage.

The lack of sleep, despite the pills, despite the alcohol, made things manageably blurry. Then came the hangovers, as much from tiredness as anything. He'd wander through the office jet-lagged, needing a line in the gents, along with a double espresso, to function.

He might have become a little slipshod.

But he desperately wanted this job; he worked all hours, aimed for further advances. His earnings, how many people work under him, how large his bonus each year, whether his BMW is upgraded; these are all yardsticks of excellence. Yes, it is important to him, like coming first in a school sports day race might have persuaded his mother of his worth.

But things are slipping away from him, as if he's the last survivor of a shipwreck, clinging on to debris in icy water.

It can only take you so far, looking the part, being tall, presentable, in possession of the correct CV, the correct accent. At some point, you have to deliver.

Whispers around the office – *promoted above his ability*.

The 'drift', as he thinks of it, is accompanied by a welcome numbing of the painful parts. Incrementally, fatigue, cocaine, despair, whatever, have started to numb other parts too. That didn't worry him unduly until the numbness started swallowing him up.

Part of him wants to slip under the ice. Give in to it. A relief. Part of him wants to torpedo through it.

Either way, there will be collateral damage.

26

4.47 a.m., 24 December

Lulu is panting, squashed into her basket. He watches her staring at him warily until he can't bear to look at her any more.

When Deborah finally shuts her ugly mouth – following a full two and a half minutes of bile, her accusations of animal cruelty sliding into general vitriol in language so crude it is *wearing* – all he can think of is how much he needs a drink. She's sweating. It is not attractive.

'Move.'

When she doesn't respond, he says it again more emphatically. 'Move!'

He stands immediately in front of her and she both pulls herself up to her full height, all five-two of it, and squashes back against the cupboard. He reaches past her for the vodka bottle.

'What! You can't be serious? At this time? What about the kids? They'll be up soon. What the fuck are you thinking—'

He opens his mouth, freezes, like a glitch, then in a voice without colour he says, 'I just can't—'

'Can't? Can't what?'

He is unable to communicate. He starts to slosh the spirit into the glass.

'What—'

'I have to ... finish this.'

'The vodka? Don't be stupid!'

She lunges for the bottle. He snatches it back. She grabs for it. He swings round, his other hand catching the glass, which spills over and rolls, rolls, teeters – pauses – then smashes on to the floor.

Deborah flinches. Lulu also jumps, then shrinks further inside her basket.

Marc does not react. He hasn't for months.

27

Seven months ago

Last Christmas was lovely. Fantastic presents. He really made an effort: playing with Pat-Pat and Dolly, taking Lulu out for walks, listening to her tell him about the gym. He'd even chatted to her sister on the phone. She'd allowed herself to hope things could stay like that.

Since then, Debs has watched with increasing irritation as Marc slowly shut her and the kids out of what passes for his home life. Back to his old habits.

Dolly's face broke her heart when he dismissed her with a sullen, 'Show your mummy, there's a good girl,' as she offered him her latest drawing of Lulu riding a unicorn.

The next day, 'Put that down! NOW!' as she picked up his work phone. Dolly was shocked into uncharacteristic silence. No cuddle was offered in apology.

If Pat-Pat bothered him, Marc would say, 'Not now, soldier.' And if he persisted, 'Patrick, please stop whining!' Then he'd lift him and thrust him towards Debs to deal with, as if the child might detonate. If the kids continued to demand his attention, he'd leave the room, shutting his office door on Dolly's pitiful (if theatrical) tears and Pat-Pat's furious protestations. The irony is that photos of his daughter in her tutu and Pat-Pat in his *Star Wars* costume have pride of place in that office. Pat-Pat makes an excellent Stormtrooper.

The tentative, unspoken peace treaty between husband and wife requires Debs to manage the fallout from these skirmishes, rather than battering down his door and punching him in the face.

She enfolds Dolly in her arms and rocks her until she quietens. She kisses Pat-Pat on his head and distributes sweeties, feeling guilty for resorting to that.

Twice she's taken the kids to McDonald's as a treat, to get them out of the house, to get them away from the bleak atmosphere Marc creates. To stop herself causing a row about it. She's kidding herself that the kids won't notice.

Debs is hurt by Marc's silent treatment. If pushed, and she always pushes, he gives single-word answers. She sometimes tries to shock him out of it, shouting at him, jabbing him with something hurtful, although she knows that just makes things worse.

He looks gormless most of the time. Slovenly. Slack-jawed. Then suddenly, jittery. Wired.

She guesses what he's up to. She says nothing, because she can't face the fallout.

On the rare occasions he comes home before she's gone to bed, he'll slump next to her on the sofa, sipping vodka, facing the TV but not really watching. He never gets so drunk that he's out of control. She's never seen him proper arseholed, so she can't really complain. But before very long, he'll plod over to his study/bunker and shut the door on her.

In the middle of the night, that's where she can usually find him. In the past, she didn't want to knock in case she disturbed his work, but now, if she sticks her head into his home office, she'll likely find him playing on his stupid Xbox, like some overgrown, monosyllabic teenager.

He's left her to fly solo. And she's so tired, she's losing it.

'What animal would you be?' asks Dolly, apropos of bugger all, which is the way of most of their conversations.

'Why, love? What would you be?' says Debs, giving her daughter perhaps a quarter of her attention, as she struggles to work out how many classes she teaches using music featuring original artists so she can pay her music licence. She can't abide licence-free rubbish, although it pains her to give two quid per class to the likes of Madonna. A phoney Madge or Kylie sound-a-like might pass, but there'll be no fake Rag'n'Bone Man on her watch. She had to listen to enough of that tinny tripe before she could afford the real thing. Before Marc.

'I'd be a unicorn,' declares her daughter.

Predictable.

'And what would Pat-Pat be?' says Debs, scrabbling for her credit card in the black hole of her rucksack, the washing machine rattling her nerves on its outraged spin cycle.

'He'd be a—' Dolly thinks hard. 'A wino!'

This tickles Debs. 'A rhinoceros?' she checks, just in case Dolly's gone psychic. 'And what would I be?'

'You'd be an orangutan!'

Debs knows she'll never be a slinky puma, and given her colouring, of course her daughter would think of a red-haired ape. But she gets up and puts the Jaffa Cakes away in case it's also an unintentional dig at her belly.

'And Daddy would be a stallion!' Dolly rears up and gallops around the kitchen.

The next time they play the game Dolly is, yet again, 'A *ponycorn*!' Pat-Pat's a brontosaurus (more bull in a china shop, think Debs as her son careers around the lounge in his pedal car because the garden's too wet) and Mummy is a dancer.

'That isn't an animal,' smiles Debs.

Dolly ignores her. In her world a dancer, so very obviously, can be an animal.

Debs asks, inclusively, 'And what would Daddy be?'

Dolly will not answer. The look she gives her mother is withering. Daddy is no longer part of the game. He's fallen off the family radar.

28

Two months ago

It's been a hard shift. She did three PT clients back-to-back, listening to their worries, thinking about what exercises would be best for them, modifying any they found too difficult. Showing them again because they weren't listening the first time. She taught her own aerobics class and covered for JJ's conditioning session. Then she had to clear the upstairs studio after the ditzy instructor leading the Movement for Actors course failed to put anything away, or wipe anything down, as per usual. Debs stacked mats and mopped up the sweat, neediness and broken dreams of the wannabe thespians. By the time she gets home, she's as wrung out as the gym mop.

He's working late at the office. Again.

After her shower, she wraps up in the big purple dressing gown her sister bought her and slumps on the sofa. She spends a lot of time like this at night, after the kids are in bed, knackered, hugging Lulu to stop herself feeing lonely. The silence is disturbing, a shock after the cacophony of music and shouting in classes and the noises at home: Pat-Pat's shrieks and bangs; Lulu yowling along to Dolly's singing.

Debs yearns for the quiet murmur of civilised adult conversation, an occasional meal together. Is that too much to ask?

She misses her evening Pilates classes. Marc paid for the course after Dolly was born. When she started teaching, even though the isolated moves were a challenge for someone so used to high-energy sessions, she found she enjoyed the company of other young mums like her trying to get their bodies and pelvic floors back in shape. An hour all to themselves.

Initially, he was supportive, staying home with his daughter while she was working at the gym, cooking for her. But then his meetings might overrun, or there'd be too much traffic – or, or, or – and he'd not get back in time. They had a big row about him letting her down. He reasoned, his hands not hitting the table, yet making emphatic chopping movements towards it, that his time was not negotiable, that's how he earned the 'big bucks', suggesting she should simply give up teaching because it wasn't like they needed the extra income.

She shouted back, 'Not everything's about bastard money!' although, obviously, most of it is.

Then, thanks to an armistice – a holiday with Dolly in the Algarve, at a family resort with a babysitting service and mojitos on tap – Pat-Pat came along. Evening classes were 'put on hold' and have been 'on hold' for three years.

Lulu has become her companion in the long hours after the kids are settled. When she was little, Debs wanted to be a vet. Now she realises she just wanted to cuddle animals, not cut them up. Stroking Lulu calms her. The dog gazes up at her with adoring eyes, which both affirm Debs' wonderful heart and soul, yet also enquire, *Might there be any sausages hidden about your person?*

She didn't want babysitters looking after the kids so she could go to work in the evenings. She and Kelly had spent enough time ostensibly being supervised by some random teenager (usually more intent on grappling with a boyfriend on the sofa than keeping an eye on them) when their mam was out doing her shifts. Eventually, they started living above the pubs where Mam worked, which meant she could pop upstairs now and then to check on them.

Debs misses her kids when she's not with them.

Marc agrees about the babysitters. He's not used the word 'lonely', but everything he's told her about the nights his mother 'tootled off' to the theatre or the opera, leaving him by himself to play his videogames, has made her promise herself that they will both be there for their kids.

They've never talked about it as such, but then they don't discuss a lot. He imposes no-go areas in conversations. There have been all sorts of misunderstandings thanks to their different views on parenting.

For instance, she'd suggested Dolly might go to private school later on, because she'd heard from one of her clients that the nearest secondary was full of drugs, albeit better-quality stuff compared with what she and Kelly had had access to growing up, but he'd put his foot down.

'And we will never' – hand chop – 'ever' – hand chop – 'send either of them to boarding school!'

'Well, yeah, obviously,' said Debs, who'd never even considered it.

She'd loved his fingers then.

Now she has to make all the decisions. She can't engage him

when it comes to the kids. Recently, she can't interest him in anything much. It's like he's disappearing.

And now she's so lonely and so wrung out.

She's settled in front of the telly watching that god-awful *Sex and the City* film, the second one, risking DVT so as not to disturb Lulu, who's crushed against her side with her paws hooked over Debs' right leg.

Too tired to go to bed.

She mutes the adverts when they come on – that's how shattered she is, she's watching it on pleb TV – scrolling through her phone for a bit, before giving in and laying her head against a cushion. And it comes across her again, the weird foreboding.

The fear begins in her chest. It always does. Her lungs constrict as if under some external force, like a hoop of iron tightening around a beer barrel. Her head starts swimming. The muddied feeling of dread intensifies.

And she senses the thing behind her.

The feeling is so strong she daren't turn around. She gnaws at her nail, deliberately staring hard at the TV screen, as the atmosphere charges with some odd static interference. The pressure in the room seems to plummet.

Suddenly, Lulu hurtles off the sofa yapping like a maniac, nearly giving her a bloody heart attack and she whirls round to find ... nothing.

There is no boy.

When she's off her head with fatigue, she imagines she

glimpses him in her peripheral vision. Blond. Skinny. Nothing like Pat-Pat. When she looks, there's nothing there.

But the absence is intense. Something *was* there, she knows.

29

4.53 a.m., 24 December

Worried about Lulu's paws and her own bare feet, Debs scrambles for the dustpan and brush in the cupboard under the sink, sweeping up the scattered shards of glass like she's in a race.

He watches her for several seconds before turning away and pacing four steps forward and four steps back, the length of the kitchen.

Lulu trots towards Marc, wary, but ever hopeful of an outing. Are they going for a walk? Yes? Yes? *Walkies?* Her whole body wags.

'No Lulu! Basket! Jesus, Marc!' He's oblivious of the dog. He continues his silent march. 'Will you grab her? She'll cut herself. Give me a hand. For fuck's sake. Come on! Please?'

And there's something so Cinderella about the scene: her on her knees in the middle of the night, cleaning up his mess!

So, after she clambers up from the floor and has wrapped the glass in a wodge of kitchen towel and an old carrier bag and rammed it in the overpriced bin from the Conran Shop (who the hell needs a designer bin?) and he's still stalking around the kitchen, useless, absent, she says, 'Sort that!' and flings the dust-pan towards him.

He punches it away. Then he's right up in her face again, demanding, 'How dare you! What do you think you're playing at?'

She doesn't reply. She can't reply because as she turns away from him, she notices what's on the worktop, just along from the bottle of sleeping pills.

Dolly and Pat-Pat's mugs. Her fairy princess mug, his Thomas the Tank Engine one. Old school, her kids. The jar of Green and Black's hot chocolate, a spoon. All in a neat row.

The way the items are laid out, lined up on parade, awaiting inspection, makes her knees weaken.

30

Five years ago

Their social life withered after Dolly came along. Of course it did. They still entertained his business contacts, but they had precious little quality time for themselves. Debs started nagging about date nights, trying to make the best out of losing her evening classes. When Marc ignored her, she refused to host any more client dinners unless he took her out.

'It's part of the job, Deborah. You know that.'

'Hire a chef, then,' she snapped. 'Or get yourself a trophy wife to butter your mangetout and a girly on the side who'll bite your balls and call you Daddy while you're at it. If you want someone to bend over backwards for you, I'll get you some numbers from the Pole Fitness class.'

'That's not what I want.'

'What do you want then?'

'Just—' He deflated.

'What? Bloody what, Marc?'

'Just ... not this.'

*

He manages an afternoon. He announces he's taking her to an exhibition. She's wrong-footed. So many things it could be – ancient art, modern art.

It's a videogame exhibition.

They wander through rooms with flashing lights and inter-active bits and bobs and kids filling in worksheets and a bunch of Italian girls with their arms round each other, giggling and taking selfies.

Marc's eyes are like saucers.

Debs recognises some of the titles she's seen in his study: *The Last of Us*, which at least seems to have a story in between the predictable zombie violence; *No Man's Sky*, retro sci-fi land-scapes the backdrop to sporadic space battles.

She studies the exhibits and fails to understand. Why does he find this world so compelling? Why would he think she'd want to see this?

He doesn't say much but stands in front of the giant screens and storyboards as if they're holy relics. And he's so earnest, she realises he must be trying to communicate something.

'Do you want me to dress up like Lara Croft?'

No reply.

'Princess Leia? We can get the bagels at the café.'

Not the place to take the piss, apparently. She gives him a few minutes. She listens to a couple of geeks debate 'inherent morality' versus 'poetic intent' in *Red Dead Redemption* and rolls her eyes.

She had no idea.

*

This is his least pernicious drug of choice, something he uses to quieten his inner demons. Tiny jolts of dopamine. Worlds over which he has some control; a demigod of his own design, in worlds he helps shape. An antidote to the crushing, Sisyphean demands of the office: death by a thousand paper cuts.

She'll never understand his high scores.

Glancing at her hard-set face in the muted light of the museum, Marc feels totally alone.

Pat-Pat can already manipulate his dad's Xbox controller, but Debs isn't so worried about him getting hooked on *Fortnite* or whatever when he's a bit older, because there were plenty of things apart from videogames that gave her the willies when she was a kid. Violence is nothing new in fairy tales. *The Goose Girl*, *Hansel and Gretel*; nightmares about being locked in a barrel with spikes inside, thrown into an oven by a witch, thanks to the delightful imaginations of the Brothers Grimm.

Smashing glasses downstairs in a pub—

Debs resents the games because they take Marc out of real life, her life, where the kids need this, or demand that, and she has to deal with their shit, literal and metaphorical, every single day. Alone. What about her needs? Just once it would be nice if he asked how she was, wanting an actual answer, not a 'fine', which he takes as permission to tune out.

Men play these games, not just kids. Blokes Marc's age, some with jobs and families, married to real live women.

Videogames aren't her thing. Those worlds, violent as they are, contain nothing of the real threat closing time generated some nights. She didn't need to pretend to escape monsters when she and Kel were terrified in the flat above the pub. Glasses were thrown and men's voices boomed threats downstairs as she and her sister huddled together under the bed sheets watching flashing blue lights pulsing through from outside the window.

And, for the millionth time, she felt the bloody unfairness that only people like Marc got to play. It's fine to waste time and mess about if you're a man, blinkered against the grindingly dull, essential stuff that needs sorting. But, if that stuff nags at you – if there's no milk in the fridge, if you're a *mother* – there isn't time to play, unless you're trying to entertain your kids, which is a job in itself. She's not been able to have a wee with the toilet door closed for *years*. And if you have to scrimp and save and sweat and slave to put food in your kids' mouths, when would you have the bloody time? And, no, she's not back *there*, back *then*, but old habits die hard and it's too easy to channel her mam when she's this tired.

At the exhibition, she heard some nerd banging on about Jung and depression and the healing power of play and she felt guilty. Perhaps Marc was feeling down. So, she suggested they go for a drink and have a game of pool together on the way home, because she'd arranged for Dolly to have a sleepover and they had the night to themselves for once.

They ended up in an old-style pub in Camden, early doors, quiet. She's good at pool, but she let him win the first couple of games. He was in a top mood after the exhibition and with a couple of drinks inside them, they both softened. She knew he was watching her bend over the pool table, and she gave him the look over her shoulder and he smiled and came to stand behind her, pressing himself against her and she went all gooey.

They had another round, and on the way back from the loo she spotted Peter Andre come in with a big group of lads and rushed up to him gabbling how she could grate cheese on his six-pack, but it wasn't Peter Andre, just a random tiny Cypriot guy, and Mark didn't even know who Peter Andre was and she got the giggles and he laughed with her. They had another drink, and she sang 'Mysterious Girl' loudly and badly and Marc grabbed her and kissed her to shut her up.

She licked his neck and whispered in his ear. He joined her in the disabled loo two minutes after she went in.

They didn't say much to each other on the Tube on the way back. She laid her head against his shoulder as he played some numbers game on his phone and Debs tried to read a piece about rowing classes being the new fitness fad in the *Metro*.

Separate retreats.

It might have been an allotment, a working men's club, a shed. A tennis club or golf for the better off. Groups who absent themselves at Spearmint Rhino, football practice, darts.

Men are always missing in action.

Kelly and Debs know about these absences. Both have father-shaped gaps in their lives.

Kelly's dad had a sequence of other women, multiple families, sons and daughters scattered around Derby, Macclesfield, Chesterfield, Leicester. Birthdays were a hit-and-miss affair.

Kelly never seemed that bothered either way. Debs isn't sure if Kel's in contact with her dad, a lorry driver, any more. He didn't turn up to their mam's funeral, so probably not. They'd expected he might make an appearance on *Jeremy Kyle* one day, before that went tits up.

There were a couple of contenders for Debs' old man.

One potential candidate she actually met twice during his short periods out on bail. Then he was sent down again, GBH the last time. She was glad. It meant she didn't have to worry on Shirley's behalf. Their mam not only had low standards when it came to blokes, she managed to limbo under them on a fairly regular basis.

The other no-mark never laid eyes on her. Total absence. OD before she was born; only twenty-seven.

Circumstances dictated that she wouldn't miss either.

But she does miss Marc. She misses the promise that he'd be there for her, in sickness and health and all that jazz. She resents the time he spends in his own worlds with aliens and punks and stupid girls with giant eyes and giant breasts, in downtown LA, the Wild West, outer space, anywhere but Muswell Hill, which is hardly grim reality, is it?

She often wants to shout, 'They're drawings! Grow up!'

31

5.00 a.m., 24 December

'Were you going to make breakfast?' That'd be a first in God knows how long. 'Was it a treat, the hot chocolate?'

His anger seems to wither. She sees how he sinks back into himself.

'Answer me, Marc!'

He doesn't respond.

'Why are the kids' mugs out?'

There's no reaction. He won't talk to her, so she talks herself down. It's Christmas Eve morning. He was making the kids hot chocolate. But his silence makes her anxious, winding her up. He might as well be holding his breath like Dolly used to when she didn't get her own way as a toddler.

'Tell me what's going on.'

He won't even look at her.

She can't stop herself lashing out, 'For fuck's sake! Talk to me, or you can get out of this house right now!'

The statement shocks her as much as him.

The challenge seems to wound him. He abandons the

bottle of vodka, crosses to the fridge and slides back down to the floor.

And this confuses her. Despite the dread biding its time deep in her guts, the way he crumples elicits a deep maternal response. Against her better judgement, she goes to him, kneels, and puts her arms around him.

But then, she's always tried to save him. It's hard-wired. Just like at school. No matter that she and Kelly weren't top of the playground pecking pile, there was always some poor sod worse off than them.

Stephen Woolley in Kelly's class – Stinky Steve-o – the poor kid hit puberty before any other lad. Kelly told their mam he'd been going round showing *it* to the girls. Their mam laughed and chanted, 'Stephen Woolley had a five-foot willy and he showed it to the girl next door. She thought it was a snake and hit it with a rake and now it's only two-foot four.'

And she'd told Kel to smack it with a ruler.

Debs felt sorry for poor old Steve-o. It's not like she fancied him or anything, she was only eight, but she had embarrassing dreams where she'd brush and cut his hair and clean his glasses, which were always filthy and crooked. She imagined him in the right sort of clothes, not the baggy hand-me-downs he got from his older brother William (Willy Woolley, for Christ's sake). It was that sort of family.

The Woolleys lived in a caravan on some waste ground near the bike factory. 'Over my dead body,' vowed Shirley, would Debs and Kel be allowed to doss down in some caravan, 'like a bunch of sodding gypsies.' With a soothing lungful of Silk Cut, she added, 'If we get to that stage, just shoot me.'

Debs would secretly watch Steve-o at school dinner times, being pelted with bits of cheese and baked beans and bread, wishing she could help him. She had to stop herself going over to his table to hug him.

Marc wraps his arms around her now. He hides his head, nuzzling into her neck and hair.

A bird trills somewhere outside. It's still a couple of hours before dawn, but it's already singing its heart out. Streetlights confuse them. Debs wonders if they die of exhaustion. She wonders if she might go the same way.

The sweetness of the sound makes her want to cry. If she can hold on for the dawn chorus, nothing will feel so bad then. Daylight will make it all seem better. But it's only just gone five. How long will it be before the sun comes up?

She knows she's kidding herself.

She used to play the same game as a kid, hope rising with the smoke from her mam's first fag of the day; Debs and Kel munching the morning's toast, marge and jam (white bread, banned by Marc), laughing at their mam bleating on about her 'banging head', believing the morning sun might shine on them along with the righteous, and that day would be a better day than the one before.

The weight of Marc is heavy against her chest as he clings to her. She tries to shift position, but slips, tumbles on to her side and then they're both lying on the floor, Marc half-sprawled on top of her.

And she could go to sleep right there.

Two years ago – maybe even one year ago when things seemed to be getting better – she might have laughed. He might have laughed. A different life.

But now she feels him harden against her. His need – always more insistent than her own. And her heart hardens in response.

32

5.05 a.m., 24 December

Dolly smiles in her sleep as the dream unfolds.

'Play with me.'

Lulu can talk! Dolly holds her paws and says, 'What do you want to play?'

'Princesses!' says Lulu.

'Boring!' shouts Dolly. 'Let's go to Tamara's and play *The Greatest Dancer.*'

Lulu stands on her hind legs and they rock and roll for a bit like Nana Shirley showed her.

Then she sees a unicorn in the garden. She's not supposed to go on the grass when it's wet because it gets her shoes dirty and then she leaves footprints on Mummy's floor that she's *only-just-bloody-cleaned*. But it's a real unicorn!

She unlocks the door and the sun is shining and it's not wet at all.

'Hello, Dolly!' says the unicorn.

The unicorn can talk like Lulu! It must be magic.

But then the bad thing starts. She sees a dark giant at the

bottom of the garden looming against the black bark of the twisted tree and it's night-time and there's a scary noise and she tries to hide as the unicorn runs away.

Dolly is actually Dolores, although no one has ever really called her that. Even Jeanne greets her with, 'Well hello, Dolly!' thinking herself mighty waspish.

Marc insisted on the 'proper spelling'. He almost campaigned for the name. He became misty-eyed when he gazed down at the prune-like alien in Debs' arms and pronounced 'Dolores!' like a prayer.

Debs loved the old-time glamour the name evoked, but mainly she thought of Delores De Lago, the toast of Chicago, one of Bette Midler's inventions. The image from her mam's video, when Bette makes her entrance dressed as a mermaid, whizzing on stage in an electric wheelchair with her tail folded neatly beneath her, still makes Debs chuckle. Her mam loved both Bettes, Davis and Midler.

Dolores actually refers to Our Lady of Sorrows – Debs googled it. Hardly fitting for the bundle of energy and pizzazz that's her daughter. Dolly is a performer at heart; much more the Divine Miss M than Our Lady of anything.

Why Marc chose the name she doesn't know. At the time he said that he'd just 'always liked it'.

Debs will never discover that it has something to do with his ex-fiancée, the ethereal Hetty: a snatched holiday; whispered passionate promises in a Spanish church. Broken promises.

*

Do not be fooled by the princess dress. Inside the pink-packaged poppet, Dolly is, as Nana Shirley called it from the off, 'A. Little. Madam.'

When she was smaller, long before Pat-Pat's arrival challenged her rightful place centre stage, Dolly's toddler tantrums were displayed by holding her breath. There must have been a pearl diver somewhere in the ancestral heritage, because Dolly could do this for A Very Long Time. Debs was once reduced to slapping the back of the child's knees when she felt her daughter, going puce in the face, might burst a blood vessel, immobile and apoplectic on the pavement outside Marks & Spencer. They went straight home without stepping inside the store, Debs wobbly, fearful of terrible judgements and retribution (in Muswell Hill terms, a Paddington hard stare or passive-aggressive tut).

Her daughter skipped all the way back.

That phase passed and Dolly became the apple of her daddy's eye; her mummy's funny little friend. She would twirl around the house trilling nonsense words and Debs thought, *If you could bottle that energy, that joie de vivre, you'd be a millionaire.*

But after her brother came along, a cloud obscured the joyful rainbow child. She pivoted to full-on nightmare mode for a while.

When Pat-Pat displeased her, she planted her feet in perfect Mary Poppins configuration, her hands on her tiny hips, and shrieked at the top of her voice. She was clever enough not to do this in front of her daddy, but she had no such compunction regarding her mother. Her wrath knew no bounds. She competed hard for attention.

Now Dolly rarely throws such fits. When Lulu arrived, she became infinitely patient with the dog and she started mothering her little brother. Her current 'favourite thing in the whole wide world' is brushing his hair. To be fair, Pat-Pat will sit for almost forty seconds at a time to endure this. Thankfully, when he's had enough, she can then brush Lulu's fur and the animal will lap that up for hours.

Dolly also learned not to snatch things away from Pat-Pat's fists, realising he'd hit or bite in retaliation.

Unfortunately, since Tamara, her new 'bestie,' inserted herself on the scene, Dolly seems to have re-cast herself as some reality-show diva, exaggerating demands and confrontations as if starring in her own drama. Luckily, she can't keep this up for long, turns on a sixpence, and reverts to sweetness and light, snuggling up on the sofa with Debs, Pat-Pat and Lulu for a 'big squish'.

Debs loves these moments, but Marc is annoyed by them, somehow. He watches them on the sofa and his face changes. Sometimes she wonders if he's a bit jealous.

Dolly once asked her Nana Shirley, on one of her grandma's rare trips 'down south', why she talked 'funny'.

'Because I'm common, duck,' said Shirley. 'Rough as old arse-holes, me.'

The girl laughed, delighted. Dolly and her gran were like naughty kids playing together.

'Mam! Please don't swear in front of her.'

'Ooo, hark at Miss Hoity-bleeding-toity. Din't do you and Kel any harm.'

Perhaps not, although Debs finds she has to constantly edit herself, reining in her language when she's teaching classes, instructing her PT clients, and at all times in front of the kids, their friends and the yummy mummies at the school entrance.

'Mam! Please don't smoke in the bloody house!'

Shirley pulled away from lighting a fag on the Bosch gas hob, making a 'Who, me?' face.

Dolly sang 'arseholes-arseholes-arseHOLES' on a regular basis for weeks after that visit.

Dolly and Pat-Pat have transcended Kelly and Debs' heritage. A different class and miles away from their gran, Debs has created a brave new world for her son and daughter – full-on Enid Blyton: balanced nutrition and reading; shoes that don't pinch their toes; long-haul flights; developmental milestones. The kids don't even talk with the same accent as Debs does.

All those lovely opportunities Dolly and Pat-Pat will have in London; opportunities Debs fought for tooth and nail. Better start and all that.

Pat-Pat, God bless him, is an altogether simpler proposition than his sister. Strong and loud, bombing around like a super-charged Duracell bunny – a straightforward, robust boy. It's not that he doesn't like glitter and pink, but he shows a distinct lack of interest in unicorns and mermaids, and his colouring approach, unlike Dolly's careful drawing-inside-the-lines style, is, as Marc puts it, 'A tad de Kooning.'

Mind games are not Pat-Pat's forte. Her lad asks for what he wants. Cries if he doesn't get it. Slams down a brick or a fist in displeasure. Flings himself into your arms if he feels upset in any way. If only he had a volume control, he'd be a dream.

His ambitions often outrun his physical abilities. Cuts and bruises are a regular occurrence. His sister has a kind heart in these instances. She'll sit with her brother and rock him, kissing it better when he's hurt his knee, his elbow, just as she'll sit in Lulu's basket to stroke and soothe her when she's anxious.

She also senses when Debs is down and gives her a hug, and when her mummy is really sad, she climbs on to the sofa to give her an 'extra big squish'. Sometimes Debs pulls a sad face just to indulge in these sessions. Recently she hasn't had to fake it.

Marc used to be enamoured with his daughter. She could make him laugh, back when such a thing was possible, before the promotion, before Whitley Bay, before everything went to shit. During one ballet school performance four years ago, in a chorus of Easter bunnies, Dolly's tights slipped down so her fluffy tail dangled, swinging between her legs like a single testicle, and Marc had laughed so hard there were tears in his eyes.

The closest Debs ever saw Marc come to losing his temper in public was during a rare trip to the supermarket *en famille* (before Pat-Pat) in the large Sainsbury's on the edge of Newquay as they stocked up for a week's break in Porth. A group of lads dressed as dinosaurs (most probably on a stag do, but in Cornwall you can never be sure) were racing trolleys laden with beers around the busy aisles and one of them clipped Dolly with his tail as he scooted by. Their girl went down squealing.

If the whole gang hadn't rallied around the offender, offering effusive apologies, Marc may well have erupted. The lad bought Dolly a 'sorry' Cornetto, so she was well chuffed.

Debs had been so shocked by Marc's aggressive reaction that time – a volley of threats and out-of-character profanities directed at the youth – she'd forgotten to lash out herself. But that doesn't mean she wouldn't kill anyone who tried to hurt one hair on her daughter's beautiful head.

Dolly might appear small and thus cute and harmless, but the bonny curls, like Debs' own, suggest a pinch of rebelliousness. Her soft little belly belies the pure steel within. Debs' heart is gladdened that her daughter appears to be so resilient. Sturdy. It bodes well for her future. But it means she's sometimes a bloody nightmare to wrangle, herd and generally muster.

The key to Dolly is to get her onside, via whatever psychological tools you have to hand. Too clever now for straight-up blackmail or bribery, you somehow must convince her that an action is her idea before she'll do it.

Might do it.

Debs admires her child's will. But this is not the child you want in the scene right now.

And right now, Debs sees her beautiful, brilliant daughter standing in the hallway, staring at her mummy, who is wide-eyed, messy, splayed underneath her daddy on the kitchen floor.

33

5.09 a.m., 24 December

'Mummy—'

Debs flinches like she's been tasered. She feels Marc go limp against her.

From her tangled position on the tiles, she manages, 'Dolly Dumpling! What is it, sweetheart? Did you have a bad dream?'

The girl ignores her saccharine act and says louder, 'Mummy?'

Quite rightly, her daughter has a good bullshit detector. She wants to know why Mummy and Daddy are wrestling on the kitchen floor in the middle of the night.

Debs tries to modulate her voice. 'What are you doing up so early?' She slowly extricates herself from Marc's leaden arms.

'I wasn't earwigging, Mummy,' protests Dolly, 'I promise.' She yawns widely.

Her new favourite phrase. Debs has seen her telling off both her brother and the dog for 'earwigging'; one of Shirley's expressions. Dolly is at the age of secrets, although hers are innocent.

But, oh, her Dolly Dumpling – the best part of her; the part where nothing bad has ever happened, or ever will. Not on her watch. She's everything she'd hoped her to be. Fierce and funny and fearless.

And Debs wishes with all her might, as she stumbles to her feet, that her daughter might just un-see this unholy mess and go back to her old life upstairs.

Dolly doesn't move from the doorway. 'Are you playing?'

'Yes, love. We're playing.'

Debs had loved the snow when she was a kid. It was bloody brilliant. She'd thrown snowballs with Kelly, skidded on it, made snow angels, rolled in it.

When she was a bit older, it was a great excuse to flirt with the lads as they stuffed handfuls of cold excitement down the back of her neck, everything alive and vital and thrilling. The light on those snowy mornings! Brighter, full of promise.

In London, there's rarely proper snow. Dirty slush is the best it offers. Too many dogs, feet, car exhausts; ice to catch you out.

And the snowflakes don't do snow, do they? Any excuse for a duvet day, the poor, tender little souls she trains. She and Kelly had yomped through blizzards to schools that were never shut, shoving each other into huge snowdrifts on the way. The buses always ran, but even if they didn't, you still turned up. You just left a little bit earlier and walked, that's all.

A snow flurry nowadays is another layer of stress. Will the car start? How much time does she need to wrestle the kids into extra layers and manage their high-octane enthusiasm on the way to school and nursery? Will school and nursery be open? How many clients will cancel?

She wonders how it was that her mam had never seemed pissed off with her and Kel on snow days. She'd not minded when they mithered at her to let them mess about in it. She'd let them go out whenever they wanted, then shove their gloves and boots next to the radiators to dry when they got in, perished and giddy.

Or she'd be out with them, yawping and laughing and throwing herself in the drifts and chucking snowballs at them and building a snowman with a carrot for a willy and playing and playing and playing.

What happened to Debs to stop her playing?

Nothing's fun any more.

'Yes, we're playing.'

She repeats it in case she can convince herself.

34

Two weeks ago

A couple of weeks before the schools break up for Christmas and both kids are gearing up on the excitement scale. Dolly is currently gyrating around the central island, singing enthusiastically and tunelessly.

And suddenly, Debs hears, 'My pussy is on fire!'

She stops wiping coffee grounds out of the double sink. 'What did you just say, love?'

Louder this time, 'My pussy is on FI-RE!'

Debs' first thought is cystitis. Her second, *Where the bloody hell did she pick up a phrase like that?* She attempts to keep the surprise out of her voice to ask, 'What do you mean, chick?'

If Dolly realises she's provoked a reaction she'll probably keep on at it.

Her girl doesn't answer and doesn't stop twirling. 'I'm giving you body-ody-ody!' she trills. There's lots of hair tossing. And then she plunges to the ground, announcing, 'Slut drop!' flinging one arm in the air and grinning.

On a hunch Debs probes, 'Does Tamara say that?'

She's ignored. She waits a few seconds as Lulu joins Dolly to roll around the kitchen floor that, for the third time that morning, needs a good clean.

She ventures, 'Did you watch something at Tamara's like that?'

Her daughter looks blank. The moment has passed.

Debs thinks, *Shit, shit, shit*, but of course doesn't say it. She's trained herself not to swear so much in front of the kids. She does well most of the time.

Lulu pads over and makes Bonio eyes at her.

'Can we go out and look for chuggy pigs?'

'It's too damp, love.'

'Pleeease!'

Dolly flings both arms around her waist and Debs caves after the fourth 'please'. She peels off her rubber gloves, pulls Pat-Pat into his miniature duffel coat while Dolly puts on her bright-red ladybird mac. Dolly grabs her brother's hand and swings his arm back and forth to make him smile and sings 'Pat-Pat-PAT, Pat-Pat-PAT,' to the tune of *Postman Pat* and they trudge out into the misty garden, which is looking more than a little frayed round the edges. Like Debs herself.

Later, she tries to discuss Dolly's new language issue with Marc and is dismissed with a curt, 'Your department, I think, darling.'

Of course, it's Tamara. It's always bloody Tamara, thanks to Tamara's bloody mother Ruby, a pink-haired, right-on Earth Mother, who gets right on Debs' tits.

Since Nasreen, Dolly's previous best friend, was branded

'basic' by Tamara and consequently shunned, Tamara's been the love of her daughter's life. Nasreen's terrible sin? Wearing 'boring' clothes, according to guess bloody who. New prejudices are blossoming in Dolly's playground, not on the basis of skin colour, but on what adorns those skins. Social pariahs thanks to a fashion faux pas. Debs can't remember it being that bad when she was a kid, at least not at that age. They're not even tweenagers yet and it's full-on *Mean Girls*.

The next day, negotiating the school gates free-for-all, she asks Ruby what the girls have been watching on TV lately. Dolly goes to play with her friend for an hour on Tuesdays after school, when Debs sees her regular PT client, Annie (postnatal, comfort eater, block bookings), who she's trained right through a couple of broken relationships, full-on Bridezilla mode, pregnancy and recent motherhood.

'Dunno really,' drawls Ruby.

Debs takes a breath and pushes down the urge to smack Ruby in the mouth. 'Might they have seen anything inappropriate?'

'Oh, Zig and I believe they monitor their own level of appropriate.'

Zig is Ruby's equally useless partner. They share a taste in tribal tattoos and idiotic parenting theories. Anti-vaxxers.

'But you wouldn't let them watch porn!' snaps Debs.

'No. We don't agree with the sexual politics of most mainstream porn,' says Ruby, hoisting her hessian shopper on one shoulder and her enhanced sense of self-righteousness on the other.

Debs snaps, 'You think!'

She bloody hates Dolly going round to Ruby's house, which she secretly dubs 'the Tofu Shack'. Marcus shares her aversion to Ruby and Zig when their paths cross (infrequently) at a school parents' evening or sports day. Plus, he doesn't like having Tamara at theirs on the rare weekends when he's home, rather than away on some work jaunt. 'Perhaps I'm allergic to her,' he grumbles when challenged. And Debs understands. She can't stand the girl. She hopes Tamara doesn't notice but assumes the kid is too self-obsessed to notice anything much. Like her bloody mother...

Ruby is ignoring all Debs' attempts to draw her on the TV shows the kids are watching. The only thing for it will be to try to rearrange Annie's personal training session, because she's not having Dolly's lack of supervision playing on her mind; she's up to her full quota of worries.

And if she loses her client as a result, that will be another resentment on the growing, festering pile, because bloody Marc could come home early on bloody Tuesdays. Instead, he makes time for his weekly squash game with one of three chaps in his management group. It's a 'team-building exercise' and thus sacrosanct.

Some days she feels she might as well be a single parent.

Last Christmas, Marc's big 'making an effort' suggestion was a trip to the North Pole to meet the real Father Christmas, but they'd agreed to wait until Pat-Pat was older. He'd also helped a bit with the shopping and cooking and went way over the top with the gifts. But that was the only time. She's usually the one in charge of Christmas for the kids. This year it's more noticeable.

Dolly and Pat-Pat are overwhelmed with wall-to-wall pre-Christmas parties and hyped-up expectations. She has to deal with them when they're tired, mardy and demanding, recovering from the latest seasonal cold, or the consequences of over-indulging in the Roses and Quality Street that get passed round playgrounds like crack cocaine at this time of year. As well as ferrying them around, she's also attended the school and nursery concerts (nothing as simple as a Nativity nowadays) with no sign of Marc. He's been pretty much absent for the last six months.

When Kelly phoned and asked, 'You okay?' as she does every time she calls and at some point in the conversation added out of politeness, 'How's knob-cheese?' in a different, not-really-giving-a-toss tone, Debs ranted, 'I bet he still thinks there's a fucking Santa Claus. And why wouldn't he, Kel? The presents appear by magic, all wrapped and labelled. They're laid under the tree that I bought, and I got delivered and I bloody decorated.'

Her sister made 'there, there' noises from Nottingham.

'And his name miraculously appears on all the Christmas cards. I even have to buy something tasteful, by which he means expensive, for his cow-bag mother and big him up like he's split the fucking atom if he manages to sign his name on the gift tag. I swear, sometimes I could bloody stab him!'

Now she's almost too tired to rant. Instead, the anger lies simmering deep in her stomach, along with the leaden weight of grief.

The first Christmas without her mam. The first Christmas she wonders if she'd be better off without him—

He's been useless about her mam dying. Precious little eye contact. No questions. A ninja in passive-aggression and avoidance techniques, Marc creates a force field around himself, in case he's called upon to comment, or volunteer support, or simply acknowledge the emotional arena. But then, empathy is never top of the list of requirements for the armed forces, is it?

She has clients like that. They don't have the balls to say, 'I don't want to work with you any longer because you're too loud, too tough, too in my face.' Some don't even have the guts to cancel. They simply don't turn up one day, send a text, and she never sees them again.

It riles her, cowardice, running away.

But that isn't as bad as the men who 'pop out' for a packet of fags and execute the grand disappearing act.

And, yes, it usually is blokes. Men fuck up more than women, they just do. Equality doesn't come into it. Most murderers are men. Men are guilty of more violence of any kind however you look at it or juggle the figures, however right-on you are.

Marc wouldn't have a clue what Santa's bought his kids this year. He won't have to fake a surprised reaction when they open the gifts.

But it's worse than that. His sullen silence, the looks, the judgements, it's become a war of attrition, like Chinese water torture. Only it wasn't Chinese, was it? Some bastard Italian invented that, some bastard bloke.

Drip, drip, drip. Wearing her down.

*

Marc's been even more hands-off with Dolly this year. Ever since her ninth birthday party back in May.

Dolly invited the usual group of friends around for her birthday do, plus the *amazing* Tamara. But Dolly did not want the suggested mermaid party. She announced that mermaid parties were 'for babies'. So, Debs had a rethink and planned the event for a Saturday when Marc wasn't at the office, so he could lend a hand. Not that he did.

Anyone might have thought it was Tamara's birthday as she conducted the proceedings, bossing around her devotees – the queen bee and her wannabes – the others traipsing round after her, agreeing to all her suggestions. Dolly was enthralled by her new glamorous friend.

Debs would love to be a fly on the wall when Zig and Ruby discuss their daughter's style, although she guesses they allow all forms of self-expression and the thigh-length boots adorning Tamara's skinny legs were probably ethically sourced vegan leather, aka plastic.

The games weren't a huge hit. The girls were much too sophisticated for Pass the Parcel, even though Debs had spent ages the night before wrapping glittery pens and hair slides in between every layer of tissue paper and then manipulating the music to stop so every child won something.

The thing they loved best was the disco. Debs had cleared the lounge, hauling furniture to the outside edges, and she'd hired a bubble machine and coloured lights that flashed in time with the music. Not only did the girls dance, dodging the obligatory helium balloons, in the shape of a golden 9, a pink 9, a multi-coloured cat, and two unicorns, they shrieked along to the lyrics, from 'Dancing Queen' to 'Single Ladies' and 'Shake It Off', an eclectic playlist featuring some of Debs' most popular Zumba tracks.

At some point, Tamara plugged in her own iPhone and Nicki Minaj blasted out 'Anaconda'.

The girls, who had been doing childish hand movements to 'Baby Shark' only minutes before, suddenly transformed into a troop of jaded lap dancers. Cue much twerking and grinding.

Marc somehow wandered into the room at the exact wrong moment, and stood startled, stock still as a maypole, as eight tiny harlots gyrated around him. Tamara was the most exuberant. She pouted. She thrust her tiny bottom in the direction of Marc's trousers. She flicked her long, pale-blonde hair and licked her lip-glossed mouth.

Watching this unfold, Debs realised she'd forgotten to breathe. Her mam would have known what to do, although, more likely, she'd have twerked along with them.

Marc stalled until Dolly joined her friend in his general crotch area and that broke the awful spell. Blushing, horrified, he somehow pushed the children away almost roughly and stumbled out into the kitchen. He hissed to her, 'Shut this down.'

'The party?'

'This *exhibition*. Yes.'

But Dolly—'

'Now!'

Debs was infuriated, although relieved that Dolly's wobbly tooth had survived the day.

*

123

The next week he banned Tamara from the house, branding her a 'terrible influence'.

'We can't stop Dolly from seeing her best friend,' reasoned Debs. 'It'll break her heart.'

'She can see her at school. I do not want her here.'

'But you know her mother's hopeless. She lets them watch anything they like.'

'Patently. You need to assert our boundaries with her.'

'I've already had a word. Ruby doesn't listen. She doesn't see a problem.'

'Your department. Deal with it how you see fit.'

End of discussion.

She can't remember doing anything like that dancing when she was Dolly's age. She and Kelly went to youth clubs and danced provocatively, but that was when they were teenagers. Okay, perhaps Debs was twelve. And she and her sister had both been a little promiscuous, at an age she really didn't want Dolly to start with all that.

She wonders if that was because she and Kel had helped their mam serve in pubs and collect glasses. Was it just where they lived, how they lived? Wasn't it just the way things went back there, back then?

Surely, one of the things she can protect her daughter from is that sort of shit. What's the point of sticking with Marc, working hard, saving, trying to get her into a good school, if not that?

*

Debs decides to tackle her daughter.

After dance class, Dolly ascends to her room like an empress, shedding netted petticoats, glittery shoes, sequined shrug and shiny, rainbow-hued backpack in her wake. Debs scurries behind collecting these accoutrements like an indentured servant.

As her daughter changes into her comfy tracksuit with the squishy unicorn horn on the hood, she tries to broach the subject, handing Pat-Pat the iPad to keep him quiet for a few minutes.

'You know when you dance like Tamara?'

'Like what?'

'Like they do in the music videos. That sort of dancing...'

'Like Cardi B?' Dolly launches into a routine, shaking her unruly curls and shimmying her tiny shoulders as they descend the stairs to the kitchen.

'Yes. Like that.' Debs can't help but smile. 'Can you not do that outside the house?' She pours the kids an apple juice each.

'Why? Not even in the garden?'

'I mean it's okay to dance like that here, in front of us, but not in front of anyone else.' She pours some filtered water into both glasses to dilute the sugar.

'Why?'

'Because it's ... some people might think it's not very nice.' Debs knows she's not handling this well. 'Some people might get the wrong idea.'

'What idea?'

She hands Pat-Pat his plastic beaker, deftly shifting the iPad to a place of safety in the same move. How can Debs tell Dolly without terrifying her?

'Will you promise me you won't dance like that outside the house, love? Just for me?' She braces for an onslaught of 'Why's.

'Okay, Mummy.' Dolly pirouettes away with her glass.

Sometimes Dolly likes to blindside her mummy by doing the unexpected.

35

5.10 a.m., 24 December

'Mummy and Daddy were having a cuddle, that's all.'

Marc rolls away to prop himself up against the fridge, like he's bloody magnetised. He says nothing. Even now he leaves her to deal with their daughter.

Lulu pads across from her basket to fuss Dolly. Debs strokes her daughter's hair. 'So, shall we go back up to bed?'

'I had a dream,' says Dolly. She doesn't so much as look at her father.

'What was it about, love?'

'It was a bad man in the garden. He'd come to hurt us. A giant—'

Debs guides her back towards the stairs. Realising she's being pushed, albeit gently, Dolly stops moving.

'Yes, love? What happened in the dream?'

'A big bad man who ... No.' She twirls her hair round her finger and pops a strand into her mouth. 'You've stopped my strain of thought.'

That's how Debs feels right now, *strain of thought*.

'Sorry, love, never mind, hey?' Debs resists the urge to tell her to stop sucking her hair. One of her mam's sayings comes to mind, 'It'll wrap around your heart and kill you stone dead.'

'Okay. Well, you go back to bed, hey chick?' Dolly doesn't move. A stand-off. 'If you do, I'll read you a story.'

She considers. 'Really?'

'Really.'

'A long one?'

'If you like.'

'You won't forget.'

'No, love.'

Her daughter still doesn't leave.

'I'll be up in a minute,' promises Debs, with no idea if she will. 'And then you can give me a big squish on the bed, hey?'

Dolly sighs pointedly and throws one of Debs' lines back at her: 'We'll see.' A dagger to her mother's heart.

She ushers the child out of the kitchen, kisses her on top of her head and watches her slowly climb the stairs with exaggerated steps, as a queen might ascend to the gallows.

When Debs comes back to the kitchen, she's hit by a smell – Marc's stale sweat and a whiff of Lulu's stress-pee – which turns her stomach. The dog looks guilty.

Debs takes a breath, tries to think. Marc's still on the floor, tuned out.

Again, her eyes are drawn back to Dolly and Pat-Pat's mugs on the side. And one horrible fear detaches itself to float clear of all the other messy fragments.

What have her kids got to do with this?

36

Ten years ago

'What do you mean?'

No conversation that starts with, 'What do you mean?' in that tone, ever ends with, 'Ah, thank you for explaining. Now I see more clearly what you mean and understand far better. Cup of tea?'

His pale eyes fix her with that grey assessing stare. Unreadable. Yet she can guess what he's itching to say, 'I know full well what you mean, I just can't fucking believe it!' although he wouldn't put it like that.

When they started dating, she insisted on having one dinner every so often where she paid, which means they're at Zizzi rather than somewhere he'd prefer. Somewhere more discreet, old school; somewhere charging a fortune for the vile cuts and offal they'd had to eat out of necessity when she was growing up: tripe and liver and other shite like that.

After an excruciatingly long pause, he continues, forcing questions out of a narrowed mouth, 'Are you sure?'

'Why would I say anything if I wasn't sodding sure?'

'Isn't it too early? You know, to tell?' He sits ramrod straight. His face remains chillingly still.

'Are you going to ask if it's yours next?'

'Don't be absurd, Deborah.'

He must be really narked, addressing her by her full name. It reminds her of her mam calling her in when she'd discovered she'd not done the dishes before gadding off to play.

But she's bloody angry too. Angry and a bit ashamed and scared. She fiddles with her water glass. 'I did a test.'

'Oh.'

'Yes. Fucking "Oh."'

He lowers his voice in case the couple at the next table can hear. Always considerate, always private. 'I didn't mean...'

She takes a gulp of water.

He takes an emphatic breath. 'What do you want to do?'

'It's hardly good timing, is it?'

'No, but—'

'But, if I decide to keep it, you'll stand by me and love it and all the bells and whistles?'

He pauses, mouth open, then splutters, 'Yes. Of course! Yes!'

And she realises he's not angry at all. He's fighting back tears!

He grabs her hand and kisses it – a move so old-fashioned it startles a laugh out of her.

And he bursts out, 'We're having a baby!' loud enough to make the woman sitting near them look up from her pizza. He takes a gulp of his wine, hand shaking. 'It's just a shock, that's all.'

She laughs. 'You can say that again.'

'I've always wanted children,' he says, sincere, emphatic. He rubs his eyes with the napkin. 'I've always imagined a boy and a girl. A family unit. Doing it right, you know? Being there for them. Giving them the best. A good start. But ... are you okay with it?'

Their neighbours have both stopped eating now, all ears. 'Okay with it? I'm spitting fucking feathers!'

And, right on cue, fat tears of relief splutter out of her stupid eyes and he leans across the table to kiss her, knocking over her water, and they're both laughing and crying and causing a scene but neither of them care.

Of course, he said and did all the right things.

He always did his duty.

'En-trap-ment,' said Jeanne, emphasising each syllable.

They had a row when she suggested a DNA test. 'Pay her off,' she added with a wave of her hand like she was wafting away a bluebottle. Well, not an argument, as such. He walked out. He'd taken enough flak from that bloody woman.

His mother called the next week suggesting a rapprochement. It was a rare occasion when she initiated contact, not like Deborah and her sister on the phone every single night, sometimes for hours at a time.

Civil, frigid relations were restored between mother and son.

He never admitted to Jeanne, or his future wife, that he felt a little ambushed.

The wedding is a small deal, on account of Debs' belly being a really big deal by then. A cheerful early spring wedding. A shotgun wedding. They've been together only ten months.

Kelly's partner Boz drives down Kelly, Shirley and Penny, his seven-year-old daughter from a previous relationship.

The night before the ceremony, the 'Northern contingent' tipsy in their Novotel, Boz dreams that he and Jason Statham get in their cars, a Ferrari and a Maserati, and tear up downtown Hong Kong or somewhere oriental with all them neon signs. Then they go to a bar and have tiny, graceful girls all over them. His looks a bit like Kel but with Debs-sized tits.

He doesn't mention the dream to Kel. She's always been jealous of her sister's bazookas. For a time, she considered getting hers done, although in the end they saved the money for IVF.

He was pissed off about the wedding, knowing Kelly would get misty-eyed about the frock and the whole shebang and start pushing again. Never going to happen. Once bitten and all that. Bloody ironic, given that he'd never wanted Penny in the first place. Not now, like. He loves the kid now, although her mum can fuck right off.

He can't stand Debs' bloke. Doesn't trust him. Poncing about with him and his squaddie mates on some ski slope was not his idea of fun, so he told him to shove his stag do, but polite, like. He doesn't fancy a cold holiday. A beach is more his cup of tea. And he doesn't like skiing. Well, he's never tried, but the slopes are full of snotty twats like Marc. Plus, he can't afford it. That's the excuse he used, and it's true. Every bit spent on the IV-bloody-F. For Kel, weren't it? He's got his Penny.

Boz still feels bad about the wedding. Not that anything was said. He's pretty sure Marc didn't mention anything to Debs because Kel's not said a word. Debs tells her sister bloody everything.

He'd had a bit to drink. They all did – it was a fucking wedding, weren't it? – and there were two or three of Marc's army mates totally cunted, like Shirley, who was a riot, as usual. Deb and Kel's mam went round the reception introducing herself as 'the Milf!' coughing and laughing, unlit fag in one hand, drink welded to the other.

A right laugh, Shirley. Life and soul.

No one on Marc's side seemed to be pissed in a good way. And things were said about 'pork-swording the old trollop' and how one posh twat wouldn't touch Shirley with the other one's dick, and Shirley, while a bit of a wildcard, was solid, salt of the earth, so Boz got involved and there was a bit of pushing and shoving and he told Marc to 'Fuck off out of it,' when he intervened and they'd squared up to each other, as much as he could with the great lanky twat looming over him.

One of the army knobs had pulled him back. Another led Marc away.

It wasn't as satisfying as lamping him would have been. But at the same time, he's sort of glad, because there'd have been consequences: Kel on at him for spoiling her sister's big day, perhaps. But also, because what he saw in Marc's eyes that night, drink aside, was something ... well psycho. Not hot rage like he felt, something cold. Like he'd bite your ear off for fun.

Later, he went outside for a fag, and he'd seen Marc surrounded by his chums. He heard one of the blokes say, 'Lay her right tonight and you can walk over her for the rest of your life.' They were all laughing. Then they were chanting, 'Do it! Do it!' and Marc was shaking his head and backing away but they were pushing and pulling him, but jokey, like, and he bent and snorted a line. He pulled away and rubbed his nose and caught Boz staring. They eyeballed each other but neither said a word.

And then Marc turned and out of nowhere punched one of his mates in the throat, so hard he buckled and collapsed, choking.

Debs couldn't drink at the reception. Didn't need to. She was high on the occasion.

Marc had stepped up. Didn't have to.

She always knew Dolly would be a dancer, how she bounced around inside her belly as she and Marc took the floor for their first dance, a few bars of Engelbert Humperdinck's 'The Last Waltz', segueing into a rousing rendition of Black Lace's finest three minutes, Debs leading everyone in the routine. It went down a bomb.

The first time Marc saw Debs rehearse a new track for her Zumba class, back when they first met, he was startled. She was so ... uncontained. She sweated and made mistakes and it didn't seem to matter. Debs didn't take herself seriously, but she was professional. She practised her tracks. She explained it was so she didn't have to think about the routine, so she could watch her participants and chivvy them along. She cared about her classes.

When she saw Marc watching, she took both his hands and

sat him on the sofa to wiggle her bum in his face, all the while giggling and singing and playing the fool.

He'd never been one for slapstick, but the way she enjoyed making fun of herself made him chuckle. Had he ever really chuckled before?

When he remembers his childhood, he can't remember lots of laughs. Nowadays, he'll smile at a particularly biting comment on *Have I Got News For You* or suppress a snigger if one of the office underlings makes a joke about the top brass.

He didn't mind it much when Debs teased him. It was always in private. She didn't take a pop at him in front of other people. She'd simply jolly him along to stop him taking himself too seriously. She liked to make him smile.

She decided they'd do a novelty dance at the wedding. 'It'll be funny with my bump and your left feet,' she announced.

And she'd actually persuaded him and rehearsed the puerile choreography with him.

He had no idea that everyone would join in at the reception. So many people seemed to know the words and they either recognised the hand movements or picked them up much quicker than he'd managed.

'Ag-a-doo-doo-doo, push pineapple, shake the tree!'

His mother-in-law really went for it. As wild as Debs was enthusiastic. Seeing Jeanne's reaction as she watched this mass display of unbridled glee, he actually threw back his head and guffawed.

Shortly after this most untraditional first dance, Jeanne claimed a headache and departed with an air kiss that barely grazed his cheek. That night, he genuinely didn't mind acting the fool in front of his friends and colleagues. Most of them were so wasted, they'd never remember.

It was all a revelation. Like Deborah's 'mam'. He'd never encountered anyone quite like her. Shirley looked nothing like a mother-in-law should, her dress indecently low-cut for a wedding, showing way too much cleavage and sunbed-crinkled skin. She blithely announced she was 'on the pull'. Twice he had to prise her fingers away from an old army chum, where she was affixed liked a cheap necklace, and steer her back to the bar.

'You'll look after her, right? Promise me.' Shirley's fingers dug into his wrist, surprisingly strong for hands so scrawny, the yellow nicotine stains harsh against the lurid pink nail varnish and over-sized plastic rings.

He answered, 'Of course.'

She spat back, 'Because if you don't, I'll hunt you down and tear your fucking heart right out your fucking ribcage.'

Then she laughed. His mother-in-law's mouth blurry, smudged, like the rest of her.

She was terrifying.

Yet, whenever he thinks of Shirley, he has to smile. That comment to Jeanne before they went into the church:

'Ooh, lovely hat, duck. I saw one a bit like it on the market. Good job I didn't get it, hey?' She blew a lungful of smoke into his mother's appalled face. 'We'd have looked like sisters!'

He and Debs didn't make love on their wedding night. They were both too tired, too content, almost. Yes, there'd been that unfortunate incident with the brother-in-law, and the wearing jokes about 'martial' and 'marital law', but that had soon blown over.

He had never felt freer in his life.

37

5.15 a.m., 24 December

Debs hears herself say, 'You know what Dolly's like. She might settle down again. But she might not. She could wake Patrick—' Babbling. He's brewing something in the silence, she can tell.

She tries, 'She might come down again.' And if she does, Debs needs to be prepared.

As she tries to walk past him, he grabs her ankle.

'No. Let me go up to her.'

She pulls her foot away and inches back. He gets to his feet, lumbering towards her. How drunk is he? How dangerous is he? He's bigger than her. Stronger. But he's got half a bottle of vodka on board and his reflexes are dulled because he's not slept properly in however many nights.

And he might have been trained with guns, but he didn't have fights like she did; so many scraps, grappling matches with a procession of little toerags who thought they'd give it a go, feeling her up, trying their luck – at the youth club, in the art room, in the girls' bogs, while another scumbag kept watch – because they reckoned they could. Because her mam was 'Shirley the

Shagger', the local 'bike'. Because her sister was known to put it about a bit.

Because Debs wore what she wore and swore what she swore and danced however the fuck she wanted.

He's not had six years of weekly kick-boxing lessons with Ali from the gym.

Debs knows what men can do when tanked up. She knows the signs.

Unsteady on his feet, he leans against the cupboards as he reaches for another glass. She doesn't say anything as he sloshes in vodka. He grabs a lemon from the fruit bowl. He reaches for the knife rack.

'Marc!'

Hearing the challenge, he looks at her. She sees how his lip curls. She clocks the eyes going hard and small as he squints to focus. He means to do her harm.

But he's not thinking clearly and her mind's suddenly sharp as the fucking knife he's now waving around. He's mumbling incoherent fragments – 'Don't understand ... can't...' Everything alive, aware, alert. Because she's just noticed his knuckles. Raw and bloodied. As if he's smashed them into someone's face.

What has he done?

She shadows his moves, a snake following the charmer's rhythms. She does not take her eyes off the knife.

38

Four years ago

When they visited – for Jeanne rarely came to them – Marc would sometimes chat to his mother in French, which Debs thought was not only bloody rude but also pathetically pretentious. The mother-in-law had studied the language before she became 'an international air hostess', like there's any other kind.

Debs didn't do French for very long at school but has enough to know the woman was a bloody great *vache*.

Yet Marc always sided with his mother. Even when Debs tried to support him in an argument – although Marc and Jeanne's spats could hardly qualify as arguments, they were so well mannered, like an achingly polite game of darts with each other's psyches as the board – he'd agree with his mother. She could make snide remarks about Debs or pull Marc apart, and still he'd agree with her. Bloody collaborator. It was awful to watch.

Jeanne described Debs' second blossoming bump as '*Un peu trop*'.

And so what if Marc's little wife looked annoyed at that? It was annoying for *her* to have them shove the new pregnancy down her throat. So easy for Deborah, motherhood. Jeanne's own pregnancy had been horrific. And, despite that, she'd had a desperate urge to have a baby brother or sister for Marc, which, thanks to Dudley, never happened. Then there had been the challenging time after Dudley abandoned them; the doctor described it as a 'breakdown', which Jeanne considered overly dramatic.

As Debs' belly expanded, so did Jeanne's distaste. Favouring the trim waists of her French role models like Carla Bruni and Brigitte Macron, she thought most British women obese and slovenly at the best of times.

Hetty alone, Marc's former fiancée – a pale girl with the perfect pedigree, pronunciation and posture – had been the only one to win Jeanne's approval. Even after the split, they went out to lunch together and Hetty still sends Jeanne cards to show she's thinking of her. So kind.

Marc sometimes dreams of Hetty. Not so much the whole person, he mainly fixates on her hair: flaxen and somewhat thin like the rest of her.

He carried a torch for her since university, from the very first time he saw her outside an Economics lecture. When she split with Teddy, her long-term boyfriend, Marc cast himself as the shoulder to cry on. Late-night sessions where she'd sniffle and analyse what Teddy had said, what Teddy might be doing, who Teddy had been doing it with, concluded with a pat on the shoulder, a hug, incrementally progressing to a kiss on the head, on the cheek, a brotherly peck on the lips. Subtly encroaching. Gaining territory.

They only made love five times, the first during a brief weekend in Madrid when he proposed. They cried in each other's arms.

Then she 'jilted' him, as his mother put it with a heavy sigh, as if it were inevitable, as if Marc had failed to measure up. She left him to return to Teddy. Hetty and Teddy, the Blonde Bombshells. Theirs was the great love affair; a union forged by their respective mothers over Henley picnics; a marriage as favourably starred as the portfolios their fathers compared at their club. Marc was reduced to a footnote in that grand romance.

Each time he thinks of Hetty, there's a contraction deep in his bowels rather than in his chest, where his heart might be.

Six weeks after the 'jilting', he met Deborah.

Hetty shared certain values with Marc. They spoke the same language and aspired to similar, expansive futures. How unlike Deborah's small-minded, old-fashioned working-class sensibilities, the ones that nag and pester him to 'save for a rainy day' and 'reel in' the spending. Because she has to feel safe and the children must have 'things of real value', like 'shared experiences', 'quality time', 'reading books' and other such nonsense.

Yet he must placate his mother with the opposite – all the normal symbols of success and wealth and achievement – to prove himself worthy of her fragile crystalline love, for didn't he ruin her figure and, after Dudley ran off, her prospects?

A rock and a hard place.

Debs has never heard of Hetty. It surprises Marc that his mother hasn't flung the former engagement in her face. He imagines Jeanne's biding her time, waiting for the moment that weaponised fact will do the most harm.

He imagines she might present Hetty's engagement ring with a flourish (stored in one of his archive boxes in his mother's attic, along with the letter containing fourteen *terribly sorrys* that accompanied it on its return), to demonstrate that the diamond is in fact larger than the one in Deborah's own ring.

The more startling thought is that his mother might have said nothing as a kindness.

39

5.17 a.m., 24 December

'Put that down, hey?'

He seems to hear her. He catches himself. He lowers the knife and whispers, 'I have to tell you something.'

'What?'

He swallows.

'What, Marc?'

'Something terrible ... truly appalling.'

She laughs. She doesn't mean to, it's a nervous reaction. It's a red rag to a bull.

She makes a dash for the door, but he lurches towards her, blocking her in the kitchen.

'No, Marc.'

He grabs for her arm and she wrenches it away. He tries to pull her to him, spinning her round and his elbow catches her sharply in the chest. She winces.

It's not that she wouldn't run now, or that she wouldn't consider trying to placate him, but her system doesn't even broach either possibility. The pain spikes her adrenalin and to her primitive brain that's the attack signal; her body is ready to fight tooth and claw. And before she knows or considers it, she's drawn back and slapped him hard, hurting her palm where she connects with his cheek. He immediately retaliates, backhanding her, his wedding ring smacking her lip into her teeth.

She tastes blood.

He didn't mean to catch her face. He was trying to push her away. The alcohol and drugs in his system confuse him. But he doesn't have time to explain, let alone say sorry, because she launches herself at him, punching at his ribs and kicking at his shins with her bare feet.

'You bastard! You fucking piece of slime!'

This is how it escalates. It was an accident, but Deborah always goes on the offensive. He tries to ward her off with his left hand. His right hand seems to be holding a knife.

The dog starts whining in her basket.

He backs away from Deborah's fury, moving around the kitchen as she continues advancing.

'Make you feel good, does it, hitting a woman? A big man, yeah? You fucking cunt!'

Always so combative. Her language is wearing.

40

Nine years ago

They never had a holiday without the kids.

They took Dolly, a babe in arms, to Venice, a delayed honeymoon of sorts. Italian shopkeepers and waiters fussed over the child, particularly when Marc was carrying her; the handsome man and the beautiful baby. They basked in the attention, amazed by the tiny, swirly-haired miracle they had created together. Darker than Debs, thanks to Marc's genes, but a few glints of Debs' fire in her colouring.

She noticed the looks women gave Marc in the Venetian shops. Their eyes would slide to her and the assessment would be clear on their faces. Usually, this attention grated on her. You think she doesn't know what they see? Dumpy Debs and the film star; punching above her weight.

Only, when Dolly was so little, she didn't care. Those looks and judgements slid right off her. For once, she was happy. Almost smug.

It was not a traditional romantic break thanks to Dolly, but it was the best time they ever had together.

Sated on her milk, Dolly slept and slept. As a baby she only seemed to have two modes, sleep and smile. They took turns strapping their daughter to their chests and wandered through opulent churches and exquisite squares, looking at miraculous paintings and statues of historical note. Debs, not being one for guides and history, was content to listen to Marc's voice burbling on – telling her things, educating her – lapping against her ears. Letting it all wash over her. Instinctively drawn to some frescos and not others. Loving him for knowing so much. Loving the ice cream more.

To be honest, her favourite times were back in the hotel, the part of the day after they'd eaten and strolled back in the pleasant warmth for gentle, lazy sex in a room overlooking some canal or other, dappled light lulling them into afternoon bliss, as she nipped his shoulder, his fingers in her hair. Watching him change Dolly, cradling his baby daughter, holding her against his chest, made something primal ping inside her. Seeing how happy he was, how he took charge of their child, she'd never wanted him more. Wide open and slippery; his tongue lapping against her—

She felt mildly drunk throughout that week, even though she only sipped long glasses of water and tiny, strong coffees. Her muscles finally relaxed for the first time in God knows how long.

She'd taught right up until the week before she gave birth, loving the new Merengue and Reggaeton Zumba tracks, simply modifying some of the moves, keeping it low-impact and cutting out the sit-ups after aerobics classes. Marc had protested, over-protective, but back then, she held her ground.

'Pregnancy's not an illness! I'm fine, love.'

In Venice, as they bobbed around on the city's canals, blood-warm, like amniotic fluids, she felt blessed.

Contrary to expectations, she did not worry every second they were out on the *vaporettos*, or on their one obligatory hilariously expensive gondola ride, anxious that their child might slip from her arms into the tepid, polluted waters of the wondrous canals.

With Marc, she felt protected, buoyed by hormones, safe in her new bubble. A *proper* family! A new, freshly minted family; one she had created with this fine, strapping man who walked holding her hand.

Look at her!

In the brilliant, early August sunshine she felt invincible. And if fortune should turn on them, if anything bad tried to break in to shatter the bastion of her joy, she knew Marc would see it off.

She stopped biting her nails during that trip.

She sang, 'If they could see me now!'

41

5.19 a.m., 24 December

'Shut up. Shut up! Shut up!' Hissing through gritted teeth, his voice is menacing despite the low-level whisper.

Her mouth stops of its own accord.

Some weird vibe is coming off him, making her retreat towards the worktop.

He comes after her. Then he's right up in her face. For a bizarre second, she imagines him biting her cheek and she pushes at his chest with both hands.

A step back, then he's looming over her again.

She shoves him away. 'Just fuck right off, Marc! Why don't—'

The move is both impossible and predictable; he swings for her with the blade.

It's half-hearted, a lazy 'get out of my face' action, a clumsy move. He just wants her to stop. He doesn't really mean it.

Does he?

He is not that person.

Was not.

Now he knows he is capable of much worse.

Her reaction is as swift as the slash of the knife towards her. She ducks under his raised arm, but as she does so, she accidentally knocks the metal mixing bowl off the cooker where she left it, meaning to put it away last night. It clatters to the floor bouncing once, twice, three times and Lulu woofs, three short yaps.

She shushes the dog. They can't wake the kids. What if Dolly comes down again and sees her father like this? She backs away to the other side of the central island, putting a barrier between her body and her husband, watching him as if he's some crazed animal.

He should try to explain he wasn't thinking; he simply forgot he was holding the knife. He should apologise. He does neither. He grips the knife tighter.

42

5.20 a.m., 24 December

The robot is huge. Huuuuuuge!

He loves robots. But this robot is scary.

It's coming towards him, red neon eyes blazing. Guns and rockets firing bombs and bullets on each side. Bang, bang, bang. Three bangs.

Pat-Pat hides. He can't shout. The robot will hear him.

But he wishes. He wishes with all his might – *Mummy!*

He wakes. Noises downstairs. Bang, bang, bang. But he's tired, so he closes his eyes again. He might go straight back to sleep.

A high-pitched yelp. He sits bolt upright in bed.

It is not the dog.

43

Nine years ago

They had a December break on Antigua when Dolly was seven months old, where they'd found a small, secluded beach and she'd got her kit off to sunbathe and stuffed Dolly in her stroller under a parasol. Not that she wasn't self-conscious about the wobbly bit of belly that had housed her daughter, but she was also a little bit proud of it. Battle scars. And nearly everyone was naked on that beach, from toddlers to grannies.

Marc tenderly smoothed sunscreen on his daughter's chubby thighs (the only time rolls of fat are adorable), then suggested Debs cover up, pointing out the rules on a beach sign. She ignored him and ran down to the sea to swim.

A couple of local boys appeared from between the rocks and followed her round the shallows with snorkels and goggles. When she finally came out to dry her goose-pimply skin on the beach towel, Marc snapped that the lads were getting 'a good eyeful' under the water and she laughed and said, 'Oh, let them! Who cares?' and she could tell that had become the wrong thing to say.

Now she was the mother of his child there were new expectations.

He used to like it when she 'paraded' around the house naked. She doesn't do it so much now, not even when she comes home to shower. She'd never take her kit off in front of class members in the changing room. Her body a road map of birth, weight gain and loss, and bruises from the gym; mainly from the gym.

He hated it when she fed Dolly in public. He hurried to drape a muslin over them, although she told him to stop fussing. He'd been fine in Venice, but over the months, he seemed to become more self-conscious about it. In bed he gave her nipples a wide berth.

They took their daughter to see his mother, and he asked Debs to feed Dolly in the kitchen 'in case of accidents'.

'What, in case Jeanne has a bloody fit?'

'No, of course not. In case Dolores is sick.'

She complied. But only because she didn't want the Ice Queen watching her.

'The bottle is much more hygienic,' proclaimed Jeanne when they came back to the lounge. 'Plus, the mastitis.' She spat out the word. 'I couldn't have fed Marcus myself, even if I had wanted.'

You don't say, thought Debs as she caught Marc's eye and grimaced. She missed the fleeting sadness wash across Jeanne's face because she avoided looking at her mother-in-law closely.

Debs loved breastfeeding, not that she had agreed with all that Nazi Childbirth Trust crap. She and Marc signed up, but she only stuck it for two sessions. She still sees a couple of the mums at Dolly's school gates. They smile at her with that holier-than-thou look, no doubt popping out their Tamsins and Georges after floating round birthing pools on fresh air and affirmations. She'd had epidurals with both Dolly and Pat-Pat.

Shirley wasn't a fan of natural births either. 'I was out my head when I fell for you and our Kelly, so I had all the drugs when I was shoving both of yous out. Deffo go for the epidural. It's like shitting a fucking football!'

Turned out this was good advice. Patrick was nine pounds.

'That's not a babbie, that's a bastard turkey!' laughed her mam when she phoned her with the news.

Marc was there for both births, but resolutely did not look down. His gaze remained fixed on her face. She had to squeeze her eyes closed to shut him out.

Debs has often accused Marc of being prudish. That's not it, exactly, although he doesn't generally look at his own body. But then he does not like his body.

He examines sections of himself – his hairline slightly receding, enough for him to try caffeine shampoo; a pouching of the skin beneath his eyes. He has no template. What will he look like when he's older? He realises he assumes he will not achieve old age. His father only made it to fifty-three. Perhaps, at best, he has a decade left.

On bad days that seems too long. Almost unbearable.

He wishes he could simply slip away. A heart attack might be easiest. The drugs that provoke the battering in his chest make that eventuality more likely. Or perhaps the bad feelings inside him are harbingers of cancer. That might not be the worst thing, although he does not want to linger. He has no intention of being a burden to his family.

But it would not be a dereliction of duty; his life insurance policy would take care of his family. He has checked the small print – in the event of something self-inflicted.

He suspects the pain in his gut is merely evidence of him rotting from the inside out; a dark putrid cesspit bubbling deep inside. His body's responses disgust him.

44

Four years ago

Kelly's Boz, professional electrician and amateur herpetologist, keeps two snakes in the house. Debs is not at all keen on them. Their terrariums are beautifully clean and warm – a real feature against the living-room wall. But still.

Boz never feeds the snakes or gets them out if Debs is around because he's not a total twat. Also, his dogs aren't keen either. Joey's the sort of mastiff-cum-boxer who'd definitely have a go at them, but Debs' money's on Muffy, a Frankenstein experiment of a mutt – part terrier, part fuck-knows-what – if it came to it.

Kelly doesn't seem to mind the snakes, and Boz's daughter, Penny, is a big fan. Although now Penny insists on being called 'Raven' and has started to look a bit like Kate Bush, if Kate Bush got her make-up from Superdrug and slapped it on all in one go.

The boy snake (Debs has no idea how you can tell), is a ball python called Rocky, patterned like a white-and-camouflage artwork. 'Piebald,' explains Boz, proudly. The girl, smaller, a sleek, pale rosy boa, is called Cinderella. Penny/Raven got to name her when Boz first brought her home, before she went goth – Penny, not the snake who was born that way.

'They don't do much,' explains Kel when Debs asks her how she can bear them. 'They're peaceful, like.'

Debs has gone up on the train, almost eight months pregnant with Pat-Pat. Her sister might have come down to see her and do some shopping, but she's not too keen on Muswell Hill or Marc these days.

'London: where the streets are paved with arseholes.' Less of a joke now.

Marc doesn't join them. He says it's work, but Debs knows he finds it difficult to see how close she is to her sister. He's always chivvying her to finish phone calls to Kelly; not that he says anything, it's just what his face does. She wonders if he's a bit jealous.

Debs hopes it's not too hard for her sister to see her like this. She sits, almost apologetic, hugging a cushion in front of her huge belly.

Boz and Kelly have only just stopped trying for kids. Never happened. Kelly agreed to give up after the last round of IVF. Five miscarriages altogether, counting the ones before the treatment. Now they're broke.

Kel's a good stepmother to Penny/Raven. She's an easy enough kid, happy to share stuff with Kelly that she'd never tell her mum. It's not quite enough but it'll have to do.

Boz dotes on his girl, the dogs, Kelly and the bloody snakes. Possibly in that order. Sings to them, according to Kel. Wraps them around his shoulders as they watch *Game of Thrones* and *Breaking Bad*.

'What if they escape?' says Debs.

'They never have,' says Kelly.

Doesn't mean they never will.

Five-year-old Dolly is off at Netto with Boz and Shirley. She shares the shopping gene with her gran, does Dolly. Debs is sitting there, munching ginger nuts, and yes, she knows she shouldn't, supping a proper builder's tea, although there's no sugar in that, and she laughs at something Kelly says and it must be the way her ponytail swings or something, but the white snake launches itself at the glass. From epic stillness to full attack mode: jaw gaping, unhinged, fangs bared, aiming to sink themselves deep into Debs' face, which is too close to the glass.

Her heart hammers in the old way.

She never sits near the terrariums again.

'They're vivariums,' Boz corrects her, smiling indulgently like an affectionate dad.

*

These days Debs has a similar, low-level, creeped-out reaction when Dolly's friend Tamara is round theirs. The child's hair is too pale, her eyes too intent, her movements too deliberate. Watching Tamara wind herself round Dolly, fiddling with her hair, sitting so close on the sofa she's almost on her knee, crooning to her, puts Debs in mind of a serpent Cinderella.

45

Six months ago

'Look, there's no choice. Ruby's had to take him to hospital.'

Zig's had an accident. He fell out of a tree he was pruning in the garden. It must have been a pathetic specimen if it couldn't hold Zig's wispy, 'grade four vegan' body, but perhaps that's why he was trimming it, thinks Debs.

Ruby called and asked her to look after Tamara, which wasn't a huge deal because it was Debs' turn to collect Dolly and her friend from school anyway, although usually she'd drop the girls back at Ruby's. She'd have already taken Pat-Pat to his little mate's house by then and he'd stay there until she fetched him on the way back from the gym, before picking up Dolly and driving them both home. (Debs wonders at which point her life became this exercise in advanced logistics.) The issue, which is what she and Marc are arguing about at the moment, is that she's got a client at four-thirty and there's no way they'll be out of A&E by then, and Ruby says she can't leave Zig because he's concussed. *How they can tell?* wonders Debs.

Their next-door neighbour, Sylvia, sometimes watches the

kids for her, but she's having her bunions done. Debs considers taking the girls to work and sitting them outside the studio with a couple of books or Tamara's phone or something, but they wouldn't be covered by the gym's insurance. Also, there was an incident the time Debs took Dolly in when she was a toddler and they'd joined Em (the super-sexy pole dance teacher, like there's any other kind) when she was rehearsing for her evening class. Dolly bloody loved it. She'd bounced around to the music and grabbed the pole, swung round and struck the poses and made the faces, mirroring Em. And Debs had laughed so much, Dolly got overexcited and pooed her pants. Em didn't mind, even helped Debs clean it up, but the boss frowns on that sort of thing.

Debs doesn't even mention the idea of taking the girls with her now that Marc's arrived like the cavalry – that is, if the cavalry simply blundered home early for once – it's become a matter of principle. Tamara will have to stay at theirs. End of. He can sort things out for once.

'Can't they go to Patrick's friend's house?'

'No. His mum's got enough on her plate with Pat and her lads, plus I owe Ruby for all the times she takes Dolly for me.'

In the end Marc concedes because after a day at work that turned a tad *Glengarry Glen Ross*, he hasn't the energy to fight on.

When Debs has left in a flurry of hurried 'goodbye's and 'be good's, Marc switches on the flatscreen and Tamara selects MTV – surely that will be fine pre-watershed? – and he checks the increasingly disturbing work emails in between playing number games on his iPhone. He glances at Tamara, checking nothing inappropriate is happening on screen, and she shoots back looks his way that seem… *knowing*. She's acting like a nine-year-old; like an actress might play a nine-year-old.

The girl makes his skin crawl. Her hair reminds him of Hetty.

He wonders why Dolly isn't annoyed by her friend, who's forever plaiting or twiddling Dolly's curls round her fingers or, like now, stroking her. There was a time he'd have scooped Dolly on to his lap to get her away from those intrusive fingers, but his daughter is too grown-up for that sort of thing these days.

'Can I use your bathroom?' asks Tamara, all politeness when Marc's around. She never bothers asking Debs, treats the place like her own, although she hasn't been invited round for several weeks, not since the birthday party.

There's a peaceful interlude where Marc catches up on a few work issues, before realising the girl hasn't reappeared. She's been absent for at least ten minutes.

He stands at the bottom of the stairs and shouts, 'Everything okay up there?'

'Yes thanks, Marc,' says Tamara in a sing-song voice.

He's annoyed he's not 'Mr Johnson', but the girl calls her own parents 'Ruby and Zig' rather than 'Mummy and Daddy'.

He can tell she's no longer in the bathroom. He hesitates. But Tamara is obviously in his daughter's bedroom. He does not want her snooping around their home.

He leaves Dolly watching the TV and walks up the stairs quietly, although he is most definitely not creeping around in his own house.

Tamara's standing with her back to Dolly's open door, examining items in his daughter's ballerina jewellery box. The ballerina doesn't twirl any more, broken by Patrick last year (Dolly screamed for almost eight straight minutes when it happened). Tamara puts a ring back. She takes a necklace, examines it and puts it in the pocket of her skinny jeans.

'Tamara?'

She whirls around, an angry nymph.

'I'm just taking it to Dolly.' Almost rehearsed. She stares, daring him to challenge her.

The things aren't worth anything, just plastic. It's the principle.

'Have you taken anything else?' He vaguely remembers Deborah saying things have been going missing.

She ignores the question and tries to push her way past him.

He puts his arm across the doorway. 'Tamara, I asked you a question.'

Her face reddens in fury more than embarrassment. 'What do you mean? Leave me alone!'

'Show me what's in your pocket.'

She stands defiant for a few seconds, jiggling her leg, before shouting, 'Stop it!' Then louder, 'Dolly!'

'Just calm down. Show me what's in your pocket, now please.'

Dolly emerges at the bottom of the stairs, craning to see what's happening.

'Daddy? What are you doing?'

'Nothing, just—'

'He's trying to make me show him stuff!'

There's a bristle of adrenaline. His impulse is to hit her. It's a primitive response to a threat, that's all.

There is the barest of struggles as the girl attempts to wiggle past, her arm catching his zip as she does so. There is a twitch. He has no control over that.

'He's trying to make me show him stuff!' screams Tamara.

And Marc puts out a hand to stop her dashing past him down the stairs. He pushes her back, as much for her safety as restraint, and she screams louder, 'He wants to see, to see ... to see my *vaj-jay-jay*!'

And Marc feels like she's punched him in the gut. His arm falls, stricken, and she slips past him. He stands shocked and slightly nauseous. He has to put both hands on the doorframe to stay upright.

Her word against his. His daughter a witness. These days the victim must always be believed.

Tamara – the *victim* – gallops down the stairs.

When Marc can gather himself, he follows. He walks slowly, shaken, entering the room as you would hostile territory. Neither girl looks up.

Dolly seems oblivious to any tension. The friends are settled on the rug with Lulu.

It's as if it never happened.

And Tamara empties her pocket of the Hello Kitty necklace and two bracelets and with exaggerated, deliberate care, puts them on Dolly. Whipping out her phone she wraps her arms around her friend, angles the camera, pouts up at the screen and takes perhaps her twelfth selfie of the day.

His daughter gives a gap-toothed smile.

As Tamara chooses a filter, the dog nudges her hand. She pats Lulu as if she might be sticky and shoots him a look of pure evil.

That night he dreams of driving his fist into the child's face.
The next week, Dolly starts using the word 'vaj-jay-jay'.

46

Fourteen months ago

Debs remembers the first few times she went back to Marc's flat, and he'd booked her a car home in the early hours. At that time, if she was lucky, a good black cab could make it back to her flat in forty-odd minutes, without too much of the racist verbals, or the sneaky sizing up her cleavage through the driver's mirror. Sore and smug from the sex, too wired for sleep, she'd watch London rush by, the city entirely hers in the small hours. She'd felt like the queen of bloody everything!

Harrods all lit up like a fairground ride, Piccadilly with a few German-looking tourists taking photos next to Eros, Soho still zinging with life and the whiff of naughtiness, up to the ghost town vibe around Warren Street, towards Camden, past the eager kids outside that club at Mornington Crescent back to hers.

All of those streets and lights, all that buzz and promise – hers!

Now her world has shrunk to the rat run: home, school, nursery, gym, shops, home again. Sweaty Betty for the occasional treat. Round and round. Rock and roll.

The house – so many rooms, so claustrophobic.

She's generally too tired for fights, so her rebellions have taken on a quieter hue. To mess with him she might leave the dish that had contained potato dauphinoise in sudsy water to soak and deliberately forget it. She might stack the dishwasher in 'a rather slipshod manner'. Or leave a knife in the washing-up bowl.

The first in her family to have a dishwasher.

But underneath those quiet *fuck-you*s the fear took root.

Having kids made her more fearful. Having kids made her a little messy. And apart from certain sex games, Marc doesn't like things messy.

There were reprisals in the bedroom.

Lulu is over-grooming. She nibbles her nether regions in an enthusiastic manner, which makes Dolly shriek with glee. The dog scratches at herself with such wild abandon that Debs' own ears itch.

The vet says she has a fleabite allergy. Debs feels like an unfit mother.

'But we use the flea-nuking stuff every month,' she protests, wondering if she's missed a dose, what with everything else.

'Look, it happens. Don't beat yourself up about it,' says the lovely, smiley vet, a young girl with a great bedside manner. 'Just make sure you thoroughly clean the bedding and carpets.'

'We don't have carpets,' says Debs. 'Well not downstairs. She's not allowed in the bedrooms.'

Although how many times has Lulu been found in Dolly's room, with a plastic tiara plonked on her head to play princesses?

'Tell your cleaner to use hot water on the floors before spraying,' says the vet, revealing an assumption based on the clientele.

'We don't have a cleaner,' says Debs.

She should have a cleaner. In fact, she once did. But when Elke left to join her girlfriend in Hungary, she couldn't bear to go through that whole mortifying interview rigmarole again. Having a cleaner made her feel guilty; dirty, hopeless and guilty. And she didn't want to be one of those women who bitch about what a rough job their cleaners do. She has clients like that. Some poor cow sweating over their surfaces at home while they pay Debs to make them sweat in the gym. It feels bad. She almost hates them for it and makes them do burpees.

Her mam had scrubbed enough floors and cleaned enough toilets, serving punters drinks by night, cleaning up the sick in the bogs the next morning. Not that her mam had minded Debs having her own cleaner.

'Jesus, don't be such a daft cow!' she'd laughed. 'If I could afford someone to do for me, don't you think I would? Me and Bradley Walsh would have our trotters up with a cuppa every afternoon if I had a cleaner.'

She can almost hear her mam taking the piss.

Then there's the language thing. Clients grumble that they can't communicate with their cleaners, so under the beds and sofas remain a no man's land. It makes Debs feel stupid when she can't understand what someone's asking her. Then there's the cultural stuff. Apparently, Romanian cleaners think cats are evil and some Muslims think dogs are filthy, which they are. But—

Anyway, Lulu's nervous enough when the Hoover's out, without a strange new person wielding it anywhere near her.

'I've given her an antibiotic injection and a steroid to help clear it up. After you've cleaned, spray this around the house but keep the dog and the children well away from it,' instructs the vet, handing her a comedy-sized spray can. 'Anyone pregnant? Other health issues at home?'

'I have asthma,' says Debs weakly.

'Get your husband to spray, then,' says the vet, tapping something into the computer.

If only it were that easy. If she tells Marc about Lulu having fleas, their home harbouring fleas, it's another reason for him to judge her. And she couldn't bear a campaign to get rid of the dog.

The vet pats Lulu, who has already forgiven her for the injection thanks to a dog treat. 'We need to manage these scabs so they don't get infected. Poor thing. It's an over-reaction to lots of tiny little bites. They drive animals mad.'

Debs is asked to bring her back for a check-up in two weeks.

Lulu mithers at herself all the way home.

So does Debs.

All those tiny little irritations, needling away at her day and night. She too feels scratched raw.

'Mummy, why is Daddy taller than you?'

'He just is.'

'But why?'

'Because ... he eats more sausages.'

'But I'm bigger than Pat-Pat. He ate more sausages than me last week.'

Yes, the little bugger did, and then he brought most of them back up again. 'You're older than Pat-Pat, chick.'

'But Daddy's not older than you.'

'No.'

'So why?'

Letting the side down, making her girl into a bad feminist, Debs sighs and tries, 'Probably because he's a bloke.'

'But Pat-Pat's a bloke—'

But, but, but, why, why, why? On and on.

She used to find it funny.

Patrick releases a loud wet fart and grins seductively, awaiting praise.

Dolly laughs with abandon and tries to compete with a forced burp.

Marc says, 'Don't, darling.'

'But why, Daddy?'

'Because it's not nice.' Sometimes he feels like he's turning into his mother.

She tries another burp.

'Dolly!' The tone is a warning.

She reaches across the table for another slice of bread with a perky, 'Scuse *me*,' then bounces up and down.

'Darling, don't do that.'

'Why not?'

'It'll make you feel sick.'

'But I don't feel sick. I'm trying to trump like Nana Shirley.'

'Please don't.'

'But why?'

'Because it's not polite.'

'But I like trumping!'

On and on. Why Deborah can't shut this down is beyond him.

*

Marc requires, *demands* that she run 'a tight ship'.

She used to counter, 'When were you in the bloody navy?'

She doesn't say anything now.

When she lets things slide, when she becomes a lax mother, like her own, or someone who takes their eye off the ball, like Ruby with Tamara, Marc notices. He comes down on her heavily.

It doesn't bother her so much, but she's afraid what the poisonous atmosphere might do to the kids.

The guilt, the anxiety ... it always comes back to the kids.

Those who say the fear of the unknown is the worst thing are talking bollocks. The unknown shows a lack of imagination. Nuclear war, dirty bombs; cancer; poverty, hunger. Debs wishes she didn't know what she's most afraid of. She wishes her mind didn't devise tortures and horrors that could befall her daughter, her boy. If only she didn't envision how their faces might look as they struggled for air. How their eyes would frantically search for her as the life was squeezed out of them.

But she can't not know, imagine, how it would be for them. And she knows how it would be impossible for her to carry on afterwards.

What if the thing she's afraid of isn't some threat lurking out-side the safety of this cosy home, clawing at the doors, peering into her double-glazed windows, its breath frosting the panes?

What if it's right here in the kitchen beside her?

Her fear has a shape. Her fear has a story. She's read stuff in the papers. What if Marc is one of those headlines? Are the sleeping pills and vodka meant for his final disappearing act? That's one fear.

But that's not the worst.

Beyond words, unnamed, stirring below her conscious worry for her husband there's a sick feeling; a constant nagging dis-quiet. What are the kids' mugs doing next to the sleeping pills?

What if her husband is one of those men who take their whole families with them?

47

Two weeks ago

'What are you planning for Christmas?'

She hears that a dozen times a week, the question from clients who are off to ski, travelling to a charming cottage in the Cotswolds, jetting away to lie on a beach frequented by well-preserved peacocks like Duncan Bannatyne and Simon Cowell, parading money and mahogany torsos alongside nubile new partners.

Debs, like most poor sods, faces negotiating several circles of festive family hell.

Those staying at home for Christmas like Kelly might be planning a seasonal Netflix-and-sugar marathon. Boz and Kel are having Raven round for Boxing Day. The kid might big up Cradle of Filth and Christian Death (well into her vintage goth, is Raven), but she still wants her dad and her Crimbo presents.

Kelly needs a fair few phone calls to help her through this season of glad tidings. It's a hard time for her sister.

*

'It's just ... the little baby Jesus and all that crap,' sobs Kel down the phone. 'It. Sets. Me ... right off.'

'I know. I'm sorry, chick,' says Debs.

She's been listening to Kelly for forty-odd minutes. Thankfully, Dolly and Pat-Pat are in bed.

'But I feel so bloody stupid! I can't stop bloody crying.' Her sister takes a wobbly inhale. 'And I feel so fucking *defective*. I mean, *why* can't I be a mum! It's not fair, Debs! It's not fair.'

'I know, chick, I know,' croons Debs.

'My stupid bastard body!'

'It's not your fault, Kel. It's just one of them things. Biology's a bitch.'

'You know, I've only got to hear Boney sodding M's "Mary's Boy Child" on the radio and I proper lose it. And don't get me started on Silent fucking Night. I just, I just can't—'

'Put the kettle on, love. You'll be okay in a bit. This'll pass. Take a few big breaths.'

'It's shit.'

'I know it is. Are you on your own? Is Boz there?'

'No. He's at the Kings having a few bevvies to warm up. Him and the lads have been up at Mapperley Reservoir with the drone all day.'

'The *drone*?'

'Yeah. Stupid knob. His bloody Christmas present to himself. He opened it early, like.'

Debs hears the faint smile in her sister's voice and knows she'll finally be able to say goodnight and put the phone down without worrying about her too much.

*

Debs is currently gearing up for an audience with Jeanne, which goes against all her protective instincts. She usually keeps the kids well away from the toxic old trout, which seems to suit all parties. Not so lucky this year.

Apart from the obligatory birthday or Christmas, Debs never volunteers family visits. Jeanne absents herself on these occasions more often than not, travelling to South Africa with friends, alternatively issuing adult-only invites for late-night soirées. If they do visit, on Marc's instruction, Jeanne directs comments above the children's heads, both literally and metaphorically. She never tries to engage with them.

Debs takes a small, mean delight in getting Dolly to call her 'Granny Jeanne'. Pat-Pat won't say so much as 'hello' to her. He becomes weirdly subdued in her presence.

Jeanne's staying in Britain this year, thanks to an unfortunate touch of bronchitis, which means they're supposed to make the jolly little pilgrimage across town, although they've not yet been summoned with an exact date or time. Jeanne likes to keep Marc on his toes, acquiescing to her every whim.

The anxiety is already eating away at Debs – not so much for the actual visit, which is merely uncomfortable, wearing and ultimately soul-destroying – but in case Jeanne mentions something about losing her mam back in April and how she may well react if the tone is the wrong one, as she guesses it will be. And how Marc will react and how he might take it out on her afterwards. And how she might then lose it completely and stave in his skull with the cast-iron skillet pan.

That's what she's planning for Christmas.

If it was up to her, she'd take the kids up to Nottingham.

Claim sanctuary; leave Marc and his mother to it.

But if she went now, wouldn't her sister sense something's wrong? And what would Debs say then? Would she be able to explain what it's like, how the marriage has sort of caved in on itself? Could she tell her how bad it's become; explain what makes her stay?

She has only herself to blame.

48

Five years ago

Their sex life changed. Naturally, it changed. She understood. It's hard to see your woman as both a mother and a slut.

As Marc's work became more demanding – texts and emails at all hours – he became distracted, stressed, exhausted much of the time. More tentative in bed. Their sex life slid into once a week, then once a fortnight.

Not willing to grieve for that part of her life, not then, at least, she offered to 'try new things'. Experiment. Explore their fantasies.

She might have had those kinds of fantasies back then – rolling Tom Hardy in chocolate; a threesome with Tom and Henry Cavill – but her favourite fantasy now is a good night's sleep and a lie in.

The shift happened by stealth. A little rough and tumble here and there. The odd slap. Not hard. She didn't object. The dressing up. 'What if you put this on? What if you use this...'

She'd heard stuff like that at work. 'Trying something new. Mixing things up a little.' It usually meant she lost a class as the boss 'freshened up' the timetable by getting some kid in to teach the latest fad for half the money: Yogalates (yoga and Pilates), Piloxing (that well-known combination of boxing, dance and Pilates), BootHoop (hula hoops and press-ups to techno beats).

But she loved Marc, so she went along with it. She felt she could control it, put the brakes on.

It had its own momentum.

She'd already had an inkling about the sort of porn he liked, an acquired taste, which demanded variations of debasement to achieve the desired effect.

But now she needed to tell someone. When she felt things slide towards the unmanageable, she decided she'd try to talk it through with her sister and organised an overnight visit to Nottingham.

When Debs and Kel invite Shirley to come with them for a coffee, they're shot down with, 'No, ta very much. All that froth? You're paying for bloody fresh air, you silly twats!'

Their mam never could get her head round paying three quid for something she could make at home for pennies. Shirley refuses to pay over the odds for anything. She takes her own flask of booze-infused coffee to Bingo, smuggling it in her Tesco Bag for Life alongside the essential kit of Silk Cut, 'dobbing pen' and her best high-heeled 'sitting-down shoes'. So, as Debs and Kelly mooch on down to the Costa in the precinct, Shirley settles in with Ben Shephard. 'Lovely little body, that one!'

Unlike Shirley, Kel's a big fan of all things caramel and macchiato, the mega-hit of caffeine and sugar sometimes providing the highlight of a slow day. Like getting her nails done (gel, Queen of Hearts red) a coffee made by some other bugger is a non-negotiable treat.

Debs is glad they've got a bit of time on their own. This trip has been fraught with discussions about their mam's great coughing jags and how little ground their stereo nagging is gaining. Shirley sometimes fires up a fag just to spite them and they then have to listen to her hacking up her guts on Kelly's back patio.

It's not the only thing on Debs' mind. She blethers on for a while about inconsequential bits and bobs, trying to find the right time to ask her sister what she really wants to ask.

She tries the opener, 'Boz still sniffing round Mags?'

Mags is the ex; not Penny's mam, the one before.

'I reckon he's keeping it in his pants.'

'Any more dodgy texts?'

'Nah. He's knocked that on the head.'

'Do you think it went any further?'

'Than the sexting? In his bloody dreams.'

Debs picks chocolate chunks out of her sister's muffin.

'Do you know what I reckon, Debs? He's a coward. He thinks he'd like a rematch just cos she's had her lips done. But he'd run a mile if she took him up on it.'

'What's she look like ... since?'

'Like they all do, half blow-up doll, half fucking haddock.'

They both laugh.

'Mind you,' says Kelly, pulling her plate away from her sister's thieving hands, 'you can't blame her. I'd still like a bit of work done. Lipo here and *here*...'

'Don't be daft.'

'Go on, you liar. You'd have a few tweaks, you know you would.'

'No, I wouldn't.'

'You would, though.'

'No, I would not.' Debs necks a glug of her extra-shot cappuccino. 'If I started, I'd never bloody stop.'

'No different to a perm,' sniffs Kel, who specialises in pensioner specials with her mobile hairdressing gig, and so is more attuned to shampoo and sets than balayage.

The topic's deflected. Debs reckons on trying again later.

'Shall we hit the shops?' says Kel.

'You know, I went to buy some camouflage pants last week – couldn't find any!'

Her sister punches her on the arm.

After a trip to Primani, where Kel tries on three dresses – one too big, one too small and one just right, because it's exactly the same as the one in yellow that's already hanging in her wardrobe – they get back, say tara to Shirley as she sets off back to her own flat, and crack on with the prosecco.

So, Debs gears herself up and when Kelly starts talking about the snakes, she tries to introduce the topic, clunky though it feels.

'Does Boz ask you to do anything weird with them snakes? You know, get you to dance around with them, or owt?'

Kelly gets the giggles. 'Boz? No! Are you insane? For fuck's sake!'

And wouldn't it be lovely to leave it there, with a laugh, but Debs has to push on as it's needling her. It's the reason she came up to see Kel. Marc had been well narked about looking after Dolly by himself for one sodding overnight. He's called her twice already – a meltdown in the Baby Ballet class and when he lost Dolly's sacred Dora the Explorer colouring book.

Debs tops up their glasses. 'So, he's not into anything a bit weird, like?'

'Nah.'

Kel catches the look on her sister's face.

'Why? Marc?'

'It's just the stuff he looks at online, it's—'

'Oh, they all do that. Don't mean they want to do it with you.' She takes a gulp from her generously filled wine glass. 'What's he into, then?'

'A bit of S and M, like.'

'Aren't they bloody all. Are you up for any of it?'

'Some of it.'

'Don't you do owt you don't want,' says Kel, rootling out a couple of packets of crisps to go with their drinks. 'I take it it's not him getting tied up.'

'What do you think?'

'Do you get off on it?'

Debs considers. 'Doesn't really do anything for me.'

'Tell him to shove it, then.'

'I will.' She won't.

Kel takes a wild guess. 'Has he bloody hurt you?'

'No! Course not.'

'Because if he has—'

'No. No. Nothing like that.' Exactly like that.

'You'd tell me, wouldn't you?'

'Course. It's just—'

'What?'

'The stuff he watches. Choking stuff...' And the rest.

'Long as he don't try it on with you.'

'And the weeing stuff...'

Kelly pulls a yuck face, so Debs leaves it at that.

She doesn't tell her how he spat in her face.

When she's on the train back, Marc calls to check what time she gets in, offering to collect her from the station. Telling her he's 'missed her', bless him. And she convinces herself that next time she'll just tell him no. Put a stop to it, the other things; things she doesn't want to say out loud.

The solution to the anxiety is to pull back her shoulders and just get on with it. And no, Marc, it isn't 'one's shoulders' because she's not in the fucking army and yes, fucking is a crude word so just get over it!

Of course, she never breathed one word of those internal conversations she rehearsed so often.

The slaps became harder. More enthusiastic. The bite marks on her breast. At one time she'd been well into that, right on the border of pain and pleasure, but then it hurt so much she wondered if she'd have to go to the doctor's.

But he bloody loved it when she was 'naughty'. And she liked to think of herself as adventurous.

There was stuff she wouldn't do. Even with his study door

locked so they wouldn't be interrupted, she couldn't face some of the things if Dolly was home. She started to dread it when her daughter was out at kids' parties and play dates and Marc wasn't at work. But sometimes, even with Dolly upstairs in bed, he insisted, so she swallowed back both sounds and worries.

But then he was so lovely after they'd tried the new things. Lots of kisses and compliments and a bath together that never quite left her feeling clean enough. Presents. She hoped it was just a phase.

Each time, despite her better instincts, she talked herself down. It happened subtly, over months, over years. Week by week it amped up. He pressed on. And she was like a frog in a pan slowly, slowly coming to the boil.

His demands rooted inside her. And his words, which were worse than the physical things sometimes, lodged inside her mind. Vile words deployed with the clinical skill of a sniper.

She found new ways to hate herself.

49

5.22 a.m., 24 December

There's a pregnant pause. Her tongue probes the cut inside her mouth; her mind probes the anxiety, but before she can grasp why it all feels so wrong – not that it hasn't been wrong for a long time – he mumbles, 'I'm sorry. I'm sorry. I'm sorry. I'm sorry.'

He shakes his head, then his chin collapses on to his chest.

Is this just one of his games that has got out of hand? Is it the drink? Or has the pressure at work got too much – has he flipped?

But didn't he just wave a fucking knife in her face? Didn't he just hit her? She's making excuses for him because she can't cope with the alternative. He's the father of her kids, for God's sake.

As her mind does its jig, deep in her bones she knows the truth. She has to get out of here.

She heads for the kitchen door. Lulu, wired on the strange atmosphere, makes a dash for it at the same time and Debs' legs get tangled around the dog and she trips. She manages to stop herself going over by grabbing the side of the washing machine. No harm done, just a small jolt as she comes down on one knee.

Marc's instantly by her side, concerned, clutching her arm, as if he's saving her from drowning.

She doesn't want him touching her.

He tries to hoist her up, but she jerks her arm away from him and as he lets go, she falls flat on her bum.

There was a time when they might have both laughed at this. It's not the first time she's made a fool of herself, clumsy, like Pat-Pat, if she's not concentrating. Marc's face changes. But it's the saddest smile in the world.

Something lightens; something defuses.

She sits where she is and Lulu climbs all over her. It should be soothing but all of a sudden, Debs feels like she's on fire, instantly slicked with sweat. It's not like the sweat whipped up by a good high-intensity class. It's a fever which flashes all over her body, like a witch going up in flames.

He steps over her and pours himself yet another vodka. He says, 'I'm sorry.' It sounds different how he says it, less an apology, more an admission. And he reaches for the pills.

50

Four months ago

She's only forty-one. Too young for all that menopause malarkey, surely? But it happened to her mam when she was even younger. It's part of the reason Kelly can't have kids.

Weirdly, Debs misses her periods, even that wearing, dragging-down sensation where she feels her womb might drop out in the middle of demonstrating squat thrusts in her Lift class.

Hot flushes are the least of it.

She starts forgetting the names of people in her sessions, clients she's known for years. Words for other things just disappear like smoke. Older clients tell her that's normal, but how come she can remember the phrase 'menopausal aphasia', yet loses the word for 'elbow' when setting up triceps dips? The gaps are like the blind spots, whiteouts she used to get with migraines as a teenager; migraines now back with a vengeance – another lovely gift from the hormonal soup sloshing around her body. Perhaps it's a brain tumour, not just the end of her fertility, the end of fucking everything.

She's full of morbid thoughts like these since her mam

died. Months on and she's still choked up when she thinks of Shirley. Her asthma, along with her emotions, is in no way well controlled.

When she was carrying Patrick, one doctor branded it a 'geriatric pregnancy', which made her laugh. But now she stands in front of classes where she's old enough to be the mother of most of the participants. She ups her game and makes sure she works harder, lifts heavier and keeps going for longer than anyone else. Yes, she's often knackered, but so are many twenty-year-olds, particularly those with a couple of kids to look after.

The new fear in the wee hours is that her own mortality is upon her.

'Don't be daft,' says Kel when she admits she's scared. 'At four in the morning, everything's bloody toe cancer.'

She makes excuses when things go missing. She's not concentrating, she's too tired, she's forty-odd. Better to doubt herself than acknowledge her womb might be shrivelling up. She loses her house keys and has to have a new set cut from Marc's, so he makes his cat's arse face. She misplaces her Jo Loves grapefruit perfume. It turns up in the bathroom two weeks later, although she could have sworn she'd already searched the cabinet.

Dolly's fluffy Minion-shaped journal dematerialises. The book is full of her doodles and 'po-yems'. Dolly locks it with a miniature key each night, although, not thinking it through, keeps that key in the same drawer. They find the book under her bed, with pages torn out. Of course, it must be Pat-Pat, although it's out of character. She can imagine him crumpling one page in his fist, but her daughter's drawings have been torn into tiny little pieces which litter the floor, a cruel confetti.

The chaos in her son's room is generally undisturbed, but her things and Dolly's things are sucked into a widening black hole.

'But Mummy, it was right here!' sobs Dolly when her favourite skirt is nowhere to be found.

Debs remembers ironing and folding and putting the pink frilly 'pretty lady skirt' as Dolly used to call it back in her wardrobe. Recently her daughter has re-categorised the skirt as 'sickening!' as in wonderful and sexy and Cara Delevingne cool.

She sees her actions in her mind's eye. She knows where she put it, but now it's not there and Dolly swears she didn't move it.

It's a creepy feeling.

The next week, ballet slippers enter the Twilight Zone.

'Are you sure you packed them after the class?'

'Yes. YES!' shouts Dolly, inconsolable.

Debs asks the dance teacher, but she's told they've not been handed in. She almost says, 'Are you sure?' but the look on Ludmilla's face shuts down further questions. Miss Ludmilla runs a tight ship.

She's thinking of knocking the ballet on the head anyway. Tamara's already on the dancer fast-track to an eating disorder in Debs' opinion. The girl never so much as looks at a biscuit in their house. She's worryingly gaunt. Dolly's little pot belly plumping out her leotard when she and Tamara set off to dance class together is noticeable in comparison.

Ruby's no Skinny Minnie, so she can't imagine the child gets it from her. They're a veggie family, but there's no meat in ice cream or chocolate. Zig's scrawny, but he's full-on vegan.

Small amounts of money seem to disappear from Debs'

purse. She can never be absolutely sure, it's just that she thought she had a pound coin or two and now the pizza lad's at the door (Marc allows deliveries from the organic pizza place) it's no longer there, and she has to rummage round in the change tin and it's embarrassing to give him a tip of only seventy pence in a cluster of pennies, ten-pees, and three five-pence bits.

She tries not to bother Marc about these losses. He's got enough on his plate. Promoted two years ago, and now it's always a 'challenging time' at work. But she thinks this would be a bloody good way to gaslight her. And she doesn't tell Kelly about the memory stuff. She doesn't want her sister to worry about her.

Then she can't find her earrings, the gold hoops. It's not like she wears them much as they get tangled in her curls when she's teaching. This time she knows she left them on her dressing table. For sure. She'd seen them there and thought she might wrap them in tissue paper and stuff them in a card for Kelly, not that it's her birthday or anything, just because it's nice to get something that you're not expecting.

It's better to think Dolly's friend is taking stuff rather than admit she's losing her mind. She feels embarrassed when Tamara comes around. She watches her closely and feels guilty – does she suspect her just because she doesn't like her? But then, sometimes Lulu or Pat-Pat demand her attention, or her phone buzzes, or she's just the usual amount of distracted.

She makes a point of asking Dolly if she's seen the earrings in front of her friend, to check for a reaction, but there's nothing. Tamara sits alongside Dolly threading beads on to ribbons to make necklaces, both wearing their Ariana cat's ear headbands.

When she notices Debs watching, the girl looks up and graces her with a smile.

She thinks about it but decides she can't ask Ruby straight out. She rehearses phrases like, 'Could Tamara have picked up my earrings by mistake?' or, 'The girls were playing with some of my stuff earlier, could you check her bag to see if my gold hoops have got mixed up with Tamara's things?' But every which way sounds like she's accusing the child of being a thief. Which she supposes she is.

But it could be her mistake, her hormones plummeting, losing the plot, which is just as bad.

Sweating for a living, she didn't clock the hot flushes at first. And her periods sometimes stop when she's stressed out.

She doesn't want to admit she's cantering towards the menopause – she's narked enough as it is – although she definitely does not want another child. But neither does she want to feel redundant, put out to pasture.

Those worries seem so long ago now, eclipsed by more pressing fears.

51

5.25 a.m., 24 December

'Marc. Don't. Please. Come here.'

Amazingly, he puts the pills down. He shuffles over and sits next to her. Lulu scoots away. He wraps his arms around her and whispers, 'Sorry,' into her neck. It might look tender, this embrace, if it were not for the knife he's still holding.

She lets him hug her but she can't relax, because as he cleaves to her he holds her tighter and tighter and she can't take a full breath.

He's holding her hard against his chest, trying to keep himself from flying apart in a hundred different directions. Clasping her to him like a drowning man.

And it does no good, because he knows she's afraid of him. He has made his wife fearful. He recognises the animal smell of the fear on her.

But then, she should be afraid.

52

Seventeen years ago

You drink to impress at the Officers' Ball. You eat a good meal beforehand, line your stomach. Poor Preparation leads to Piss Poor Performance. And that's what this is – as much as a drill, as much as an inspection – you put on a show.

You brush up well. Smart. Impressive. You look the part. A photo at the beginning of the night would make your mother proud. If you had that sort of mother.

It's a long night. Banter. Not bullying, as such; banter. You drink into belligerence.

Hostilities commence.

Lance-Corporal What's-his-face, black chap, whining to the Service Complaints Commission. Case dismissed, naturally. Medical discharge. PTSD. Every fucker who's been to Iraq has PTSD. Shut the fuck up. Stop whingeing. Get on with it. What did he expect, silly cunt? A suntan?

Nasty laughs. Baying laughs. Pack mentality. You join in. Safest.

The evening starts coming at you in slices.

You might lose the professional smile. You might stumble.

But these are your comrades, your friends, your peers. They have your back.

They have you on your back. Wrestling. Young bucks. Rutting.

Blanks. Firing blanks. Just banter. But—

All you hear is *cunt this, cunt that*.

Out of hand. You try to protest.

Your dress trousers are round your calves and you've been sick down your white shirt and they push you into the shower. Your head smashes against the wall. The pain is blinding.

And you don't see who it is. You can't look round. Someone's holding your neck. Hard.

Soap in your eyes. And, improbably, someone's cock in your mouth.

You thought you wanted to cry out then.

But suddenly the soap is rammed up your rectum. Harder.

Again. Again.

Later, someone finds you unconscious.

The medical report lists contusions and abrasions around the wrists and neck, a dislocated shoulder, which still aches deep under the scapula when it's cold. The head wound appears superficial – sixteen tiny stitches – but the concussion is more severe. Blurred vision for several days.

The rectum is damaged. Torn. Bright red bloodstains decorate your pants.

You're prescribed senna, advised to eat prunes to allow the loose passage of stools during the healing process. You are warned of future prolapse. Given a leaflet on safe sex and HIV. Naturally, you don't formally report any of it.

Bruises fade. Another blooms internally.

Perhaps, secretly, in the next weeks and months, you might wonder, a childish, irrational thought, swiftly dismissed, if it was because of your father. Although no one here could know that.

This wound is not addressed.

It is never addressed.

53

One month ago

She realises she's losing it when she starts snapping at clients, participants, people in shops. Not Marc, so much. She's not stupid.

She feels strung out, like she did after that one time she tried speed with Kelly. It didn't suit either of them. If anyone needed something to take off the edges, smooth them out, it was Kelly and Debs. What they deffo did not need was something to ramp up the anxiety. They were born jangly. They didn't try it again.

Debs couldn't afford to do as much weed as Kelly did back then either because she always got the bloody munchies and, being so much shorter than Kel, there was always the constant battle with her waistline.

They didn't get into the booze in a huge way either, not after the first few years. They'd seen what it did to their mam. Not that she was an alky or anything, Shirley just liked a drink now and then. And sometimes she really, really liked it.

Debs doesn't need any external stimulant to provoke her, she's gearing up to erupt as it is.

'We need some form of identification.'

She knows this. She has it ready. She passes the girl her credit card, balancing the phone by her ear with the other hand.

'We need photo identification.'

'Sorry, Kel, hang on— Pardon?'

'A driving licence?'

'Why?'

'You paid by PayPal.'

'Yeah. With this credit card.'

She has no idea where her driving licence is – somewhere at home. Her rucksack weighs enough at the best of times with the resistance bands, and her notebook to log her client's progress and list their exercises, and wipes for the kids and for herself after classes, and her phone and the charger, and face-towel, and purse, and make-up bag, most of the items from that having escaped to roam free amid the rest of the junk, it seems—

The girl stands looking at her, making no move towards the credit card she's holding out, or moving her lazy arse to get the parcel Debs has come to collect.

'We need photo ID.'

'Photo ID?' echoes Debs. 'For a bread bin? Just a sec, Kel—'

Her sister is distraught. A row with Raven. The death-knell, 'You're not my mum!' flung her way after a campaign for a tattoo was vetoed, even though Kelly and Boz and Debs and Shirley all have a fair selection themselves.

Debs thrusts her Waitrose card towards the desk to no avail. The girl would make a good poker player.

Debs does not respond well to Groundhog Day scenarios, especially when she only has twenty minutes to collect the bread bin, a replacement for the one Pat-Pat jumped on last week – from a chair, don't ask – ordered from John Lewis because it said online you can collect from the Waitrose down in Crouch End, which she's planned to do on the way to the gym from her client in Highgate (Josie, recent hip replacement, can't get to the gym yet) and eat the little tub of coconut and drink the pomegranate juice (because she's trying to be good, weight-wise) before her next client, then tear back to pick up Pat-Pat from his nursery and prepare for her afternoon Mums and Tots Park Workout session.

'My name's on the card,' she offers. 'I don't carry my driving licence with me.'

'A passport?' reiterates the girl, half-heartedly now, obviously losing interest.

'Actually,' says Debs, knowing full well this could escalate just by hearing herself utter that word, and also knowing she's not going to get anywhere, yet pushing on regardless, 'I don't have my passport with me because I'm not planning on taking the bread bin on holiday.'

She feels slightly smug that she's managed not to swear.

'I'm afraid we can't give out goods without proper identification.'

'Computer says no?' counters Debs.

The girl doesn't respond.

And this goes round and round, winding Debs up at every convolution, until she has to walk away without the impounded bread bin, otherwise it will get ugly, and she'll be late for Mike (sixty-odd, old knee injury, high blood pressure) who always comes early and requires some soothing to keep that blood pressure in check.

She slinks back the next day with her passport and thank God it's the young guy with the dodgy fringe and pimples who retrieves her precious package from quarantine without incident.

And that should have been the end of it, only she dreams of punching the girl who wouldn't serve her, punching her hard.

It's displacement fury. She knows who she really wants to punch.

54

5.29 a.m., 24 December

She stays absolutely still until Marc's breathing becomes softer and he seems to tune out. His arms relax a little.

Debs' mind ricochets between puzzling what might be going on in his brain and thinking that she has to get herself together before the kids wake. It's nearly half five. She hopes they'll sleep past seven, knackered after a late bedtime.

But when she starts to shimmy away, Marc grips her tighter.

'Let's get sorted for breakfast.' She says it softly so's not to disturb the peace.

'No.' His voice is also quiet.

Lulu doesn't stir from her basket, not even when Marc brings Debs down to the tiles, arranging her beneath him. He straddles her, leaning into her chest, squashing her breasts and ribs. She can't twist away. It's a bad position to be in. The bastard gets off on this. The weight of him is crushing air out of her lungs.

He rears up. His face contorts. She reads the signal. He starts to undo his zip.

'No. Marc. Stop.' She hisses, 'Stop! Dolly might come down again. Pat-Pat—'

He pauses and for a second she thinks it will be okay. He leans back on his heels and the pressure lifts a little. Then he strokes the side of her neck with the tip of the blade, his moves slow and dreamy.

She holds her breath.

'Take it off.' He gestures to her dressing gown.

She considers but does nothing. She notices a blackhead on the side of his nose. There was a time when she'd have loved to squeeze that. There was a time he'd have let her. But now she's too busy cleaning sleep out of Pat-Pat's eyes and trimming Dolly's nails, and squishing fleas she's teased out of Lulu's fur.

Kelly gets it, this grooming behaviour. She jokes, 'I'm only with Boz for his crop of back spots.'

Debs couldn't touch Marc that way now. It seems wrong; too intimate.

She doesn't move, but when he begins to pull at the front of the dressing gown, she clutches it together. He stops yanking the material and brings his hand around her throat, gently caressing, squeezing a little, then a little harder, like he's in a dream, kneading sourdough, then digging in his fingers, as she tries to prise his hand away, but he increases the pressure, tighter, tighter and she panics and croaks, 'Stop!' but he won't, curling his lips into a snarl like an attack dog, his grip tighter, harder, until she gasps, 'Stop! I might be pregnant!'

He's suddenly alert.

55

Ten months ago

When she first moved in with him – after he'd put the deposit down on the house that looked like one of those you saw in glossy magazines, a proper family home with a garden, something she never really believed would ever be hers – he'd paid for a cleaner and a gardener and they'd eaten out a lot.

He'd pulled his weight for a time, tidying up, doing the laundry, shopping. Incrementally, all that came under her job description during her 'maternity leave'. A joke: self-employed, she daren't take too long off work, otherwise she'd lose clients. She had the energy when it was just Dolly, but with two, plus Marc's incremental campaign of domestic retreat over the last two years, she's pretty much dead on her feet most of the time.

'You could always drop a few clients,' is his solution, like a slap. 'You work too hard, darling. Have a break, don't push yourself.'

She's sure he'd be happier if she gave up work altogether, but that's never going to happen. That's one line she's drawn and stuck to. Shirley taught her that much: 'Keep your own money, duck, for when the fuckers fuck off.'

Debs dropped other things instead, like hoovering and cooking. Anyway, she wasn't very good at cooking the sort of stuff Marc liked. She was happy eating beans on toast with the kids. If he wanted fancy food, he could sort it.

In the olden days he'd been hands-on with the kids. He'd read them bedtime stories and take them on outings at weekends. He'd play with them as soon as he got back from work.

He'd organised picnics when Dolly was little. She remembers him laying out the rug with a flourish, unpacking egg sandwiches he'd made from scratch; smoked salmon and chilled wine for them, juice for Dolly, strawberries and cream for all.

That time Dolly waddled over to a dog that was sniffing round the ham Marc had thrown to it. 'What's his name?' she'd asked the dog's owner, an old boy in socks and sandals. 'Pat. Pat the dog,' he'd replied, grinning.

Brilliant.

They'd have popcorn and film nights at home. Marc hugging her tight on the sofa. Dolly marching round with a tea towel on her head singing the *Star Wars* theme tune.

Later he supervised bath time with Pat-Pat, splashing and singing 'The Grand Old Duke of York'. He did nappy-changing duty with both kids. He taught Dolly how to tie her shoelaces.

Now all basic training and maintenance of child life-support systems is left to her. Yet it doesn't stop him making pronouncements from on high, like some general safe in his bunker – his study the equivalent of a Whitehall war room – far away from the grim realities of life at the front. He's been particularly intrusive regarding Pat-Pat's on-going toilet training, wrinkling his nose at the occasional accidents.

'Big boys do not wet their pants, Patrick. Now, how shall we sort this out, soldier?'

'For Christ's sake, he's not even three,' she'd snapped at the time.

'Dolly had this all done and dusted when she was two,' he replied, for which she has no answer, apart from the thing she can't say: boys are sometimes bloody hopeless.

Pat-Pat's more into his Transformers, any technology, rather than focusing on cues from his bladder. He can be mesmerised by the microwave. His superpower is having the energy of a supernova. Eyes open, instant fifth gear. He tears around making nonsense sounds and expresses himself physically rather than verbally – a kick or a slap to signify displeasure or frustration, running at full pelt, flinging his whole body into your arms when he's happy. He doesn't possess the skill to recognise internal signals, or to tell her when he wants a wee or a poo.

It used to be funny watching Marc try to negotiate with this force of nature.

'What did you do at nursery today?' he'd ask his son. And Pat-Pat might roar. Or he might spin like a top. He simply did not have the words.

The way Marc has started chipping in about Dolly's weight is another bone of contention. He'll poke his daughter's tummy and say, 'What have we here? Have you eaten your brother?'

He used to enfold his daughter in his arms; he used to tickle and kiss and blow raspberries on that tummy. The way he pokes it now isn't entirely kind.

After Dolly skips away to play, she says, 'You'll give her a complex.'

But he won't let it go. She can see he disapproves of the photos of his daughter in her tutu from the dance school's latest end-of-term showcase. She can see the shadow of Jeanne in his face when he advises her to cut down on the child's treats.

'Who's got the qualification in nutrition, Marc?' she challenges.

Jeanne labelled Dolly 'chubby' when they last visited, and Debs wanted to smash her bloody face in.

Marc's disciplined when it comes to his food. He calculates calories and portion size. He does not allow himself sweets of any kind. He's committed to his weekly squash, morning runs and gym sessions; he monitors energy input and output, as she advises some of her clients to do, but with a far tighter rein. He has a state-of-the-art fitness tracker. He has a *spreadsheet*.

How he works the amount of booze he puts away into his weekly calorie counter, she's not sure. She imagines it balances out the times he's coked up and shows no interest in eating.

Of course she knows. She just can't face a huge blow-up over it.

Kelly calls.

After the 'You okay? The kids okay?' litany, the phone call moves on to another constant: the weight issue.

Kel says, for the hundredth time, 'I've got to knock the chips on the head. I've really chunked up again.'

'I know what you mean,' says Debs, without thinking, because this is always the wrong thing to say.

'Fuck off. You're not fat, Debs.'

'Okay, not medically obese, but sometimes I feel like a bloody walrus when I'm teaching.'

'Oh, for fuck's sake!'

This is Kelly's favourite argument, an argument Debs is involved in against her will. Whatever her sister says, it doesn't change how she feels. She wishes she didn't, but that doesn't make it go away.

There's no convincing Kel that being a size twelve, at Debs' height, is too big, not when Kelly's at least a fourteen, on a good day with a following wind.

'I'd give my right arm to be a bloody twelve,' moans her sister.

But there's no getting away from the fact that, in London terms, Debs is big for a fitness instructor. In the land of Instagram models, posing in their bloody bikinis alongside their plates of perfectly arranged papaya, she is a bit porky, like British actresses are total heifers next to the micro women of Hollywood.

Kelly tells her sister she thinks she's gorgeous. 'You remind me of Kylie in that musical where she looked like a green Tinker Bell, the one where Ewan McGregor embarrassed himself singing.'

Debs always wanted to be taller like Kel, always admired her figure, although her sister has indeed bulked up quite a bit in recent years, thanks to both the IVF hormones and the self-harming with great slabs of Cadbury's when it didn't work.

Debs knows the media obsession with looking a certain way is all bollocks, but you just can't win as a woman. The other day, seeing a slim young punter stretching into beautiful yoga poses on a mat in the gym, she'd gone up to her and said, 'Great flexibility!'

And the girl had looked up, flustered, and said, 'I'm sorry.'

Debs said, 'What? Why?'

'I wasn't showing off.'

No bloke would ever, not in a million manspreading, mansplaining years, have said anything like that.

Don't get her wrong, she has a couple of boy dancers who come to her Monday Zumba who have a toehold on the self-loathing spectrum. But they're not the usual.

She hates it in herself, this desire to be smaller. She's all about being healthy. But the narrow path she treads between feeling lumpen and shite, or feeling she's presenting an achievable, sensible role model to the girls who come to her sessions – and Dolly will become one of those girls one day very soon – is a rocky road with steep edges of self-disgust and panic on either side, all within about four or five pounds/a couple of days on the chocolate eclairs.

Most of the time Debs thinks she does some good in her job. She likes to help people. But quite often she wonders if she's not letting the side down thanks to her own fuck-ups around size. And this is the toxic world her daughter will inherit.

She rants to her sister, 'You know, Kel, there'll be no equality until straight men do fucking Christmas and women stop this constant bloody fretting about how we look and what the bastard scales say.'

'Yeah, but, like ... how do I lose a bit?' asks Kelly.

Debs gives up, and says, 'You need to knock the wine and sugar on the head—'

'Give me a bloody break!' Kel is not up for negotiations about her drugs of choice.

'I mean it.'

'Stop nagging.'

'You asked! And people pay me to nag them.'

'Yeah, those with more money than sense.'

'That's not fair, Kel.'

'I know. I didn't mean it.'

And after a bit more gossip about the current size of Adele, her sister ends the call with, 'You really okay?'

'Yeah, fine.'

'Twat-features behaving himself?'

'Yeah.'

What else can Debs say?

The way Marc fixes her with a stare during some of the *discussions* about their daughter's weight is sometimes worse than the words. The way she feels he judges her parenting skills makes her shrivel.

Then there are his comments about the state of the house, like she's some 1950s housewife. She understands that he's fastidious and that military training might serve him well in the office, but it's verging on squeamish, if you ask her.

She's had more than her fair share of cleaning up shit, with the kids and with her mam. It wouldn't kill him to give her a hand now and then.

She does her best and she does it on her own. All he does is have a pop at her, again and again.

Words suggesting she's a failure as a mother. Words telling her she's worthless. Lethal words in the bedroom, branding her a dirty bitch who deserves all she gets.

Each word, each tiny snag, each shallow cut stings. A word, a look, a sigh. One after the other after the other, all in a row, like the teeth on a bread knife. Tiny, tiny serrations.

Eventually, they could slice you in half.

A pressure builds in the house. Not like summer thunderclouds, more the glowering approach of snow. Light seems green-tinged. There's a prickling on her scalp. The atmosphere is brittle. Some sort of current crackles. Words have sharp edges. Debs worries how this stress will poison the kids. Years of therapy ahead.

Tiny little anxieties building and building. A hair might break the camel's back.

A pile of individual grains of sand, scratching at her eyes. A dune, a drift, settling heavy on her chest.

For years she felt becalmed. Now she's going under.

She sees the boy twice in the middle of the night, just for a second or two.

She's not ruling out that she's asleep.

There's something like a shimmer, a vibration across her eyes.

She can't make out his expression. There's no gesture. Just a terrifying emptiness.

She always knows it's not Pat-Pat. The child has fair hair, whereas Pat-Pat's is dark. But he's someone's boy. He wants her to help him, but she doesn't know how. She feels the need radiating off him as he stands stock still and silent.

She knows he's not really there. But sometimes she shuts her eyes and keeps them closed tight, just in case.

56

Nine months ago

By the time their mam dies, Debs is ripe to totally lose the plot.

But first, she and Kelly have to step up and help the Macmillan cancer nurses wipe their mother's arse and give her tiny sips of water and slivers of ice cubes and collect the morphine from the local chemist's, which they've not been in for years.

Shirley's a model patient. It's the only time she's been fussed over quite like this.

The sisters have discussions over endless cups of sweet hot tea, conversations you never want to have. A hospital-style bed is brought to Shirley's flat by a nice specialist delivery man who shows them how to set it up. The earnest GP, who's actually met their mam before, which is a bonus, perches on the new bed's inflatable mattress, to discuss what it will be like for her to die, in physical terms at least.

Shirley gasps out, one word at a time, 'Do. Not. Resuscitate.'

And when Kelly says, 'You sure, Mam?' she gives them a weak thumbs-up.

If they resuscitate her, she'll have to go back to work, and she is 'dog-fucking-tired'.

Shirley hears the kettle boil again. Then she sleeps/passes out/slips under. It's hard to tell.

Awake or asleep, sober or pissed, it's the same thing she wishes for, dreams of – a bit of a laugh and a decent life for her and the kids.

Perhaps they're playing on that wide beach, a sky for fucking days, the Tower behind them, and she has her feet up and a Baileys or an ice cream or both. They do Baileys Magnums in Asda now – what a time to be alive!

By the end that's all she wants, a nice day out at Blackpool with her kids. 'Take me up the Tower!' the old joke.

Nothing like those dreams up until a few months ago, when it was all about the blokes: Idris Elba, Denzel Washington, that young lad from the fish and chip shop in town with the lopsided grin. Dreams with lots and lots of lovely shagging.

She opens her eyes to watch Debs sleeping alongside her in the chair. Her youngest is drooling. Shirley might smile if she had the energy.

She worries about leaving her girls, although they're proper grown-up now. Don't really need her no more.

Pain. Light. More pain.

Dark.

She sees her hands gripping the rail around the bed, the

weird bed, not her own bed, hanging on for dear life, her fingers slipping off one by one. Her hands are going numb. She can't feel her face.

She's fought for every breath, every step of the way. Now she's so tired.

She thinks, *I'm sorry*. She's not sure exactly what for, but as a mother you've always got plenty of stuff to be sorry for.

The bed creaks and makes strange hissing noises as it shifts position, all by itself, like it's possessed, to stop Shirley getting bedsores.

As it turns out, there's not enough time for that.

57

Eight months ago

From the initial diagnosis to the death certificate, three and a half weeks. Another week and a bit, then the funeral.

It started in the lungs. Of course it bloody did. They didn't need a medical degree to guess that. Shirley's dedication to Silk Cut was a sure-fire winner on that front. Secondary cancers in the liver. They don't get the official results of where it started until they're in the middle of probate hell, sorting out the bank and the electric and the landlord being shitty about the deposit and battling with Mario, the latest useless wazzock of a boyfriend who happened to be shacking up with their mam at the time, who claimed they'd been planning on getting wed, so he 'should be entitled to something'.

Kelly threw a mug at him and Boz warned, 'Mate, you'll be entitled to this Toby jug rammed right up your jacksie, handle and all, if you don't fuck the fuck off right now.'

They'd not seen hide nor hair of Super fucking Mario when they camped out in their mam's flat, Kelly on the sofa and Debs on a chair next to Shirley with her feet up on her overnight bag for most of the time. It felt too weird for either of them to sleep in their mam's old bed, which Boz helped them drag into the living room to make space for the clinical version, which she hated, but needs must.

Now and then, Kelly would swap with her, and Debs texted Marc from the living room. She couldn't bear to call him, pretended she didn't want to disturb Shirley.

Watching her mam slip away felt profound, inevitable and mainly, in the end, a relief. She'd been unconscious for a couple of days by then. That's when Debs felt closest to her, because she'd seen her like that often enough. It was sort of soothing.

The grief was altogether messier.

Kelly's emotions seemed cleaner somehow, lots of straightforward tears. Debs cried a bit with her sister, but most of the time she was spitting feathers, not sad at all. She was narked with the florist, the undertaker, the man who came an hour late to take the hospital bed away, like she had somewhere else to be. She was angry with Marc for not being there, even though she kept telling him she didn't want him to come. And she was furious at her mam: for smoking, for drinking, for fucking dying. She was ashamed of herself for those feelings.

Mario turns up to the funeral, a bitterly cold day in some godforsaken crematorium up near Worksop that Debs never knew existed. She has no idea why Shirley wanted it all done and dusted there.

Boz announces, 'The chancer cunt's here, asking for a slap,' and Kelly has to talk him down.

Boz has been a diamond, helping them clear their mam's flat and providing the fuel to do so with cups of tea and too many packs of cheapo biscuits that Debs hates herself for eating.

Marc was conspicuous by his absence during the funeral planning, the paperwork, the hauling piles of shite up to the dump, hurriedly shoving Shirley's 'bedroom toys' into a bin liner.

She's relieved he's not been around. But he does shepherd the kids up on the train for the big day.

They're so smart, it stings. Dolly has a new black coat to match her shiny black shoes. Pat-Pat, tall for his age at nearly three, seems so grown-up in his miniature suit. Debs can hardly look at them or she'll properly lose it.

Marc carries his suit well and attracts admiring glances. A couple of Shirley's old mates twitter round him before the (thankfully) brief service. Boz's Raven is indistinguishable from the other mourners in her goth get-up. But beneath her flapping black coat, she wears a vintage *Jesus Is A Cunt* T-shirt, so Boz hisses at her and makes her keep it buttoned. The girl looks aggrieved.

Shirley's wearing her best turquoise frock in the coffin, which is just *there* in the aisle. Small. So much smaller than she was in real life, because their mam had so much life in her. She's wearing her favourite ring, the one Dolly loved, a giant plastic flower ring that looked like it might squirt water in your eye.

'If she'd laid off the vicious fuck-buckets, the booze and the fags, she'd have been grand,' says Kelly, although not in the eulogy.

Shirley's older sister, Aunty Pearl, misses the crem but polls up for the drinks after. Debs has only met her once, but she's seen a couple of photos.

Shirley's photo album, with the cracked white plastic cover and the few faded snaps from when she and Pearl were kids, always made Debs shiver. Her mam would slowly turn the pages, chatting about the day they did this or that, and Debs would tense, waiting for that one creepy picture of the other sister, Aunty Mona, the eldest. She'd never met her.

The photo still haunts Debs. For some reason Kel's kept it.

It shows Mona, who looks too young to be a mother, cradling her baby daughter, smiling shyly up at the camera through her fringe. You can't really see the baby's face as she's clutching her tight to her ample chest.

Shirley told it like a ghost story: the chilled, foggy day; the scribbled note left behind in the kitchen.

Mona went off the top of a multi-storey car park in Leeds the year after that photo was taken, not that she ever lived in Leeds. And the worst thing: 'She took the kiddie with her.'

Her toddler, Jenny, fourteen months, was in her arms when she jumped.

She wasn't in her arms at the bottom.

The thing that got Debs was that, as her mam told it, Mona had wrapped little Jenny up for the cold weather. The kid was wearing mittens.

Probably manic depressive, bipolar as they say now, or as Shirley called it, without one single ounce of empathy, 'Round the fucking twist.' She spat out the words as Debs shuddered.

'No matter how shit your life is, you do not take the fucking kiddies with you!'

It's not like there are many photos from Shirley's life but every one of their mam shows her laughing, beaming wide at the camera. Even those where she's squinting into the light, gaps showing between her teeth, she looks so bloody happy.

Marc has to get back for work, so they don't stay over after the funeral.

Dolly leans against Debs' shoulder on the train on the way back. First class. Free coffee. Pat-Pat crashes out in his dad's arms on the other side of the table, as Marc tries to surreptitiously check his phone. Lights stream by the windows like the Blackpool Illuminations.

Dolly asks sleepy questions about where Nana Shirley is now. Debs can't bring herself to say 'heaven' and settles for, 'No one knows for sure, chick. But she'll always be with us in our memories,' announcing that little gem like she's on Radio Four.

She thinks a minute, fighting the slew of nausea from the egg and cress sandwich and three brandies she's managed to get down her. To be honest, she adds, 'Or it might be just like going to sleep. Without dreaming. Like nothing, really.'

'Will I have a funeral?' says Dolly, chewing on a piece of hair.

Debs pulls it out her mouth, hearing her mam say loudly, right next to her ear (although she knows it's only inside her head, she knows it's not real), 'Will you bloody stop that! It'll get wrapped round your heart and you'll drop down dead, mark my words,' and she worries how this day might impact on her girl. She tries, 'Not for a very, very long time, love. Only poorly, old people die.'

'Oh.' Dolly sounds subdued. Debs strokes her head. 'That's a shame,' she adds. 'I liked all the flowers.'

Shirley wanted some of her ashes scattered on her own mother's grave, which was a turn-up for the books, given that she didn't have a lot to do with her when she was alive, some, even more inexplicably, on Dave's grave – contestant number one in the *Blind Date* sweepstake for Debs' sperm donor – and the rest up the park where she sometimes sat and had a ciggie on the way back from the Co-op.

Afterwards, Debs goes off the rails a little. Who wouldn't?

She not only ups the kick-boxing sessions with Ali at the gym, because – God bless him – he refuses to charge her for the extra hours she books so she can work out her need to hit something hard without being arrested, she also succumbs to his kindness and flattery, and doesn't go home straight from work. Let bloody Marc look after the kids for once while she has a night out. Fuelled by righteous anger at Marc's detached coolness and the four random unplanned gin and tonics after her shift (she doesn't even like gin), she gives in because she's too numb and tired and weak and pissed and pissed off and pathetic not to.

And it's not like it's the first time she's messed around behind someone's back. She's got form.

She creeps back home in the early hours. A hasty wet wipe in the bathroom before she slides into bed next to Marc, holding her breath.

'What, that knob-cheese from the gym?' says Kelly when she calls her. 'The one who looks like a boiled egg?'

'I know,' sighs Debs.

Ali had a shaved head at Debs' wedding. Kel wasn't too impressed with his ostentatious display of dancing at the reception, which knocked over two chairs and three vodka Red Bulls.

'Pie him off,' advises her sister.

'I will,' she promises.

To makes things worse, Ali seems grateful. Out of politeness, there's a rematch before she does manage to finish it.

When she tells him, his face crumples like Pat-Pat's when he drops his biccie on the floor.

That's the only time Debs feels a bit guilty.

Has Marc ever cheated? She doesn't think so, although she sometimes wishes he had, as that would make it okay to hate him more.

The next week, Ali begs her to come for a coffee at the café around the corner from his gaff. She biffs him off until he says he's got something important to tell her. She hopes it's not that he's come clean to his wife, currently estranged and living back with her mum in Lewisham. Ali's perhaps not the catch of the day but surely, he's a better prospect than *Lewisham*?

Actually, he's not. Over their trendy turmeric lattes, in mugs with stupid handles that make them hard to hold, he tells her she needs to get herself checked out because he may have chlamydia.

'What the fuck do you mean, "may have"? Why the fuck didn't you tell me? For fuck's sake, Ali!'

Debs could stab him with the wooden fork she's using to shovel the walnut cake she shouldn't be eating into her stupid mouth as a soothing mechanism. She feels a wave of shame, although it might also be a hot flush.

She should never have taken the risk. Twice. Stupid, stupid cow.

Thank God she didn't have it. If she'd given that to Marc, he'd have killed her.

58

5.36 a.m., 24 December

'Pregnant?' He heaves himself up above her, pushing one hand on her sternum. 'When did that happen?'

A clever question.

She notices a clump of Lulu's fur, which has gathered under the fridge like tumbleweed, and forces herself to come up with something to deflect the danger in the question. Anything. She just needs to distract him.

'I need my inhaler, Marc.' It comes out raspy. Convincing because it's true.

There's a moment. Perhaps he's considering it.

She considers sinking her teeth into his hand which is still holding her down.

Suddenly he shifts his weight. 'Stay here. I'll get it.'

Lulu stays. She knows that word.

Watching him rise like a ruined MMA contender, Debs plans not to stay. She plans to sidle into the lounge, get her phone, call for help.

She props herself up to sitting and waits until she hears his footsteps above her in their bedroom.

Can she can leg it round to Sylvia's? Another quick glance at the kitchen clock. Isn't it too early to run to a neighbour's for help? What would she say? He's not touched her, not really. He's hurt her worse than this when the sex games got out of hand. Why is she so frightened of him now?

How will the kids react if police turn up on the bloody doorstep? Isn't she just overreacting?

Think!

Jesus – why has she let him go upstairs where the kids are sleeping?

Perhaps if she can keep him calm for another hour or so, until it starts to get light. Everything will feel better in daylight.

That's no plan, and she knows it.

And of course she's not fucking pregnant. She'd say anything to get him off her. If you lack the reach, the weight advantage, the power, you have to fight dirty.

Ali showed her that during their one-to-one kick-boxing sessions, when he'd torment and provoke and jab at her arm, her side, her solar plexus, until once she'd exploded and went fucking-ape-shit and kicked him rather than the pad and bit him on the arm – in front of members, mortifying! – so he had to wrestle and contain and finally sit on her.

She received a written warning from the Virgin Customer Services Manager for that.

Despite his army training, years ago now, she reckons Marc lacks that killer instinct. He's more cul-de-sac than street cred. And, despite everything, he thinks of himself as a gentleman. Chivalrous! What a fucking joke. Claiming a phantom pregnancy will appeal to his protective streak. It might be enough to make him quit whatever it is he's playing at.

And if he doesn't, well, he might know military strategy, he might have a theoretical knowledge of offensive and defensive moves, but you can't prepare for quick wits and unbridled violence.

He's positioned, strived for, fought for promotion. Sometimes she's felt like she's fighting for her life.

Concentrate. She needs to find her phone.

She creeps across to the lounge, willing Lulu to stay in her basket. If the dog thinks Debs is getting her harness, she'll start barking in gleeful anticipation of a walk. Shit! Her phone isn't on the table. She could have sworn she left it there. Where the hell did she put it?

She tries to re-run last night's routine. Yes! She had to pop to the corner shop because they'd run out of the almond milk Pat-Pat needed for his rice pudding. She's not so sure his 'hyperactivity' has anything to do with dairy products, but Marc insists, and it can all kick off if he doesn't see it neatly stacked, all present and correct in the fridge when he gets home.

He doesn't notice a lot of things – the new blue streak in her hair, how his marriage is falling apart – but he can nag for Britain if there's no special milk for his son. He's always been particular when it comes to what the kids eat.

She stumbles over to the coat pegs in the hall, the modern design Marc liked, the multi-coloured, eye-threatening protrusions as confusing as a science experiment. She's still frantically fumbling in the pocket of her jacket as he lopes down the stairs two at a time.

Stupid, stupid cow! She should have run for help or grabbed a knife before going for the phone.

He snatches the coat away from her fingers and grips her arm, hauling her back to the kitchen, startling Lulu out of her whistly snores.

He drops her arm like he's flinging away rubbish and she rubs the part where his fingers dug in. She waits for the interrogation about the non-existent baby. Surely, he knows she's made it up. But what if he accuses her of an affair? She'd not exactly pass a lie-detector test on that front with flying colours.

But there are no questions. A respite of sorts.

He reaches into his own pocket.

She ducks as he flings the Ventolin at her head.

Lulu's out of the basket like a waddling rocket. The Game! The man's playing the Game! She knows what to do. Tear after the thing. Find the thing. Under the chair, there! Fetch the thing. Then sit!

The man used to throw a ball for her in the garden. And she ran like the wind. She got to the ball before the girl, before the boy – Fetch! Fetch! Bring it! Bring it, Lulu! *Here*, Lulu! Come on, Lulu! – she grabbed the ball and she *fetched* and she *sat*, although she was so excited, she could hardly sit still.

And the man would pat her head and then she was Whatta Good Girl.

The man hasn't played the Game for ages.

*

Debs shouts under her breath: 'No! No, Lulu! Give it to me. Come on, *here*—'

Lulu drops the inhaler, which bounces on the floor and skids under the table. Debs hurries across to pick it up before the dog slobbers all over it again, quickly wipes it on her dressing gown and knocks back a swift puff. She knows it's not the right way to do it, but her chest feels like it's in a vice.

As she's holding her breath, he reaches across. For a moment she's surprised, thinking he might hug her. He smooths some strands of hair out of her face, then digs his fingers into her cheeks, hard, and pushes her face away.

Jesus.

She breathes out heavily, sweating again now, inching back towards the door.

She should get out now and call for help. Would Sylvia hear?

But she hesitates. Always back to that thought – his trump card – she can't risk the kids, unless she can get them out of the house with her.

And as she edges round the table to head for the stairs to do just that, he grabs her again. She starts to resist, but he pulls harder on her arm, bending it behind her so she has to back away from the door to stop the pain.

He steers her back into the middle of the kitchen, his feet coming towards Lulu, who also backs away, claws skittering on the tiles as she retreats to her basket, bewildered that the Game has finished so abruptly.

He brings Debs down to the floor. *Again.* What does he want her to do – kneel before her lord and master? She could fucking cry.

He wraps his arms and legs around her to keep her still. It almost looks like he's keeping her warm; it's almost like he's embracing her, keeping her safe.

His legs are heavy across her. She's pinned. She considers her options.

If she fucks him now, will that calm him?

She's wired, yet so exhausted, she can't think straight. How did her mind get so stuffed full, stupefied with lists of never-ending things to do? Like his neatly organised to-do lists on his phone calendar. Only his lists never include basics like *buy washing-up liquid, call vets*. Even now those external demands distract her.

How did she let this happen? Her brain isn't used to thinking straight. Now she needs it to work, she's not sure it will.

59

Three months ago

Her anxiety has been getting worse. Trips into town are now occasionally (okay, more often than not) accompanied by sweats and hyperventilating, spiralling into an asthma attack, leaning her head against the tiles in the bathroom at Costa on Upper Street, gasping.

And she's not sure if it's worse because of the perimenopause, if it's an anxiety attack, or if it's the start of something, perhaps going round the twist like her mam on the morphine, although she suspects her mam's confusion, pickled in booze, hazed in tobacco smoke, ringed with strings of fuckwit blokes, might have started before that.

Marc tried to address her worries in the old days. He'd talk to her, hug her. Back when he loved her. He liked to look after her, accompany her on outings with a reassuring arm around her shoulders, his palm on the small of her back for support. He was once genuinely concerned about her 'hyper-vigilance', before his tone became exasperated. He said her anxiety was unfounded. He loved to make it all better. To be needed.

So much so that, like a withered muscle, her will became flabby with lack of use. And when she tried to do things on her own, when she looked around and he wasn't there at her side any more, she faltered.

He suggested her worry and angst regarding Dolly and Pat-Pat was unnecessary. He told her he would be there to protect her; to protect them all.

He lied.

Since she'd had kids, all her fears have become magnified. She could write a comprehensive list of cruel, ingenious ways her children might be damaged or maimed or killed right in front of her. Like that time she'd tried to get a train so she could take Dolly and Pat-Pat, a new baby at the time, up to see their Nana Shirley, booking on the computer, which was confusing enough – baby brain, too many prices and restrictions – and then there was some issue and they wouldn't help her at the ticket office although she'd queued for so long, and Pat Pat was so heavy, even back then, her shoulders aching, and they made her call Trainline on some grubby landline at the end of the counter – another queue – and she'd been so flummoxed she'd left her iPhone next to the shitty museum-piece phone (who even has them now?) and then she had to run back for it and then—

And then she lost Dolly.

Her daughter disappeared.

It was only for a minute or so, but by the time she saw her, pouting and bored, slouched by a pillar, unaware that she'd been misplaced, Debs, distraught and wheezing, couldn't find the inhaler in her rucksack, so they'd missed the train she'd booked even though she'd allowed a good hour at the station and she'd had to pay a fortune for not having the right ticket on the right service at the right time.

Because she's just 'not up to muster'. She'd become used to Marc looking after tickets and phones and bills. Organising her, telling her what to do.

60

Seven years ago

When Dolly is just two and a bit, he has the chance to do a year in the New York office. And he simply expects her to up sticks and follow him out there.

'What about Dolly?'

'We'll be back before she starts school.'

It isn't so much what he says as how he says it that riles her, dismissing her concerns, her fears, as if they were nothing.

It means her giving up her classes and clients, which have taken years to build up. Abandoning her work for his. Just as she is back in the swing of things, getting some sort of balance between teaching and managing a toddler; just as she is finally sorting out her own body.

And she can't explain to him her visceral reaction when she visits New York for a long weekend recce. She loathes it. Too vertical. It feels like the city has reached critical mass. A bloody great black hole of a place, full of shouts and bangs and slamming doors and sirens. Things being smashed at all hours. She's on edge the entire visit.

He must have known she'd hate it. Every time she trekked down to the City to meet him in the early days, she reacted against the glass and concrete. Offices with names like Slaughter and May. The pub full of dead animals with a clientele to match. Slivers of sky choked by tons of ugly buildings looming over her, pushing in and down on her. The stench of sewage wafting upwards. It really creeped her out round Moorgate. It's all built on plague pits round there.

She could list other times, perhaps on a smaller scale, when he couldn't see, refused to see what she might need; where she was expected to bend her will to his. But it's a fair exchange, her compliance for his protection and the nice safe life he provides.

In the end, the offer falls through. Suddenly they need him in London after some crisis or other. They pull out of the house sale (it had got that far) and Debs frantically rings round everyone and is eventually forgiven by clients and colleagues. She breathes a temporary sigh of relief. But he had been willing to railroad her career off its path, derailed as it already was by motherhood.

When Pat-Pat turns one she decides to better her career by doing the Level Three PT qualification. If things go tits up, she reasons, she'll have that to fall back on.

But the exam day comes round so fast, she doesn't feel ready. There's always so much else to distract her. The trek to the physio, sports massage, rehab exercises in between sessions and still her shoulder aches with a throbbing insistence that keeps her awake.

He did that. He hurt her shoulder.

Never-ending chores. The laundry: so much sports kit alongside Dolly and Pat-Pat's clothes. Most of Marc's things are dry-cleaned, although she still has to remember to take them in and pick them up. Ironing, though the bulk of her stuff doesn't need it. Cooking, cleaning, tidying, ferrying the kids here and there and bloody back again.

By the time she gets to work, her actual job – sweating for a living, the hard graft, with the delayed-onset muscle soreness and other random aches and pains caused by wear and tear, exacerbated by age and gravity – that's the easiest part of her day.

And they say women nag, but Jesus, he's on at her for every little thing.

The latest bone of contention is a bag of clothes he's put out for her to take to the charity shop. She took it to her car, but he noticed it was still in the back seat a week later and he insisted she brought it inside lest the two Paul Smith suits and five shirts he intended to donate became damp.

The next night, when he came home to discover the bag languishing in the same place in the hall, he snapped, 'I don't understand, Deborah.'

'What's to understand? I've not had time, that's all.'

She doesn't know what else to say. She can hardly tell him the truth, because it makes no sense. She just loathes going in those shops.

As kids, she and Kel got most of their clothes from charity shops, long before stuff there was rebranded as 'vintage' and concepts like 'upcycling' graced them with moral superiority. They were just smelly places filled with old people's junk where poor people went.

She's anxious with so many to-do lists and shopping lists and exercise plans and other distractions. There's no space in her head for learning.

There's something about exams that sends Debs over the edge. At school, she'd mess them up, even though she was clever enough; even though the teachers told her she was bright and that she should breathe and think calm thoughts and just do her best, promising it would all be fine and dandy.

As if.

Too much other stuff was going on before she cocked up her exams at school. She'd missed too many lessons, learned others the hard way.

Marc apologised for the arm (an accident, she fell awkwardly, although if he'd not grabbed her in the first place...) but he's not exactly supportive about the revision. He'd promise to watch Dolly and Pat-Pat while she studied for half an hour. If she was lucky, she'd manage ten minutes before he let the kids come and pester her.

Pat-Pat spills his cereal all over himself the morning of the exam and Marc chooses not to see. After she's cleaned him up, and Lulu has lapped the remains off the floor, she finally grabs her bag and rushes out the door, fifteen minutes later than intended, although she has allowed herself leeway just in case there are any delays on the Piccadilly Line.

Dolly shouts after her, 'Good luck!'

And Debs pauses, touched that her daughter has remembered. She blows her a kiss, but as she turns to shut the door, Dolly adds, 'And Mummy...'

'Yes, love?'

'Don't fuck it up.'

Something else she'll have to tackle when she gets home.

And, unfortunately, inevitably, she does fuck it up. Not badly. Just badly enough that she'll need to do another day's assessment in order to pass. And she knows. Before the results, before the official confirmation of failure.

When she gets home, shattered and low, Marc doesn't raise his eyes from his phone when he asks how it went. He didn't get it, how doing another Level Three exam was like the Pilates qualification. Something *she* wants. Something she can be proud of.

When her results arrive, Marc says, 'Sorry, darling,' in a way she knows he isn't. Not really.

And that hurts.

But then he always prioritised his career over hers.

61

5.45 a.m., 24 December

He brings the knife to her mouth – when did he pick that up again? – teasing her with it. Gently parting her lips with the tip. The flat edge rests on her lower lip, pushing it out like Pat-Pat when he sulks. If he turns it on the side, it will slice her. She takes shallow breaths.

The knife is chilling, but his face is worse.

His eyes don't in fact look darker, although the small muscles around them have contracted. There's a slight narrowing that you wouldn't notice if you didn't already know this face so well, as well as your own, almost.

There are scores of other, barely perceptible signs that warn her of danger, beyond anything her mind is computing right now. Beyond the obvious. His smell. The rhythm of his breathing. The way his shoulders are braced. And she responds. Her focus changes in a way you might describe as an inattention to normal things and a heightened sensitivity to others.

He's more intent on the knife than holding her and she manages to shuffle away very slowly, swaying and dodging as he draws patterns centimetres from her face, her neck craning one way then another, like swans greeting each other; a mating ritual, perhaps.

Incrementally, she backs up against the bin, a slight waft of rot from within because she failed to take the bin liner out last night.

He continues the wordless taunting, the point of the knife hovering too near her eyes, so of course she flinches, as anyone would in that situation. And when he grabs her again, because this is their dance now – teeth and claws and animal instincts – she hisses bitterness and blame, anger spewing out in a hot rush.

The bastard's getting off on this.

And she snaps. She goes for him, lashing out in all directions, despite the absence in his eyes, despite the knife.

Lulu trembles in her basket.

62

Three weeks ago

Debs is shaking by the time she gets to the gym. She's never been late before. Chaos at home. Rushing into the studio, praying her pelvic floor holds up for an hour because she didn't have time for a wee, she shouts a cheery hello to the class, trying to ignore the chilly look of disapproval from Cynthia (grumbling old bitch, diabetes) and instructs her seventeen participants to start marching as she fumbles to connect her phone to the music machine, quickly scrolling through her playlists to the Seniors section.

She's relieved there are no newcomers to screen for their endless ailments and she runs through her usual 'Any injuries, illnesses, aches or pains out of the ordinary to tell me?' routine. 'Anything dropped off since last time?' gets a titter. 'Any pregnancies?' always gets a laugh, as the average age is seventy-odd.

Ethel announces she has cramp in her foot because she's 'a bit desecrated'. Debs grins and reminds her to sip water throughout the class.

You can't mess around with this mob. They come hell or high water, trekking to the Sobell Centre in all weathers. Resolute.

As she starts the protocols to warm up and mobilise the collection of creaky joints, her anxiety levels ease a little. She reckons exercise is the only way she stays sane sometimes. Forced to be in the present and focus on what's before her, she channels her adrenaline into what it's meant to do: move the body.

By the time she's on to the squats, she manages some more well-worn jokes. 'Like you're sitting on the loo, but don't get carried away, there's no mop in here!' A couple of the old girls, and Bill, who used to come with Irene but she's too ill now, reward her with smiles.

'Stick your bums out. Let's do the world's laziest twerk!'

Marina laughs. Marina always laughs because she's got dementia. She comes with her daughter (fit as a butcher's dog, depression, worn down by caring for her mum) who's in her early sixties herself.

They get their mats and the yoga blocks for arthritic necks and as she's instructing the set-up, offering alternatives for those who can't kneel and holding on to Betty's arm to help her down to the floor (osteoporosis, but she needs to practise getting off the floor if she falls) she hears her phone tone interrupt the music. Damn! She forgot to put it on Airplane Mode. She can't let go of Betty right now.

By the time she gets to her phone she fumbles and Marc's icy voice booms through the speakers. No swearing, never any swearing. But the tone! The demand, brooking no dissent. The underlying menace.

She sees the shocked looks.

Her own voice is slightly wobbly as she instructs the core work and final stretches.

As she's bagging up the resistance bands at the end of class, one of the ladies whose name she can't immediately recall (former magistrate, hip replacement booked for December) comes up and asks, 'Are you okay, Debbie?'

Debs presses her lips into a line and nods, because she doesn't trust what will squeak out of her mouth if she answers.

A brisk nod in return from the woman. 'I'm here should you need a confidante,' she says in clipped no-nonsense tones, giving her a swift pat on the forearm with a bony hand.

Debs can't look at her when she leaves, trying to catch her eye, smiling the 'supportive' look.

She can't bloody bear it.

Marc bought her a huge bunch of lilies after the first night she slept over, with a scent so intoxicating it was almost alien. She'd never experienced anything like it. She didn't have a vase to put them in, so improvised with a cardboard box and a bin liner.

The smell permeated her dreams. Usually there was only the waft of traffic fumes from downstairs and the occasional tinge of hot oil and non-specific meat from the burger bar two doors along. The scent was a gift in itself. It made her ache for something, she wasn't sure what exactly, just something *different*.

What would it be like that life, his life, where you could afford something so exotic; something so beautiful never meant to last?

Her mam once planted handfuls of daffodil bulbs in a tub outside the Black Swan. They emerged cheerful against the peeling grey paint in the weak March daylight; it made her happy to see them when she came home from school, like drawing a big smiley sun on your picture in felt-tip. After about a week, someone pulled them up, booted the flowers across the road and trashed the tub. They'd not even bothered to pick them to take home. Her mam didn't plant any more.

Smelling the lilies, she was embarrassed at herself. The first time a bloke had bought her flowers and she went all soppy.

When she was with him, she was full of cocky bluster, rude, almost. The chip on her shoulder suggested bold claims: her world was better than his, her lot laughed at themselves, were better dancers and, God, they knew how to have a good time. But when she was alone in her cramped living space, the lilies drew her in. She sat mooning over them. They became an obsession. A coded message, an offer, a promise.

She kept them until the petals turned limp and transparent like onion skin and the leaves rotted into slime.

Now she finds it hard to walk by flower shops with those lilies on sale. She's drawn to bury her nose in their flesh, to evoke that magical time, a time when he treated her like a princess. And there's often an echo of sadness percolating through the perfume, a minor note signifying the loss of hope. A betrayal of the original unspoken assurances and the spoken vows.

If only she'd ripped the heads off the bastard lilies and stuffed them into the bin or booted them hard across the road.

The nasty pollen ruins everything it touches, staining your hands and clothes rusty orange. It doesn't wash out. It's poisonous to cats and dogs.

63

5.49 a.m., 24 December

She's lost it big time. Her fury outweighs any sense of danger. The need to hurt him consumes her – a blackout of rational thoughts. Red fucking rage.

She manages to kick out and shoot away from under him, staggering to her feet, and as he's clambering up, she grabs the NutriBullet off the worktop and starts swinging it at him like a club, the lead and plug trailing in her wake.

Lulu woofles, partly in panic, partly in excitement, not sure if this is a new game.

Marc circles as Debs lashes out and then he launches himself at her, as an animal might spring for a hunk of meat. She manages to bash his wrist away – a satisfying clunk of metal on bone. He doesn't let go of the knife. He manages to grab her arm with his free hand and – Jesus! – the rage in his face. He means to stab her! When he lunges, Lulu is out of her basket to snap at his ankles in an ineffectual display of valour, and in that half second when he looks down to the dog, Debs smashes the heel of her hand into his nose.

64

Six years ago

She's always had a short trigger, but this is not the car to rant in. The eyelashes stuck to the headlights, the bright egg-yolk yellow bodywork, the white daisies along the side – they say, 'I'm a nice person; a considerate lady driver.'

They do not caution, *Push me, mofo, and I bite back.*

The clown car. She can always find it, wherever she's parked. Three-year-old Dolly adores it. They stuck the daisies on the side together and attached the eyelashes. Marc tutted about the paintwork when he saw it, trying to hide his grin.

When she drives Marc's dark-blue BMW, as she does occasionally, she'll be cut up, blocked in, beeped at and bullied, the everyday experience of life on London roads.

It's getting worse. Drivers can't be arsed to indicate any more. Pedestrians glued to their phones leap out into the road without warning. Some hurl buggies off the kerb right in front of you. And don't get her started on cyclists. All those accidents? Darwinism in bloody action.

There's a different sort of bullying when she ventures out in the yellow Beetle. Men in vans take the piss; men in general. They see the eyelashes and assume they can.

The incident at the traffic lights is where she thinks she's crossed some line.

She's been waiting to turn right. An entire green, amber, red rotation has passed without anyone letting her through. Sure, she's antsy, but she does not make a rash decision. There's a gap on the next amber and she starts to turn. It's definitely her right of way, but some wanker in a black Audi puts his foot down from fifteen metres away when it's already turned red his side and then has to screech to a halt just millimetres away from her passenger side.

It's not like he didn't notice her. You can see her bloody car from the International Space Station.

What she should do now is act like a grown-up and simply pull away. His bad. Get over it. Move on. Literally. They're blocking the traffic from the other direction. But she can't.

She sits. She glares.

The man in the Audi is shouting and swearing at her. She can't hear what he's saying, but she sees him mouth the usual obscenities.

Stupid cow. Stupid bitch.

But she's done nothing wrong. She will not scuttle away. She's tired of this kind of flak.

She takes a breath, but it's not a calm, steadying, mindful breath, it's a breath of preparation, the breath of war.

She opens her car door. She slips off her seat belt and gets out, which she knows you must never do. She jumps at a blast of car horns from a couple of drivers who can see her car has not in fact been hit or harmed in any way. Ignoring them, she walks round to the driver's side on the other vehicle, which – yes – everyone knows, you must never, ever do.

He may have a knife.

She hears the bass beat through the glass and metal, thumping like an aggressive heartbeat. He does not wind down his window. She sees his neck straining as he spits out more abuse at her. He has short dark hair, messier than Marc's. Blue, nasty eyes. She politely knocks on his window and stands with her arms folded, waiting.

Another driver sticks his head out of his Volvo and shouts, 'Come on, darling. Get a move on.'

'I'll just be a sec, *darling*,' she shouts back, waving like the Queen Mother.

She waits a lot longer than a second, but Audi man does not open the window, or turn his head away from her, or stop shouting abuse. But now, to punctuate his vitriol, he slams his hand on his horn. Bang. Bang. Bang.

She jolts as it shoots through her. Stab. Stab. Stab.

She sees him mouth, 'Suck. My. Dick!'

She turns back to her jolly Beetle but thinks better of it, swings round and kicks the side of his door. Hard. Hard enough to dent it.

The man looks stunned. His mouth stops. But he doesn't open his car window. She wonders if he's been smoking weed and doesn't want her to smell it. Drug dealers have nice cars round here.

She gives it a couple of seconds, bracing for the retaliation, forcing herself to stand her ground, before slowly, deliberately walking back to her car and putting on her seatbelt. The horns stop.

She breathes.

Before pulling away she winds down her window and flashes the V. A different horn signals a cartoon-style 'toot-tootle-toot-toot' reply, which might signify anything.

The black Audi does not follow her.

No police officer turns up on her doorstep. No insurance company gets in contact. And it's not like he couldn't identify her car.

She doesn't tell Marc.

The dreams afterwards are what worry her. The images, over and over, of punching through the driver's side window and pulling his head out to stop those words.

Grabbing his hair and slicing his neck, backwards and forwards and backwards and forwards across the jagged glass. That frightens her. It wakes her up in a sweat.

She knows she needs to keep a lid on that aggression. She's done really well since Dolly came along and she knocked the drinking on the head. But dreams like that spark the memories and take her right back to it. The nights at the pub that could turn on a sixpence, laughter growing ugly.

She doesn't like what booze does to her, what she becomes, as nasty as her mam was a right laugh.

65

5.51 a.m., 24 December

A shocking pain as she connects with his nose. *Fucking bitch!*

And suddenly he's hyped. Not at a sexual level. He's gone into survival mode. He doesn't really see her as Deborah – his lover, his wife, the mother of his children – all the old, fluffy labels. None of those apply any more.

Now she is simply the enemy.

She's thrashing her arms about, catching him glancing blows here and there. Pain stabs through his nose.

Her vile mouth is spewing nonsense words, hissing profanities, accusations and filth. An assault. An attack.

His training kicks in. He punches her just once, but it's enough.

He steps over her.

He leaves the body on the floor. A woman. Once his wife. Her adultery put paid to that.

She thinks he doesn't know. He's not stupid.

He *smelled* it on her.

He climbs the stairs, his movements jerky. Seven minutes to

six. His deadline, spurious. This needs to be finished.

He leaves the chocolate and sleeping pills on the counter. Too late for them.

Leave no man behind.

Better to end this now, so they don't suffer.

He tells himself, *I am not a monster.* He's not sure if he believes it.

He did the research. His life insurance policy would pay out if he executed the initial plan. He's been honest about the depression and post-traumatic stress and drug use, on paper at least. He's had the policy for well over two years; the clause invalidating pay-outs for suicides – *hasty* suicides – will not apply. The letter in the top drawer of his office lays out his intention.

But then he would leave his children behind. And this thought torments him.

To take them with him ... or to leave them behind...

But can he do it? Is he man enough? A brutal decision either way.

His children are cursed. Bad DNA on both sides. Can they be allowed to pass on his warped genes? He has come to realise that cannot happen.

He pushes open Dolly's door and slips inside her room, a riot of pink and purple; her small shoes lined up against the wall like baby piglets suckling a sow. On her scaled-down easel is a drawing of a unicorn. On the creature's back – standing, balancing, not sitting; she's not yet mastered how to show them sitting – Dolly and the dog. A bright smiley sun above them, clouds like legless sheep, the inevitable rainbow. Her nightlight softly illuminates it all, spraying stars around the room.

He stands over his daughter. Hears a rhythmic inhalation, exhalation.

What does he mean to do?

He had planned to—

No. The idea came upon him. He has not been able to shake it since it clawed its way up from the deepest parts of his brain. And it provided some relief.

He means to end it. He means to end them.

When he opens his eyes in the middle of the night and comes to a harsh consciousness, stained with failure and anxiety and defeat and shame – glaring shame – he's disappointed. He needs it to be over. But without him he knows Deborah will crumble. He's seen the cracks. Her recent behaviour has been worrying. Forgetfulness, mood swings, panic attacks, fury. She will not survive without him.

And then what? His children taken into care? Or let them go to her slatternly sister and the God-awful *Boz* in that sordid house full of snakes and feral dogs? He'd do anything in his power to protect them from that.

Sad, toxic families. Broken genes all round.

The unit's integrity is sacrosanct. Let no man fall into enemy hands.

Everyone breaks – SAS, Navy Seals, the toughest men and women trained to withstand all known forms of interrogation – in enemy hands, they all break.

His children will break...

Better if they both went to sleep. A warm drink, the pills, a story. Then as they dream, the drugs keeping them deep and safe below, then he could – might – do it.

The pillow over his daughter's face, the knife across her neck. Swift. A kindness.

The same with the boy.

Then he could finish the job himself.

He's never had a clear plan of what he'd do with Deborah. He's always assumed she'd fight.

When Victor's back legs gave up on him, Jeanne said she couldn't bear to do it, so Marc had to take him to the vet, to be 'put to sleep'. Not that it turned out like that. The dog fought and juddered and kicked and twitched, the will to live burning at a primitive level, until the drugs got the better of him and Marc felt that once strong heart slow and stop under his hands.

He couldn't watch. He had to turn his head away from the accusing eyes, but his hand on the animal's sunken flank felt it. Victor fought to the last breath. Noble. He wasn't a simpering bitch like Lulu.

After the awfulness, the stillness that came was sweetly calm. Meat, the only thing left behind on the examination table. The animal's spirit freed.

The first dead thing in his life, after his father. Although he never saw that. He couldn't believe Dudley was in that box with the flowers on the top.

He used to wonder if his father's death wasn't a cruel, elaborate joke. For years he almost expected to bump into him. But as the months and years passed his hope withered.

*

He watches his daughter sleep.

248

The boy and the girl are prisoners in the current situation. Non-combatants. Collateral damage. They are hostages to the way things have turned out.

He's not sure how long he stands looking down at Dolly's bed, the idea gnawing somewhere in his skull.

He is not sure he will be able to go through with it. He knows he's a coward.

In ancient times, they erected statues to people who gave their lives in war. Today, reporters hurl abuse. Citizens throw paint and tear down memorials. Governments, mortified by what they've ordered humans do to other humans, turn away. Officers are put on trial decades after their years of service. Abandoned. Vilified.

He deserves this hatred. Shame is his old companion.

He considers going back downstairs, simply walking out of the house, leaving everyone and everything behind.

But they will discover what he's done...

His children will be tainted, labelled the offspring of a murderer.

He closes the door quietly and comes back to stand by his daughter's bed.

66

5.56 a.m., 24 December

A real tree nowadays. How she's come up in the world. She can see the red and blue and green and white lights. But she can't focus.

Blue and white flashing lights.

But no ... that was then, not now.

She closes her eyes again.

How lovely it would be to go to sleep. And sleep and sleep.

Christmas Eve, the last at the Fox and Goose. She and Kelly and their mam lived in that big draughty flat above the bar, one of the rooms housing the stack of knock-off fags and spirits. Kelly was away at Granny Knees' house – her dad's mum (the constant complaining, Debs now realises, thanks to chronic arthritis) – along with several assorted half-brothers and sisters. Some Kelly had even met before.

And Debs had been back at the pub, dancing around the lounge as people clapped and smiled at her, then she sat on her own little stool by the bar (they found it in a charity shop and it was *brilliant*), and her mam sat on some bloke's knee, although it wasn't Santa. And there was tinsel everywhere.

In the middle of the room a girl was on her knees, straddling another man, the one who always played dominoes with the old fellas, who was lying on his back on the floor. Playing horsey, though she was the wrong way round. The woman put the man's willy in her mouth and Debs thought it must be dirty to lie on the carpet with all the crisp bits and spilled beer. And Adam Ant was singing 'Goody Two Shoes' and there was a big gang of blokes standing round shouting and clapping and then 'Mary's Boy Child' came on – her mam loved that one – and they all stopped whooping and it went quiet.

Later when Debs woke up it was getting light out so she knew it must be Christmas Day and everyone had gone home. She got off the coat she'd been lying on round the back of the plastic Christmas tree in the lounge, put the bolt across the pub door, otherwise they'd get in trouble, and went to find her mam.

She was asleep upstairs in the flat and Santa had been!

Her mam was a bit quiet, but then they had some Baileys together (which is sweet and burny and makes you giggly) and they put on hats from the crackers and Kelly came home with a love bite – but no, that was from another year wasn't it, she's getting mixed up – and after some singing they all did Christmas a bit and then they wished each other a Happy New Year!

67

5.58 a.m., 24 December

In the corner, next to Dolly's pink buckled shoes, there appears to be a dead animal. He stares at it until he can make sense of the inert lump of bushy red fur.

He finally identifies it as the ridiculous squirrel-tail fancy dress Deborah bought for Dolly's birthday, her favourite present for several weeks, which she insisted on wearing at every opportunity. Deborah even let her wear it in bed, which was most probably unhygienic.

Dolly shuffles over on her pillow and he sees her eyes are open.

'Daddy.' She summons him, her voice slurred.

He sits on her bed like he's sinking.

'Go back to sleep, darling.'

Her voice clogged with tiredness, she protests, 'I can't sleep!' A dramatic sigh. 'Will you read me a story?'

A memory of her in his arms as a baby. The best times.

He does not want to put the light on. If he does, he'll see her too clearly.

He pauses and she reaches across for his hand. He quickly moves it away, as if her skin is radioactive, and he announces with more clarity than he feels, 'I'll tell you a story, how's that?'

She acquiesces with a nod and a huge grin. The gap between her teeth is difficult for him to look at.

The only stories in his mind are full of witches and crones, wicked queens and evil stepmothers. He has no idea where any of these stories might end.

He stares at the pillow rather than her face.

'Daddy!' The word, a command.

'Yes, darling?'

'Why is your nose all runny?'

He reaches up to find his nose is bleeding slightly.

'I bumped it.'

'Oh.' A pause. 'The story?'

'Once upon a time, a little boy lived in a kingdom of ice. The queen who ruled that land had a frozen splinter of glass where her heart should be.'

Dolly hugs the duvet close round her, as if she can feel the chill breath.

'The queen was very lonely.' His voice is miles away from him.

There are things he does not say out loud. How the queen poisoned him and held him prisoner and stabbed his heart with a dagger of ice, over and over, and over...

'Was he cold, the boy?' asks Dolly.

'He was, darling. Very, very cold.'

'Will he get rescued?'

'Well...' His eyes track across the room to her drawing. 'He waited for a knight to come and save him, on a beautiful white horse.'

Only Dudley was no knight. His father never came back for him.

'And?'

So quiet he might hear his heartbeat.

'*And*, Daddy...'

'The boy was sad, all alone in the ice palace. When he cried, his tears turned to ice and burned his face.'

'Were there penguins?'

He continues as if he's not heard her. 'But one day he made up his mind to escape.'

'Were there unicorns? Unicorns and penguins on ice skates...?'

His mind slips away from the story.

Over there, children are used as decoys. They are more dangerous than adults. They are not children as we know them. They are hardened, ruined by conflict.

Children there are traps. Children there are weapons.

68

6.00 a.m., 24 December

She comes to with Lulu licking her hand, the side of her face cool against the floor.

She's confused. Why is she in the kitchen and not in her bed?

She feels she should get up, but even the thought is heavy. It would be so nice to go to sleep again.

A pain nags somewhere to one side. She closes her eyes against it. A second of peace.

But the pain sticks to its guns.

She puts one hand on the dog, one on the tiles and heaves herself up to sitting. It is harder to open one eye than the other.

Sometimes she's so angry as she waits for Marc to come home that she's sure she won't be able to sleep. But then her body betrays her and gives in after only five minutes or so. Sometimes he's left for work again before she wakes, the only evidence of a marriage the duvet flung back on the other side of the bed, an indentation in his pillow.

A half-memory, half-dream dissolves. There was a little boy in the house. He was so cold. He sat with the presents under the tree, his eyes wide, imploring. He wanted to hold her hand. Is he still in the room next door? What does he need from her?

The boy feels wrong. Everything feels wrong.

An instinct propels her up. And she sees the pills and the kids' mugs on the side, and she remembers.

Her kids are in danger.

The crossing nearest the gym has plastic flowers tied to the railings alongside water-stained photos of a smiling teenager in his school uniform. 'RIP Kev.' He has a ridiculously wide smile.

Debs isn't naïve enough to think Kev hadn't been tearing around on a bike, which may or may not have been borrowed. No lights. No looking back. Dark so early now.

She's had near misses on this crossing. Curses flung at the departing lights of some bloke who couldn't be arsed slowing or stopping. Once a woman, who put her hand up in supplication – sorry, mistimed it.

Kev's is the type of shrine you walk by several times a year in the city. On the railings, tied with blue ribbon, a blue teddy holding a heart.

She has to gather herself. She has to get up. Her legs aren't sure. Her neural pathways mutiny.

The image of that blue teddy forces her to try standing, grabbing the side of the cupboard to balance herself. She braces her forearms against the worktop over the washing machine.

There's no way there will be tributes and teddies laid at this doorstep. No fucking way.

Over her dead body.

She attempts to shout, 'Marc!' stumbling for the stairs, the hall rug tilting up at her, the patterns skewed, fighting dizziness and sickness and pure terror, no longer caring if she wakes the kids. She needs to wake them, then grab them and get out as fast as they can. But the thoughts are scrambled. She can't hold on to them. A cascade of colour and fragmented thoughts, like the jackpot machine in the corner of the Crown that never paid out.

She heads for the stairs, but—

She knows the boy is there, just over her left shoulder. He's standing, waiting next to the Christmas tree. Willing her to go to him.

She refuses to look. Her children need her.

A pressure grows. A dark magnetism pulls her towards the lounge, urging her to turn. She flounders forward, away from it.

Two steps up, the sensation vanishes. The absence itself so intense she wants to cry.

She half falls up the stairs and lurches towards Pat-Pat's door, simply because it's the nearest.

In the warm, slightly stuffy room, he's splayed like a starfish, half under his Buzz Lightyear duvet. The only time he's quiet, when he's asleep.

Something askew here. His miniature desk isn't in its normal place – then she remembers – she dragged it across to hide the scribble he did on the wallpaper in case his father noticed. She should grab her son and get out. But she doesn't know where Marc is.

She turns, clinging to the doorframe for balance, and wheels round towards Dolly's room. She sees the door is shut.

She senses he's inside. She reaches for the handle, afraid of what she might find. But she can't seem to get a grip. She teeters. Her hand finds air.

She can hear his voice somewhere. Why can she hear his voice? What is he saying to her daughter?

Now she's sitting on the carpet, her chest tight. She wonders where her inhaler has gone. She feels drunk. And very cold.

Suddenly, the boy's right in front of her. So close, she could touch him.

Skinny and blond. Nothing like Pat-Pat.

So sad. She could reach out her hand and...

She sees her hand reaching out towards nothing, and for an instant she wonders if she's finally lost her mind.

She needs to lie on the carpet by Dolly's door, to rest her throbbing head against the floor for just a little while...

They took to competitive sleeping after Pat-Pat was born. He was such a shock after those easy nights with Dolly. His constant squawks and shrieks were torture. They slept the sleep of the dead as soon as they get into bed.

Used to.

Now he's hardly there. And she's so tired, all the time.

She needs a break.

They'd never considered leaving either of the kids with Jeanne or Shirley for a weekend away. Debs thought about Kelly, but it seemed unfair that she'd have to take them away from her again.

If anything happens to her, her sister will take care of the kids.

Why is she sitting at this weird angle?

He's there. Close.

No.

There is no boy in front of her.

Of course there isn't.

Then she remembers – it's bad. Marc in Dolly's room is bad.

But why?

69

Three months ago

He's never been able to deal with her anxiety, the panic attacks. In the early days he tried to soothe her. When she started to struggle for breath and weep at nothing. When she jumped out of her bloody skin at every loud noise.

Then he lost patience. He'd lecture her. And she wanted to scream in his face. But that was more evidence. Then he could brand her hysterical.

She expected more of him. He pretended he could make things easier. He promised to take care of her in sickness and in health.

Now she's furious with him for being the person he is, and with herself for believing him to be someone else entirely. Wanting him, willing him to be the provider, the protector. She cast him in the bloody role. Someone she needed him to be.

She fell in love with his grey eyes. Gentle eyes. They reminded her of a horse's eyes, large, fringed with long lashes; beautiful. Only then she realised horses are flight animals. The first whiff of danger and they're off.

She cast him in a bloody fairy-tale role of the prince who'd come to save her, but whenever she needs him, he gallops far, far away.

And she hates him for that, and she hates herself for wanting the happy ending. She hates herself for a lot of things.

Sure, she admits it, underneath the bravado, she's anxious. Came out that way. Even as a kid. Mam said so.

But it's not some syndrome, some disorder, some complex. It doesn't need to be treated by years of sitting on someone's uncomfortable designer chair, splurging out her innards for seventy-five quid an hour. Hers is everyday anxiety. Normal anxiety. It's right to be on edge in the city. You need it to check if there's a bomb on the Tube. See it. Say it. Sorted. It's normal to worry if there's a nutter with a knife in an alley.

When the asthma gets really bad and she's jumping out of her skin at pretty much everything, Marc starts mithering her.

The next time her sister calls, she tells Kelly, 'He wants me to get therapy.'

'What sort?'

'Dunno. Would you do it?'

'Nah,' says Kelly, 'I've got Slimming World.'

Marc nags on until, in the spirit of 'making an effort' she agrees to a few mindfulness sessions at the local library to shut him up.

She knows it'll do no good the instant 'Greetings-I'm-Sebastian' invites her to take a seat on one of the uncomfortable hard plastic chairs and, in a sing-song nasally voice, bangs on about 'breath-*ing*' and 'ob-serv-*ing*' and just 'be-*ing*'.

After about twelve minutes, Debs very much wants to be punch-ing his lights out.

One of the mindful ladies flutters around their leader, asking lots of trivial questions at the end, and she leaves Sebastian an offering of sea salt fudge from the farmers' market at Ally Pally. Marc forces Debs to trail round there on Sundays.

The market does her head in. So far, the record is six pounds fifty for a loaf of (fennel-date-seasalt-one-million-year-old-mother-lode-bollocks-sourdough) bread.

Yomping round the stalls, refusing to buy Lulu organic dog treats despite *the eyes* and the wild tugs on her lead, Debs whines to Marc that mindfulness is doing no good, although she shuts up when she sees his expression. She agrees to download the Calm app instead.

In the end, she gives in to his pressure 'to see someone'. But only after her dreams get totally out of hand.

She agrees to see a CBT practitioner, not on the basis of any personal recommendation, but because the woman works from home, just around the corner. The convenience of living in North London.

She hates it, *therapy*. Marc discovers she hasn't been keeping half her appointments, when she confesses under protracted interrogation about what she talks about in her sessions, admitting to skiving off to Starbucks for fifty overpriced minutes.

She suspects the therapist, whom she loathes – her immense fat arse squidged over the sides of her high-backed chair, looking over the top of her glasses at Debs – reports back to Marc. Perhaps not what she says in the sessions, but definitely if she turns up or not. And that's still well fucked up as far as Debs is concerned. Although that may be a 'projection of her paranoia'.

Anyway, *he* needs bloody counselling more than her.

She always knew he was a bit on the spectrum – most blokes are, as far as she can see – but she didn't really mind that he could be emotionally unavailable. If she wants to talk, she has Kelly for that. But a therapist? Someone you have to *pay* to listen to you? How can you trust that? And she doesn't want strangers knowing her business. Sniffing out her soft spots.

She's not entirely aware of some of the half-formed fragmented thoughts spinning round her head, but those she grasps are best shared with no one. So, she makes up things in the sessions. The bloke in her Zumba class who fancies her and who she's considering fucking. The therapist spends nearly two hours on that old flannel. Ha ha! You don't need a psychology degree to know the only blokes who come to her Zumba are gay as.

But then she wonders if the stuff she makes up reveal bits of herself she doesn't want airing. What if her non-existent fantasies expose some part of her soul? Like dreams. So she starts faking her dreams as well. But don't ask her why she thinks that keeps her secrets any better.

She never mentions what happened to her and her mam.

She never mentions wanting to stab Marc.

She never mentions seeing the boy.

70

6.04 a.m., 24 December

She forces her eyes open. Tries to focus.

He's standing there, absolutely still. Like when they used to play statues, her and Kelly.

She sits splayed, looking up, groggy, confused, watching him looking down at her.

The boy is pointing his fingers at her head like a gun. Like he's playing.

The moment is almost peaceful. Her mind keeps sliding off what she has to do. The little boy looks so sad. So needy. Her head slumps.

It's so quiet now.

She feels peaceful.

Suddenly she's standing.

'Mummy!'

Debs props herself in the doorway. She must have opened the door. How did she get to her feet?

Dolly is sitting up in bed. 'Why is your face all funny?'

Debs reaches up and touches her head, brings her fingers

away, amazed. There seems to be blood from her brow, down her eyebrow, cheek, her neck. It must have soaked into the collar of her dressing gown, because that's also damp. She hopes Dolly can't see that because the fluffy material is purple, and the light dim.

He did this. He made her terrifying to her own daughter.

He's standing next to the bed. There's blood around his nose. She manages to spit out, 'Get. Away. From. Her.'

By her side she discovers she's holding a knife from the rack downstairs. No memory of getting it.

An even playing field now. Mexican stand-off.

'I said—'

He stands. He sways slightly. He comes towards her. Debs stands back to let him pass, not taking her eyes off him.

'What happened to the boy, Daddy?' asks Dolly. 'Does he manage to escape?'

Marc pauses and looks back to his daughter. 'Yes.'

'How? Does the Ice Queen let him go?'

'No, darling. He has to kill her.'

'Oh,' says Dolly, who obviously doesn't think this is much of a story. She sighs extravagantly. 'Night-night, Daddy. Night-night, Mummy.'

It's morning, thinks Debs. *Soon be light.*

'Goodnight, darling,' says Marc. And he adds, so softly she might not hear, 'Goodbye.'

71

4.23 p.m., 23 December

He has many acquaintances, work colleagues. He would not categorize these as friends, although he goes for a drink with some, plays squash with others, provides alibis for a few chancers, mainly the young chaps but also one or two habitual philanderers his own age.

Not his MO. Never has been.

There are so many bosses, so many demands at work, yet no one he could ask for support. For cover.

He would never ask. He wouldn't know how. He has no comrades. He no longer has a unit. His faceless, anonymous virtual community is the closest – Geoffers123, SearchEngineBigBalls, Black-Jack, NomNomII, MisterSnake2you – the chaps who are online in the small hours.

There's a certain amount of banter at work but it has toned down in recent years, now almost non-existent between the male and female members of the team. They know to err on the safe side. There are to be no inappropriate comments. No accusations. Teamwork here is civilised; this is no bear pit.

There remain non-verbal put-downs: eye rolling; a colleague turning his back; sneers masquerading as smiles. He is left out of the in group – those who gather in a clichéd clump by the water cooler and Nespresso machine, who sit together during briefings – and his ideas are sometimes, more often than not recently, belittled by them in cool yet eviscerating management-speak.

He knows – he overhears and guesses – some of the things that are said about him behind his back. Trigger points. The injury here is not obvious; the injury inflicted by those playground office tactics is internal. He wonders if it wouldn't be easier to take a punch.

The things he might file under paranoia grow incrementally, stealthily. A drip-feed of cortisol, waking him at three in the morning, making it impossible to get back to sleep.

Succumbing to these miscellaneous glitches makes him feel ashamed. A better man would be able to deal with them.

He's in the toilets, scrolling through his phone in a cubicle; a bolthole away from the brewing acid anxiety of the office floor, with the swirling rumours, covert preparation of CVs and whispered, hurried phone calls lining up meetings with contacts in other firms. The sleek lines of basins, toilets, urinals and mirrors make this space tolerable, despite the smells, masked with some synthetic cinnamon bathroom deodoriser. He is scouting out possible escape routes himself.

He hears a pair of his adversaries come in. Men from a different section, on par with him in the line of command. There's the usual amping up of language away from the office floor. He hears a rustle and sniff and the edge to the voices that follows.

This shared ritual, the drug itself, makes them less guarded, more garrulous, but also more likely to lash out.

Coarse talk about Yvonne, a new low-ranking employee whose unbuttoned blouse and close-fitting skirt have caught the eye of most of the young blades. Obvious signals. This might be the point to laugh and add his voice to the mix, comment on her availability, but he does not call out to alert them to his presence. He continues to sit in his cubicle. Some might say he hides. Those with suspicious natures might think he spies.

The two are joined by a third. Now he's truly outnumbered. A pack mentality. Now is the time for knee-jerk anxiety and calculations and planned exit strategies to put a lid on that fear. The adrenaline pumps faster and his legs brace. He stands, zips and waits, standing back from the door.

The laughter and baying outside suddenly cease. He guesses someone has noticed the door at the end is closed. He breathes as quietly as he is able. Footsteps come towards him. Stop.

Thud. Thud. Thud.

The door shakes as a fist bangs against it. He finds he can't make his mouth work.

From the sinks, the spell is broken with a shout, 'Having a wank in there, mate?'

He takes a breath, leans his head against the metal wall, forces jocularity. 'You got me. Just sending a dick pic.' His voice is placating. Squeaky. 'Some privacy please, mate.'

They are not his mates.

An explosion of laughter.

He almost hears the collective relief outside. With his admission he has declared he has no power to censure them and thus he is no threat.

After they leave, he gives it a minute before stepping out of the cubicle.

Deborah likes to watch nature programmes with the children, mostly gentle shows like *The Secret Life of the Zoo*. They had to turn off David Attenborough's *Dynasties*, which became as torturous as *Lord of the Flies*; chimpanzees torn limb from limb ...

He must guard against such coups.

He splashes water on his face. He squares his shoulders, pulls himself up to full height. In the mirror, a person he no longer recognises looks ashen and indistinct. An actor in his own life. He steels himself to return to his desk – deep breaths – an exercise of will.

And then he's summoned to HR.

72

6.08 a.m., 24 December

She shuts Dolly's door behind them. Waits a beat in case there's a protest. Braces herself. Breathes.

She's buffeted by a wave of nausea. Her eye socket screeches.

He stands across the landing from her. She squints to focus. Something stings and blurs her vision, so she rubs her knuckles across her eyelid. They come away red, softly illuminated by the streetlight shining through the bathroom window.

He does not say sorry.

She calculates – the distance, how much energy she has left in the tank. If she can draw him to her – open her arms as if to hug him, take half a step forward like she might, perhaps, kiss him – he could mirror that step and come towards her.

And if he did, if he shifted his weight even a tiny bit, she could use that momentum, use his height against him, round-house kick, grab his arm and haul him unbalanced down the stairs.

She's not thought much past that.

She doesn't think she intends to stab him.

Is this what it's come to? She should have legged it when she had the chance.

73

One year ago

When Debs was at her lowest – what she thought at the time was her lowest, before she really understood how low she had to go and yet still, somehow, not cave in entirely – she did try to leave.

The November before last Christmas, she packed up the kids and the dog, and drove all the way up to Whitley Bay to stay with an old friend, Susan, who'd been on the Pilates course with her. She knew more about Susan's pelvic floor than she did her own husband's interior workings.

It wasn't so much Susan as the fact that she lived near the sea that decided Debs on where, and the where didn't matter so much as the why and the how. Driving away was the point. Hours and hours up the M1, just her, the kids and Lulu, with so many pit-stops at McDonalds and KFC, banned by Marc and so a fun 'holiday treat', it took them all day and well into the night. When they arrived, she was shaking, either from fatigue or exhilaration, she wasn't sure.

She didn't tell her friend the ins and outs of it, just that she needed to get away for a bit. She didn't mention Marc was off his head most of the time – the coke to perk him up and improve his performance at work totally out of control since the bloody promotion. She couldn't let him look after the kids by himself any more. And she dreaded the interminable sex sessions where his demands became nastier by the week.

It was so bitter that far north, they risked bloody hypothermia every time they ventured out Susan's front door. After being caught in a hailstorm ('hurty rain', Dolly called it) the girls rebelled. When they prepared for another walk Lulu planted her four paws on the welcome mat and pulled hard against her little red harness, like some ancient sled dog, and Dolly wailed piteously when Susan tried to wrestle her feet into her pink glitter wellies. Even Debs admitted defeat because her time in Muswell Hill had turned her into a 'soft southern bastard'.

On the one day they actually did make it to the beach, they yomped onwards like matchstick men and dogs from the old Lowry paintings, leaning, bent forward into the ridiculous wind, a glowering cathedral of clouds above them.

Pat-Pat was in his element. He screeched and whooped and ran headlong into the gale with his flailing gait, arms whirring, two kinetic whirlwinds. And it amazed her. That will!

He sprinted off, heading straight for the sea. She'd hesitated a second or two before she realised what could happen and then tore after him, grabbing the hood on his duffle just in time. And she knew, without a doubt, that he would have continued running and the shock of the bone-cold water would not have stopped him. Even as she wrenched him back to the safety of the sand, she heard his roar of defiance, louder than the wind and the waves, and his immense strength fighting to escape her and continue forward, forward.

She'd been like that once.

In the car on the way back to Susan's house, Dolly cuddled Pat-Pat and tried to engage him in a game of I Spy.

She was kinder to her brother now she didn't compete with him on the same playing field. She was so far ahead in all areas of childhood development she was learning to let him be. It hadn't always been that way.

A year before, Debs had once found her daughter leaning over Pat-Pat in his crib, pinching him so hard he was squealing in shock. And she'd yanked her daughter's hand away and shouted, 'What the bloody hell do you think you're doing?'

And for a second she was so furious it was almost an out-of-body experience. She did nothing but shout. But it frightened her – what she might do.

When she eventually calmed down, and Dolly had stopped sobbing hysterically, and Pat-Pat was sucking on the bottle she'd expressed earlier, already over it, she asked again, 'Why? Why did you do that to your little brother?' fearing a murderous rage within her daughter, usurped by the male child, the son and heir.

And Dolly said, 'To see if he squeaked like BoBo.'

She didn't get it for a moment, then she twigged: BoBo the baby elephant, Dolly's old squeaky toy.

She went mad at Pat-Pat last week. He drove his pedal car at Dolly, completely intentionally, catching her hard in the shins.

Her daughter squealed and Debs shrieked, 'Patrick!' and Lulu barked and Marc shouted from the other room, 'For God's sake, Deborah!'

Debs was incandescent. Her son couldn't be allowed this violence. Soon he would be as big as his sister; large enough to do real harm. It might only be a few months before it started.

There's something about Pat-Pat that brings to mind Max, one of several 'say hello to your new brothers' she and Kel endured over the years. Max never lived with them, but he stayed over. His dad, Pete, came from Skeggy. Their mam met him during a Motown weekender at Butlins and while she wasn't over the moon with Pete's moustache ('It's the only porn star thing about him, duck!') staying with him made for a nice little holiday now and then, whenever Shirl could get cover from one of the other barmaids who owed her a favour.

'Maxi Pad' as Kel and Debs called him, although not to his face, was less than thrilled with two girls invading his bedroom whenever Shirley polled up.

There were only a couple of months between Max and Debs. Usually this might have led to a crush, but she didn't like his sullen mush and tuneless whistling. On the first visit she punched him really hard on the arm after a disagreement over footie teams. She was surprised when he didn't wallop her back. She also kicked him during an argument over which flavour crisp was best, but Shirley caught her that time and read her the riot act while shaking her hard, like they'd seen that Jack Russell shake a rat in the pub cellar.

There was some sort of hiatus for just over a year, when Pete briefly reconciled with Max's mum, but when that went pear-shaped, he won Shirley back by turning up with a bunch of actual roses, just before closing time, and their mam puffed up her cleavage like a pigeon.

The next visit down to the bracing air of Skeggy – 'full of ozone', according to Pete – Max seemed to have shot up half a foot at least and Debs sensed the scales had tipped. She knew better than to get into a scrap, but as soon as Kelly was off to get them a fish and chip supper, the lad launched himself at her like a rugby player and pinned her to his bedroom carpet, proceeding to jab her in the ribs. He sat on her, hand hard over her mouth, squashing any thoughts of retaliation. She just had to lie there, trying to breathe through her nose and waiting until Pete called them down for tea.

He didn't try to cop a feel or anything. But if he'd wanted to, there was little she could have done to stop him.

Brute force. It crushes bullying. It might even trump cunning.

Anyway, the biggest shock wasn't the violence, it was the words he called her, a torrent of words: 'Dirty whore, dirty cunt, dirty bitch, just like your poxy fucking mother.'

Marc tracked Debs to Whitley Bay, as she guessed he might. He turned up at Susan's, having caught the train from London. He bared his teeth on the doorstep in something that might resemble a smile if you weren't paying attention. He beamed fake charm and dimples towards Susan's open trusting face, accepted a cup of ordinary tea, which he wouldn't be seen dead drinking in other circumstances and confided in her friend how worried he'd been.

She heard him talking as she trudged downstairs, carrying the kids' bags out to the car. Resigned.

She plonked on Susan's sofa watching Marc with the kids: there he is spinning Pat-Pat round above his head like a plane, the boy roaring with delight; there's Dolly hugging her daddy's legs as he strokes her head, saying, 'I've missed you too, Miss Dumpling'; there's Marc with both kids hanging off his arms like a chair-o-plane, all of them laughing. A perfect family triptych.

And then he dragged her back, both of them pretending this had been 'a little break', a bright spontaneous treat for the children. Not a test run.

He drove them all the way down the motorway in the Beetle. Lulu lay across her lap and she worked out a knot in the fur behind her ear as the kids conked out in the back. Lulu's soft snores the only sound in the car.

At Luton he started talking. A surprising monologue of self-reflection. He admitted work had been exhausting but promised he would develop strategies to delegate. He swore he was going to knock the drugs on the head and step up, be a proper father, be a proper husband. He said he was nothing without her, that she was his world, the best thing that had ever happened to him. He begged her forgiveness.

She fell for it.

For a few weeks, months, he'd made a real effort. A great Christmas, a lavish Valentine's Day. He came home on time. He engaged with Dolly and Pat-Pat. He was solicitous of her needs in bed. She got her hopes up.

But he let her down. It was a plaster on a broken leg.

She knew he was back on the coke when she came down one morning to get breakfast, and it was obvious he'd not been to bed, playing his stupid games all night. Foot jiggling, hard eyes.

The stairs seem to pitch towards her. She shakes her head to clear it. She forces herself to smile at him. It might confuse him. She can see the blade he's holding resting against his leg, like he's forgotten he's still got it. She grips the knife in her hand tighter.

If he takes one step towards her, then she might stab him.

74

Twenty-seven years ago

Charlie wasn't the worst of their mam's boyfriends. Not at the start. He let them be for the most part. He just wasn't Debs' favourite.

She'd liked Anthony, who sold ladies clothes on the market; factory rejects from the Leicester manufacturers, where he had 'contacts' in the big factories. Her mam paraded round in nice frocks for the duration of that one. Anthony had waltzed Debs up and down the bar and called her 'my little cherub' once, so Kelly got jealous and flushed her Cabbage Patch doll's head down the loo. She'd been wearing the fairy wings her mam had made for the school Christmas party from a tatty pair of tights and a hanger. She told Anthony she was Tinker Bell, not a cherub because they were boys, but he didn't seem to mind.

'Angel, my arse!' laughed Shirley.

Debs had grown gangly since Anthony. Her mam had lost a couple of teeth along the way.

What she didn't like about Charlie, when he turned up, wasn't so much his huge, meaty arms, or his cartoon bulldog neck, but how he'd turn on a sixpence. He'd be laughing one second, their mam sitting on his pumped beefy thighs playing giddy-up, the next spilling her on to the carpet and raging right in your face with spittle.

Shirley blamed it on the steroids. Charlie didn't drink or do drugs like some of the others, but steroids were 'part of the game'. When he was in training for a competition – 'posing in his knickers', as Kelly put it, although never to his face – he was more irritable on account of the 'shredding'. The day before the contest he'd get a tan so dark he looked like Dev from the garage, and he wouldn't even drink water. They knew to keep well clear then.

As hobbies went, it was fair enough. Their mam didn't mind the hours he spent pumping weights in the boxing gym near the fire station because she worked most nights. And she liked the looks he got when he took off his T-shirt in the bar to show the punters when he'd finished. She was less keen on other lasses feeling up his biceps.

'He's been all over with his competitions, London and that,' boasted Shirley to anyone who'd listen. 'He's never won owt, though,' she conceded.

The honeymoon period lasted for about six months. Him commandeering too much room on the sofa, which sagged with the imprint of his giant thighs when he got off it. Him yawping, so they couldn't hear the telly over him. Him sucking up their mam's attention, all the oxygen in the room, what was left in between her fags.

He took the piss out of Kelly's 'face like a slapped arse' when she was mardy. He took the piss out of Debs' 'ginger minge' although she made sure he never saw that. Shirley would say, 'Shut it, Charlie. Leave them be,' but in a way that was half teasing, almost like she was in on the joke.

Then he pulled or tore or snapped something and took up residence on their sofa for hours at a time with a pack of frozen veg wrapped in a tea towel nestled on his groin, resting his leg on the big squishy cushion thing that Debs had liked to sit on till he ousted her.

The bickering with Shirley turned to slanging matches soon enough. Things were shouted. Things were flung. To be fair, their mam would start a lot of the rows.

Charlie would always finish them.

So, Shirley had a wobble, as she did now and then every few months, every few weeks. She had a lock-in. Came upstairs about half-two, reeking, arseholed, totally bladdered.

Debs half woke up to croak, 'Wrong door, Mam,' when Shirley tripped through to their bedroom rather than her own.

Charlie stormed in from his own lock-in (a poker game down the Halfway House) about forty minutes later, cursing as he hopped up the stairs to the flat. He'd cracked off as soon as he opened the door. Shirley began screeching at him and he started on with smashing things.

Then it went quiet, which was often the worst part. Eventually, their door was yanked open. 'Put the kettle on!' he demanded. 'Make us a brew.'

Debs and Kelly looked at each other in the dark, a silent agreement that they'd do it together, safer that way.

When Kelly cautiously placed the mug on the coffee table next to the sofa, his hand darted out suddenly like a viper grabbing a baby rabbit, snatching her hair. He jerked her head next to his lips. 'What are you two little bitches plotting?' His gob looked nasty, although there's hardly a way to say stuff like that with a nice smiley mouth.

Other stuff was said. Things were threatened. He didn't let go of Kelly's hair and she started whimpering. Debs didn't know what to do. It never occurred to her to call the police. Their mam was slumped, conked out on the sofa beside Charlie. Likely the gin, from what Debs could see; no obvious wounds, no bits missing. No fucking use.

It was only when Kelly started screaming 'Debs! Debs!' with her hair yanked back so hard it looked like her head was coming off, that Debs' body seemed to decide for her, and she shot across the room, grabbed the mug of tea and chucked it in his face, scalding her sister's hand in the process. All three of them screamed. Charlie pushed Kelly away and hauled himself off the sofa and hobbled round trying to catch Debs. She dodged round and round the sofa, scuttling sideways like a barmy crab, Charlie crashing after her, bellowing, 'Come here, you little bitch!' Then he tripped over their mam's leg. As he crashed down, he managed to catch hold of Kelly's forearm, snatching her to him before falling across her. And Kelly shrieked so loud that Debs thought he must have broken something, so she grabbed the Shire horse doorstop and with all her strength smashed it down on the side of his head.

Something cracked. It wasn't the horse.

She couldn't see a dent or any blood. But she couldn't see if he was breathing either.

Kel tried to shove him off and Debs tried to help but he was the size of a chest freezer and she worried her sister would be crushed to death. But then he groaned. And he grunted, 'I. Will. Fucking—' And he lumbered up on one knee. Kelly took the opportunity to scoot out from under him. 'Kill. You.' Then up on the other knee. 'You. Little. Cunt.'

The girls retreated to the front door and he stumbled towards them. Kelly got to the handle first, managing to pull it open, and he sailed through.

And if they'd been lucky, they might have just shoved him out and bolted and locked the door and barricaded the flat behind him. But he stopped on the landing, looked right at Debs, and shouted, 'You two little cunts and your mam are dead. Hear me? Fucking dead!'

Debs paused for just a second. Perhaps if she'd thought about it a bit longer, she'd have made a different choice. Or perhaps that instinct is what saved them all, because as he started on another variation of 'Fucking dead, all of you,' she made some animal noise and launched herself at him, kicking him hard on the shin and punching him where it hurts, and he made a squealy sort of yelp, stepped back on the dodgy leg and down he went.

Down and down and down, all the way to the bottom of the stairs.

They waited. And then they waited some more. But he didn't move.

'Oh shit,' said Kelly.

The girls locked the door, and they spent the rest of the night under Kel's duvet, whispering, dreading the bang at the door, or worse, his ghost sliding through the walls into their room to accuse them.

Shirley found him the next morning, crumpled at the bottom of the stairs. But not dead, thank God. To be fair, as their mam called the ambulance, they were a bit relieved about that.

Although, at the time she did it, Debs had wanted him dead. One hundred per cent.

Shirley's next bloke raced greyhounds.

The dogs always won, though.

75

6.09 a.m., 24 December

Patience has never been Debs' strong suit.

She moves, as if she's simply intending to pass him to go into Pat-Pat's room, then all at once swivels and pushes at him with all her strength. She misjudges, only catches him in the diaphragm, enough to wind him slightly, not enough to topple him. He doesn't even take a step back.

Instead, he uses her momentum, gripping the hand that's gone for him, slinging her round and away towards the stairs.

She wavers.

Her foot finds an absence of solid ground, her free hand grabs for, fumbles and misses the rail. The other stupidly tries to hold on to her knife.

Why didn't she stab him when she had the chance?

He lets go. Her excellent core control isn't enough to save her.

She screams.

And she's down, smashing her hip, her elbow, her head.

Down and down.

The knife flies away from her fingers.
At the top of the stairs, he smiles.

76

6.10 a.m., 24 December

She's already awake when she hears it. Loud bangs and a cry – a sound women are attuned to in the same way they hear a baby's demand to be fed, while a man might sleep through – the scream of a frightened woman.

Earlier she'd dreamed the awful dream. Shopping at the big M&S in Oxford Street she'd desperately needed the loo but she couldn't find it. She went up and down escalators, asked unhelpful shop assistants, the feeling pressing on her bladder, more and more urgent, but so many wrong turns and dead ends, until (finally!) she found the sign, the right place.

But there's no door. Just a toilet. Exposed. Facing the shop floor.

She rushed to the loo as soon as she woke up.

She always gets up with Dennis when he's on his earlies. Makes him wholemeal toast and a pot of Assam for them both. A hug goodbye. Then she potters upstairs with her panda mug, the one her granddaughter, Kirstie, bought her, and she reads sections from the Sunday papers she hasn't finished yet, until she dozes off again. Half day today. Christmas Eve.

She's only just lain back on her microfibre pillow when the noises interrupt any thought of sleep.

They're a nice family, the neighbours. Friendly. Well, *she's* friendly. Sylvia's hardly seen much of him, although he puts her in mind of the dark young Irish actor from that movie. The Muswell Hill Everyman was crammed when she went to see the film with her friend Julie from the book club. Not one man in the audience, thankfully, although the lad who made the coffees in the little café section seemed to be smirking at them.

The people next door don't have shouting matches or anything like that. Even their parties – rather, dinner parties – are well behaved. She and Dennis sometimes get invitations, but Dennis has to be up so early they refuse. She wouldn't want to go by herself.

Yes, the children are sometimes noisy, but she doesn't mind that. Children should be allowed to be children. She loves having them round, although it doesn't happen often.

She misses her granddaughter. Didn't even get to see her on her birthday this year. It's been months now. Her son's 'partner' moved back to Scotland to be nearer her own family when they split up. Like she's not family. They never married, thought they knew better. And Grandma Sylvia has no claims, no rights, no hope. Her Maurice – a good son, a good man, she can't understand what went wrong – gets the train up there every two weeks. But he doesn't go until late on a Friday, to come back even later on a Sunday. That's a bit too much for her and Dennis, with his work. She couldn't go alone.

She and Dennis made the journey in April. They stayed at a very nice hotel with good TripAdvisor reviews, although it's never the same as sleeping in your own bed. Both of them were wilting on the way back, exhausted by delays, and then the buffet bar ran out of milk. There'd been a row when they were there. When Sylvia tackled her, Maurice's ex said, 'Ask him what went on. You haven't got a clue what your darling son is capable of!'

The little girl next door is always beautifully turned out. And so polite! A couple of years older than their Kirstie. Well spoken.

Her granddaughter is picking up the accent now, which is a shame.

Sylvia sits on her side of the bed feeling shaky. Not that long past six o'clock. It's none of her business, but she puts on her slippers, pauses, then ventures downstairs. She pulls a coat over her dressing gown and waits a few more seconds before she forces herself to the front door. She leaves it on the latch.

Even as she steps outside, she's not sure if she will knock.

As she hurries down the path, the security light flashes on, exposing her pale startled face.

77

6.11 a.m., 24 December

'Mummy-Mummy-Mummy-Mummy-MUMMY!'

Patrick's wail jolts Marc out of God knows where.

'Daddy!' Dolly's demand joins her brother's.

Which to defuse first?

He goes back to his daughter's room, looks in and says, 'Go back to sleep, darling. Mummy's tripped on the stairs. I'm going to help her.'

'Is she hurted?'

Dolly often slips back into baby-speak when she's tired, or when she's attempting to charm you into something. Deborah has failed to address this.

'No, no. Probably just a bruise.'

'Can I have another story?'

'Mumm-eeeee!' from the room next door.

'I'll come back after I've made sure your brother is all right and helped Mummy. Okay?'

She throws herself back on the pillow in a theatrical manner. 'It's not fair!'

'What? What isn't fair?'

'You said you'd read me a story.'

He did not. He's pretty sure he didn't. Promises are important. He does not give his word and make it worthless. How to play this…

'Daddy!'

'As soon as I've settled your brother and checked on Mummy I'll be back.'

'When?'

Rattled now, 'For goodness' sake, Dolly. Will you be quiet for just a moment and—'

'MUMMY!'

He closes the door, hurries across to Patrick's room.

On automatic, 'What's all this, soldier?'

His boy's face is florid, sheened with tears and mucus. His legs thrash against the duvet like he's trying to escape piranhas. He eyes his father suspiciously and demands once more, 'Mummy!'

His son always wants his mother, a habit Marc hoped he would soon leave behind. He wonders if this attachment is normal.

What would he know?

He sits on Patrick's tiny bed and switches on the robot-shaped nightlight. Their mother gives the children these lights to banish the darkness, to see off terrors. And if nightmares wake them, she hurries to their sides, an immediate rescue mission.

How can he reassure his son?

He takes a tissue from the bedside cabinet and wipes his

face. Patrick pulls back his head in outrage and shouts again, 'Mum-MEE!'

Marc snaps back, 'She's busy.'

He is aware that his treatment of his boy is different to how he tackled his daughter at this age. Perhaps he is a little too strict with his son – Deborah's favourite accusation – but he really cannot cope with Patrick's belligerent tantrums.

He can admit to himself that his son's craven need for his mother churns up uncomfortable feelings. Of course, it's not jealousy. He doesn't have the exact word for it, but it isn't that.

She mollycoddles him. And she let the boy suckle far too long in his opinion. It used to turn his stomach watching his son gobble at Deborah's breast. When he was feeding, pawing at her, her face soft and indulgent, gazing down at the child as if he was something miraculous rather than a greedy little animal, he found himself turning away.

If he accidentally walks in on his son with Deborah in the bath nowadays, if he sees him lolling against his mother's breasts, more pendulous now after feeding the two children, he has to suppress a shudder. And if he lifts him out of the water to dry him, the boy will flail and fight, kicking and writhing in his arms. 'No! No! No!'

Totally undisciplined. She has failed to train him.

Of course, compared with Jeanne, Deborah is obviously Mother of the Year, yet he finds her methods infuriatingly sloppy. She is not a good leader. Imposing boundaries seems beyond her skill set. She employs poor strategies. Both children can wheedle round her, so she gives in to pleas for 'just one more' story, 'just one more' sweet with irritating regularity.

She spoils the boy. Every time Patrick reaches for her – when he's upset, when he's tired, when things become difficult – she swoops him up and hugs him. His boy puts up his hands for his mother like he's surrendering. It is not the best drill for his future.

Marc catches the thought – perhaps they have a future?

But he can no longer provide for that. He has failed in his duty to provide for his family. He must end this now, because he has failed as a man, as a father. As Deborah would say, he has fucked up, royally fucked up.

78

4.36 p.m., 23 December

HR. Room 101.

There's something about Agnieta's face when she tells him: the delight of a woman watching a man suffer. Schadenfreude. He knows that look well.

Gloria sits by her side, a relic from the old days, a hard-boiled old bird in a vintage Chanel jacket. Not long before she's put out to pasture. She has never risen above some sort of sub-lieutenant role. She gives him an encouraging nod, but in this game, kindness kills. He might drown in her sympathy.

He's been expecting this. Braced. Yet he didn't see it coming. Not so soon. He's heard the words ricochet around the office: 'restructure', 'reshuffle'. He's felt himself shrink, clenching against the worry. His old back problem has returned for a nasty encore. His neck is often gripped in spasm. Driving has become a liability – he can't always turn to see what might be behind him. He certainly can't see what lies ahead.

She enunciates her words precisely, her accent stripping them of inflection, all empathy. It is not without an erotic frisson. And how long has she been with the company? Less than a year. Brought in as a 'hatchet woman'. That was the initial gossip; Benson and Phillips got off on it. No doubt they imagined her in some shiny dominatrix outfit. It is not an unpleasant image.

She doesn't socialise with the team, keeps herself to herself, thus rumours grew in whichever direction fancy took them. And she rarely smiles which, given the teeth, is just as well. These Eastern European types, hard-working, certainly, yet lacking certain nuances in the social skills arena.

The clinical procedure is suddenly over. She does not say she is sorry. She wishes him well with all the warmth of a pole dancer. A copy of his personnel file is passed to him. His knuckles white as he signs away his rights. He should take the pen and stab her in the heart. He should grab the paperwork, crumple it into a ball and ram it into her mouth, smearing the gaudy plum-coloured lipstick as he forces it deeper and deeper into her fucking throat.

Marc pulls back his shoulders as he exits the room. Across the office, Benson raises his eyebrows, signalling, 'You too?' Marc is annoyed that his throat constricts of its own volition as he nods a brief assent.

He is escorted out. Bill from security saying he's sorry, trying to boost him with platitudes like, 'You'll find something else within a week, you'll see, Mr Johnson,' as he marches him to the lift and down to the foyer.

And down and down and down as he scans the topmost document in his personnel file:

Internet search history, Mark (Marcus) Johnson
Squirters XVideo
Erectile Dysfunction
Anti-depressants side effects
Loans4You
Gamblers Anonymous
What invalidates life insurance?
Paddy Power Casino
GirlsChoke.Com
Bukkake babes

He reads no further; he has no need.

He ends up in the local Davey's wine bar with Benson and one of the accountants, Karl, who wears swirly-patterned shirts and for some reason dubs himself 'Karen from Finance'. They both make noises about how deep in the shit the firm might be; how it's a good time to be getting the hell out. They buy him rounds. These gestures are offered in solidarity.

A couple of others join them after a few hours. Those left on the payroll stay late at their desks, shackled to their workloads, to make up for those like Marc who have fallen by the wayside.

An empty, noisy evening. As a farewell to the troops, it's a damp squib.

Benson overdoes it a little, as is his wont, and is refused more alcohol. Marc loudly summons the bar manager and a contre-temps ensues. They are escorted outside, where his colleague crashes into a solitary Millwall supporter, according to the T-shirt – no coat despite the chill, a wreath of tinsel around his head – who makes a few disparaging comments. Marc retaliates.

What he does not understand is the look of horror on Benson's face as he watches Marc punch the hooligan twice on the side of his face, and then smash the lout's head against the wall. He cannot compute why his friend storms off.

He leaves the other man crumpled on the ground. Walks away briskly.

By chance, as he heads for his train, tripping a little, his knuckles sore, he sees Agnieta leave the building. Her coat, cinched at the waist, sporting a real fur collar. She has reapplied the slash of plummy lipstick for her journey home.

He imagines following her, pushing her up against a wall and punching her hard in the face. Again and again, ramming his fist into her fucking face.

Agnieta knows she is not liked.

Her husband, her mother, her son, they do not like her. It is to be expected. Her son is at that age. Her mother, in pain, in decline, at another. Her husband, resentful of her career and her absence. She steels herself against this, applies herself to her work.

She is not liked at work. Almost certainly feared, which is useful; mocked, perhaps, which is not. She presents to them her professional veneer.

By the end of the day, a long day, she has dealt with several redundancies. What Marc Johnson will not see – after dealing with his dismissal and the long hours of paperwork and logistics that follow – is her descent into the bowels of the Tube, and how she changes into a pair of trainers (to save her good shoes) for the long walk from the station at Woolwich Arsenal to her friend's flat where she picks up her son, and the march onwards to the smaller flat she shares with her mother, who has problems with her eyes and her breathing, yet finds more than enough breath to nag at her constantly. He will not be able to imagine how she re-heats her portion of the casserole she prepared and froze at the weekend and checks her son's homework when he goes to his bedroom to play on his phone before he sleeps. How she irons her skirt for the next day and brushes her mother's hair before giving her her medications and settling her in the pull-out bed in the living room. He will not be there to notice the way her features change, soften, as she wipes away the grime of a day in London and the heavy make-up that covers skin pitted from childhood chicken pox. How she finishes the washing-up and then takes down and eases out her tightly-wound plaited bun before settling herself in front of the computer on the kitchen table to Zoom call her husband in Romania, who tells her that yes, he is still looking for work, '*Scorpie! Cateaua naibii!*' – of course this continues – '*Curva proasta!*' and she knows he's been drinking by the way he skims off certain words and refuses to notice the utter exhaustion in her face as she tells him she is worried that her boy, her Carol, will perhaps join a gang. That their son will perhaps take drugs, will perhaps be stabbed to death in the street, like so many other young men in this crowded lonely city of opportunity.

Instead, Marc's preoccupied, imagining the conversation that will take place if he goes home and tells Deborah that he's been made redundant. How her face will harden against him.

He will try, 'You have no idea.'

'Of course I have no idea. You tell me *nothing*! I don't know shit about fuck!'

Furious. Of course, she'll be furious.

'You don't listen.' He will try this line. An emasculating statement.

She will counter that of course she listens. But yes, she might concede, she has been a little preoccupied of late. Again she will tell him that there are only so many hours in the day, and most of them are accounted for already. By the time she's seen to the demands of the children – she calls them kids but kids are infant goats – and the needs of the useless dog and running the house and managing her clients and her classes and putting in her own invoices, not that they're for much, but it takes as much time to chase a bill for fifty quid as five hundred – *quid*, another word that grates on him – on and on, she'll list all these brainless, boring tasks for him, as if he's an ignorant child. As if he's not aware. As if, in her words, he gives a 'flying fuck'.

And her voice will become strident as she adds that she has to do the Christmas planning and shopping on top of all that, 'the straw that broke the bastard camel's back', and naturally she'll then cry, fired up with blame and self-pity.

So, she'll sneer, perhaps she doesn't listen as well as she used to, as well as she might.

Did she ever listen? Did he say anything of note? Did he ever try to tell her?

And then the money argument will start. And she won't stop. At him all the time, peck, peck, pecking in sharp little stabs. Dolly needs this, Pat-Pat needs that. The dog needs to go to the vet.

And to shock the torrent of demands into silence, he might just tell her what a pit they're in to stop those endless words spewing out of her ugly mouth.

'How much?'

'I re-mortgaged.'

'Of course, you fucking did!'

And her disappointment in him will somehow be worse than the punching and screaming and accusations that will inevitably ensue. It will be worse than her betrayal – he knows, he guesses – with some ape from her gym. Because her disappointment mirrors his own. It proves things about himself he doesn't want exposed.

And as mortifying as those imagined accusations might be, it's worse, more shaming still, because he's too much of a coward to start the conversation.

On the night of 23 December, after losing his job, Marc doesn't go straight home. Instead, he goes to his mother's.

79

6.14 a.m., 24 December

Vietnam fuelled by smack and dope and Hendrix. Hitler's army running on meth. *Panzerschokolade*. Ha! Ha! *Heil! Heil!* It's hard to do evil to other humans without a little pick me up. Purple Hearts on purple hearts, baby. Daddy's little helper.

He's a dead beat, dog-tired, dog soldier.

A quick snort, pinching the bridge of his nose, membranes screeching. Clarity, of sorts. A brittle confidence. Putting it back in its hiding place in his shaving gear on the top shelf in the bathroom cabinet. Nowhere little fingers can find it, for he is a responsible parent.

What should I do? What should Daddy do?

He has done terrible things. He has sanctioned terrible things by doing nothing. He is guilty.

Her eyes lose focus. Her lips go slack. Her muscles stop fighting. She goes limp, and you – you vile, filthy animal – you grow hard.

You want to fuck her now. Oh yes, you could fuck her now.

Your hands loosen their grip around her neck. Just a little. Take a sip of air, whore.

And just as the bitch begins to revive – gasp, gasp, gasp, like she's coming – you squeeze harder. You put her down again. Put her out of her misery. Happy memories!

That's how you treat the mother of your children.

And now you might smother those children in their sleep.

He should lie down. But as soon as he's horizontal, worse things crawl out from wherever they hide and eat away at him.

He has to see this through.

His son, his boy, is being poisoned by them all – his whore of a mother, Jeanne, all the other witches. No. He will not allow that. His job, as a father, as head of this unit, is to protect his son against that. Whatever it takes.

Something wrong is growing inside him like a cancer. A black clot of hatred.

The BUPA check-up a few months back (the last he'll be having as the health insurance is part of his management package) showed nothing untoward, apart from slightly raised cholesterol – all they gave him was inane advice about stress management. But he knows something worse is festering inside.

He almost wishes it were cancer. Then he could simply stop. He could abdicate. The godforsaken mess they're in would be out of his control.

How he would welcome cancer. A cancer might stop the worry eating away at him – it could eat away at him in its place and release him from being the breadwinner, the volunteer, the commanding officer. He's had enough of being forced to step up. He can no longer bear the role of alpha fucking male.

This language isn't him either. That's her influence. A mouth like a sewer.

'Daddy!'

She's supposed to be asleep, isn't she? Why is she awake? Why is he back in his daughter's room?

He sits heavily on the bed, deflating. 'What should I do, darling?'

'I don't know, Daddy.'

'What should I do?'

'I don't KNOW!'

'Tell me. Tell me what I should do.'

'Go away! Go away, Daddy. You're scaring me. Stop it. Stop it!'

His leg is jiggling. He is looming over her. He grips the side of the bed.

Suddenly he is clinging to the side of the swimming baths at the deep end, bastard Ed standing on his fingers, grinding his heel on to Marc's knuckles and he's losing his grip, terrified of the weight of water which will close over his head...

'Daddy!'

'I don't know what to do. What should I do?'

Dolly pulls the duvet up to her chin and squeaks, 'GO AWAY!'

His daughter, his child, afraid of him. He's become a bully.

A bully. And a murderer.

80

6.16 a.m., 24 December

Debs is aware of a sickening pulse jabbing in her temple. Time has passed, she's not sure how much. There's a loud noise she can't quite place.

Then it disappears. She disappears into stars.

There are stars on Dolly's ceiling. They glow. She has given her girl the entire universe. Dolly doesn't like the dark. Nor does she. It's very dark now. Or perhaps her eyes have closed.

She used to like the dark. She'd watch the sun set behind the rooftops opposite the Duke, the sky bleeding into dusk, staining the walls in their living room blood orange. The falling light, moth-soft, full of promise. Dusk was her favourite time because the night might not crack off into carnage, but bloom instead into starbursts and sparklers, and the people she'd see shuffling to the bus stop ashen-faced in the mornings would dance and spin round and round and throw back their heads, released from their daily grind. And they'd smile at their mam and throw money over the bar and Shirley would laugh so hard she might cry.

And they were full of joy.

A dusk full of hope. Not a night filled with fear.

She feels the weight of him on his side of the bed. The coldness he brings with him after sitting up late, working, worrying.

She stretches out her hand and lays her palm against his back, still muscled from his workout sessions. She doesn't like his gym – one of those extortionate City places – well appointed, but no natural light.

He leans across her, grabs her gently by the hair, pulls her to him and bites her neck. And her heart, her skin, her nipples answer immediately.

She embraces him with both arms round his neck, then reaches down for him. Urgent. Insistent. Her insides turning liquid. She wants him to fuck her. Let him fuck away his worries. But she feels him soften. A chill extinguishes her need.

Still, she takes a breath and asks, as she's learned to, 'What do you want?'

His lips brush her ear as his fingers dig hard into her breast. 'Fuck me.' And she doesn't want to, but she goes along with it. She always goes along with it.

Once she'd tried, 'I don't always want to be the bloke, Marc.' She'd got a right pasting for that. So now she does as he asks, taking the vibrator and lube from the little black case in the locked bedside cabinet, swallowing her distaste.

You can stick that where the sun don't shine. One of her mam's.

'Harder.'

And her own response flickers far, far away.

'I said fucking harder, you stupid bitch.'

So, she does.

And after, it doesn't stop, the terrible things he whispers as he thrusts his fingers into her mouth so she gags – she used to suck on those fingers – ramming his beautiful fingers deeper and deeper down her throat as she struggles for breath. The words he hisses affirm her deep fears, her shame, her belief that she is, as he says, a dirty worthless whore. The words spinning out as she loses consciousness.

The same voice is close in her ear now, close as a heartbeat. 'Get up.' Quiet but insistent.

And she tries. But a noise hurts her head.

A knocking in her skull. A knock outside. A ringing in her ears. The shrill of the doorbell.

'Debbie! Debbie!' Not his voice. A woman's voice. Outside. She can't compute this information.

He instructs her, 'Open the door.'

This is simple enough for her to understand. But why is he holding a tea towel to her brow?

Bright light jabbing at her. She has to close her eyes against it.

Her stomach flips and unbalances her as she attempts to stagger up. Why is she at the bottom of the stairs? He grips under her armpits and brings her roughly to her feet, pulling her head round, digging his fingers into her cheeks as he leans down and makes her look up at him.

He enunciates, 'Get rid of her.'

He props her up against the wall. He wipes the smear of

blood off her face, as she might wipe tomato sauce from Pat-Pat's chin after he's demolished a bowl of baked beans.

Almost gently.

And the knowledge is on her all at once. She fell. The door-bell will be their neighbour. Dennis's wife. She knows her name – what time is it? It's really late, or really early – Sylvia, her name is Sylvia. She might have called out as she fell. She fell downstairs.

No.

He pushed her.

Has Sylvia come to help?

'Tell her to go home. Get rid of her.'

Woozy as she is, she hears the threat, the warning, the promise.

She jerks as the doorbell rings again. Lulu starts a soft snarling at her side. But the dog isn't facing the door. Her stumpy legs are set on guard, her eyes don't leave the lounge. She's seeing off something next to the Christmas tree.

Debs refuses to look.

She reaches for the door.

81

Twenty-seven years ago

Marc lost the extra teenage weight thanks to a long bout of bronchitis. The illness wasn't so bad. He remembers fragments of sweaty dreams. The devil. Warfare. Explosions. Hitting Ed. His games bleeding through to his waking life.

It was worse for Jeanne.

He was less amazed by the feverish red blotches on her usually pale face than he was to see her natural hair emerge. Her weekly blow-dry and manicure sessions had been so long a thing of ritual, he had no idea she had springy, almost curly hair. He liked the frizzing at her temples, soft waves, some spiralling into corkscrews by her ears, but she detested them. They never reappeared.

When she worsened, he suggested calling someone to look after her and she'd rasped, 'Oh do fuck off, *chéri*.' When he persisted, she coughed and hissed, 'As bad as bloody Dudley,' one of the few times he'd heard her swear.

She batted him away when he crept into her bedroom to ask if he might bring her a drink or a cool flannel for her aching eyes. She wafted him 'out to play'. She never cared where he went, trailing round the London streets for hours. Nothing ever happened. So much might have.

When he drifted back home, he escaped into his videogames.

She never forgave Marc for seeing her in that state. As soon as she was able to make a call, she summoned to her bedside not a doctor, but her hairdresser. Marc heard her laugh as she complained to Caspian (born Neil, which wasn't nearly ritzy enough as a professional name for someone who had trained with Vidal Sassoon himself), 'The little beast nearly killed me with his vile contagion!'

She threw a cocktail party to celebrate getting well. Marc stayed in his room.

82

11.24 p.m., 23 December

Marc bangs on his mother's door. It's a dangerous time to be around Jeanne when he's drunk, when he's exhausted, when he's surplus to requirements, his career stalled, torpedoed. How bad could it be to go home to Deborah? Surely it would be better than being here, deep in enemy territory.

He feels feverish. A quick snort or two in the bar before he left. Perhaps a few lines more with the chaps, just to be sociable.

She opens the door, a pashmina wrapped around her shoulders.

'What's wrong, Marcus? You look awful!'

But he has not come for his mother's tender loving care or healing words.

'Why are there no photos of him, Ma?'

'Why would I want to be reminded, *chéri*?'

She's enjoying this. She can tell he's in pain and she's fucking loving it.

83

Thirty-six years ago

Dudley's joy was immense. But it broke his heart to leave his boy behind. He felt he was fleeing for his life. Rushing away from her, *Jeanne*, his so-called wife, as much as hurtling into the strong welcoming arms of Miro.

My lover, Miroslav; the name like cream on his tongue.

She had suspected there was someone before he told her of 'the affair', as she labelled it, cheapening the *miracle*. She was prepared to 'put up with it' as long as certain terms were adhered to. She never liked his 'messing about'. Despite their separate rooms, despite their agreement. He never enquired about *her* friends. So why was it so different this time? What was it to her if he moved to Brighton? He always provided. She always despised him.

The admission, 'I love him,' unleashed hell.

He felt, at first, he'd made a terrible mistake. He'd sob against Miro's chest, 'I can't! I just can't!' And the bitter irony was that Miro would have welcomed the child. Would have loved him, as Dudley did. Miro was born to be a parent. In contrast,

Jeanne was obviously congenitally unsuited for motherhood. She lacked both aptitude and the will to do anything remotely nurturing, shipping the boy off to prep school as soon as he was old enough, all the better to pursue what she did best – down gin and the reputations of others.

He was desperate to see his boy, but she wouldn't let him visit. The only way she would even consider it was if he gave up Miro and moved back in.

A punishment.

The thought of that half-life in the second bedroom, with her *breathing* next door, made him feel faint. Worse, the times she'd had too many gins and tried to creep into his bed, and he would reason with her, gently prising her fingers away from his body, for she knew the score. And she might *beg*. 'Please, Leigh. Please!' Awful. Or she'd say, 'Just hold me. Please, Leigh.' And he'd snap, 'My name, *Jean*, is Dudley, not bloody Leigh.' And then she'd shriek and slap at him, her face reddening as she turned the air blue.

But couldn't he endure that for his son?

Then came that amazing day, the visit to the nudist beach at Kemp Town! How could he go back to his old life after that? All the beautiful boys bronzing themselves in the unseasonal warm May air. Out and proud! It was all out, every delicious bit of them. A cock and ball story, as Miro would say. A revelation. A bolt of freedom! He discovered his sexuality, really grasped it in both hands, so to speak, at the tender age of forty-three.

Yet that aspect of himself, his libido unleashed, that itself gave him pause. Could he bring a young boy into this startling new world? Not that there was anything wrong with it, of course not, yet ... old habits and so forth. He'd denied that part of himself for so long. Plus, he was never one for a battle. And he was pretty damn sure that Jeanne would fight him, tooth and spiteful nail. Not because she wanted Marc, simply to stop him, her husband, having anything he might want.

A bright May day on Brighton beach settled his mind, if not his heart. Miro frolicked around like a Labrador, as much as one could on those unforgiving pebbles. It was a dizzy-with-daisies day, when even the scabby seagulls soar. He crunched his way along the beach, what was left of his hair blowing in the breeze. He was 'Let's Go Fly a Kite' giddy. It was bloody marvellous. On the walk back to the flat, he bounced along humming and then burst into, 'Oh we do like to be beside the seaside,' and was the happiest he had ever been.

He was home. He was himself.

But there was a terrible price to pay. He abandoned his boy. He had no right to fight for him.

When Dudley passes away in the hospice, several streets away from the seafront in Hove, the nurse one side, Miro the other, both holding his desiccated hands, all of them bathed in the insipid warmth of the weakening light, that day on the beach is his last dream.

But those shimmering images are even better than the memory. Because they're walking on those pebbles, listening to the clatter and shuck of stones and waves, and gulls and laughter, and both Mark and Miro are by his side. They're eating ice creams – a 99 flake for Miro and the boy and a plain cone for him – and Victor is trotting ahead, the dog's lovely loping run a smile in itself, his tongue lolling out to taste the joy. And his boy, his beautiful Mark – *Marc*, as his mother insists on spelling it, the pretentious old trollop – is holding his hand.

His last breath, a gentle breath, is a wave going back home.

84

6.19 a.m., 24 December

Adrenaline is potent. The survival drug. A marvellous chemical, which helps athletes perform better, run faster, hit harder, allowing the terrified mother to lift a car to save her baby's body crushed beneath the wheels.

Adrenaline is Debs' drug of choice. It has hoisted her to her feet.

She clings to the door. 'Sylvia.'

'Debbie! Oh-my-God-are-you-all-right-you-look-awful-what-happened?' Sylvia gabbles, shocked.

I've never seen her without her make-up before, thinks Debs. Useless thoughts floating around an echoing head space. She needs to concentrate.

'Yes. Sorry.'

Must she get rid of her? Could she give her a message? Think. Think!

'Debbie! What happened?' The woman's breath escapes in little white puffs like a nervous baby dragon.

Could she pass her a note? Where's the nearest pen? Paper?

Her own voice interrupts the cascading thoughts. 'I. Fell. Downstairs.' She must stay on her feet. She grasps the door frame harder. Because now she remembers: Marc. Her children are upstairs. Her husband is behind her, behind the door, pressed against the wall, pressing a knife against her ribs.

'Oh! Gosh! I'll call an ambulance.' Her neighbour's hand flutters up to her chest.

'I'm fine, really,' protests Debs, who has become the woman who walks into cupboard doors, who trips, who falls downstairs, who clumsily, accidentally strangles herself.

Her thoughts won't organise themselves. She gazes at Sylvia's dressing gown, the collar emerging from the top of the coat pulled around it, mesmerised by the busy pattern.

She can sense Marc breathing beside her. She feels the knife point insistent through the material of her own robe.

'I. Was. Sleepwalking.' She hears herself say it. A credible sentence. Some part of her brain must be working.

'Oh. That can be dangerous.'

You think.

'You shouldn't be alone ...' The statement's fishing for more information.

An idea! Debs mouths, *Fetch help!*

Sylvia startles. An 'Oh!' escapes.

'Marc's upstairs with the kids, in case they're worried. The doorbell might have woken them.'

'I heard a scream—'

'Yes. Me ... I fell. The kids ... I need to. See to the kids.'

Whole sentences. She hopes Marc thinks they're plausible. The knife digs deeper into her skin. She mouths, *Phone! For help!*

'Sorry, Sylvia, I'll have to go up. See how they are.'

Sylvia steps back. She looks confused. 'Of course,' she says. 'Sorry. Sorry! I'll leave you to it.'

Debs likes Sylvia and Dennis. Mind you, anyone would be better than the nightmare who lived next door before they moved in.

When Dolly was about three, Debs slathered the child's skin with Factor 50, plonked a floppy, over-sized sun hat on her dark curls and sat her on the lawn, which looked more like a lawn back then in the pre-Lulu days, and she set about blowing up the paddling pool. Debs has good aerobic capacity, despite the asthma, but it was a brutally hot afternoon, even under the tree and Dolly demanded she sing, 'Dory song! Dory song!'

Ten minutes later, puffing in between endless rounds of, 'Keep on swimming, keep on swimming,' Debs rolled out the garden hose and filled the inflated *Finding Nemo* pool, as her daughter watched with eyes round as marbles.

Debs took the rubber duck with the punk Mohawk from Dolly's bathroom playtime set and launched it on the surface of the cooling water, before lifting her pink, wriggly daughter into the shallows. The squeal of delight was worth the effort. They achieved two whole minutes of elation, Debs taking photos as Dolly splashed and squeaked with glee.

Then Debs smelled smoke.

Their elderly neighbour, Mr Christodoulou, was a bit of 'an issue' as Marc put it, and as Debs thought of it, a bit of a cunt.

When they first moved in, Marc had tackled him about

trimming back the diseased poplar tree that loomed and listed over the western side of their garden, threatening to collapse at any moment, a danger to their fence and their daughter. He offered to help with the pruning. After protracted discussions did not effect a response from the old man, Marc said they'd pay for its removal. Mr Christodoulou muttered something in Greek and ignored all further requests.

As their neighbour's health and temper deteriorated, the angle of the tree increased and rubbish started accumulating on his side of the fence, attracting rats. Marc opened a new parley, to little effect.

And then the bonfires started. The smoke made Debs wheeze and her eyes sting. The animal part of her, smelling danger, was always on high alert. She particularly didn't like it when she'd hung out her washing to get the best of a breeze on the rare sunny day. Chats with other neighbours revealed that, while Mr Christodoulou claimed to be too infirm to keep his own house and garden in order, he was vigorously conducting various feuds on all sides of the street.

Debs wasn't one for protracted negotiations, and, anyway, Marc was at work. Her method involved shouting at Mr C. over the fence. He feigned deafness.

On that particular day, she decided she'd be buggered if she'd scoop her girl out of her aquatic playpen when she was enjoying it so much, the splintering light dappling her creamy skin as she splashed. Instead, she hauled the garden hose to the side of the fence, turned the tap on full, and shot a jet of water at the smouldering heap of garden debris and baklava wrappings.

Mr Christodoulou shrieked. Debs stopped. They both glared.

The old man stormed towards her, his baggy shorts flapping, spitting in fury, brandishing a garden fork. Debs held the nozzle close by her side, a loaded weapon. He cursed and gesticulated at her, and even though she didn't know the actual words, *'Mouni! Skyla skatoskylaki sou! Porni!'* she got the gist, saw the curl of his lips, the sneer in his wrinkles, so she shot a quick spray right at the nasty old bastard's furry knees, making him scuttle back towards his sodden pyre. She allowed herself a small smile, hopped off the chair and turned back to play with Dolly.

Seconds later, the vicious old git was back, thrusting his shoulders through the green foliage, spouting bile, *'Na pas na gamitheis poutana!'* shaking his fist at Debs and her daughter.

'Ai gamisou skeela!'

And she realised he wasn't shaking his fist, he was making wanking gestures. At her child.

She sprang to her feet, grabbed the hose and shot a spray at his ugly face, and as he spluttered, *'Vromiki tsoulitsa!'* she kept the jet aimed at him as she marched right up to the fence, watching him retreat into his house, pursued by arching rainbows.

Dolly was in her jimjams by the time the police came. Marc dealt with it all, smoothing things over with the two male police officers, pointing out he had not been home to defend his wife and child, apologising profusely, blaming Debs' rioting female hormones caused by a new pregnancy, which, as it happened, turned out not to be the case just two days later.

Debs felt Marc sorting things with the police was a good thing, but blaming her hormones was not.

Mr Christodoulou moved out before Pat-Pat was born.

He might have gone back to live with relatives in Greece, or Cyprus, or Shepherd's Bush, or he might be dead for all Debs knows or cares.

She's just glad Sylvia and Dennis moved in next door. They look after the kids and Lulu for the odd hour if Debs is desperate. They like dogs. They like women.

Sylvia hesitates on the doorstep. Something feels very wrong.

Why is Debbie gurning like that? So dishevelled! Has she been drinking? And why is she mouthing what looks like *fuck off*?

But Sylvia will never allow herself to be accused of being rude. She's originally from Surrey. She would always rather err on the side of caution. She's a good neighbour. She *hopes* Debbie thinks of her as a good neighbour. Clearly her help is not required.

85

Four months ago

Miroslav is back in Zagreb. Back in the war. Back when they feared the Serbs – the bastards with the army, the tanks, the bombs – were going to shell the fuck out of the city's old cathedral with the lovely roof, like a drawing in a fairy tale, and rain hell upon their tiny immaculate flat with the windows taped up to contain shattering glass and kill them all.

He flew back home, walking among the murmuration of violence, tasting death in the air.

His mother weeping.

His older sister shot dead in her bed. Married to a Serb for five years. No one knows who did it. Perhaps a neighbouring Croat, angry that she'd slept with the enemy. More likely her husband, who disappeared back to Belgrade to fight for his own people.

Anyhow, what does a single domestic murder count for in a war?

Trams trundle past the dark alley. Techno blasting out its frenetic beat from the clubs; the bassline, pump, pump, pumping.

The snow littered with cigarette butts. UN guys waiting to take turns with his Aunty Dragica. Pump, pump, pump. He pretends he doesn't see as he hurries past.

Then, the miracle.

That New Year, guns firing into the sky – not in defence, but in celebration – welcoming in a giddy, fragile peace.

Yet at what price?

The desecrations. The mutilations. Churches and bodies in ruins. Photos his father made him look at, although he tried to turn his head away.

All a jumble. More feelings than story.

The anxiety and shock etched deep in the lines on his mother's face, the faces of the ruined Muslim women.

He rarely dreams of Dudley. He knew he was the love of his partner's life. And he loved him too, in his own way. As much as he could.

Only—

His heart was cauterised by those images.

A client in Brighton. Marc travels down, first class, quiet coach, with two new chaps, supposed allies, unknown quantities; friend or foe, to be determined, MacBooks drawn at the ready. His role will be advisory. Showing up as a senior account manager to signify the firm takes this business seriously. They may be putting two youngsters on the project, but that does not mean they are coming at the issues half-cocked.

They are, in fact, coming at the issues half-cocked. Marc's presence is merely set dressing. Being over six foot with broad shoulders sends a reassuring message. If the client is a straight woman or a certain kind of man, they're usually 'quids in', as his wife might say. On paper, Marc is the full package. Perhaps, on the evidence of his squash games, he lacks a certain killer instinct. He can push and triumph on court, but if his opponent is having an off day, he doesn't thrash his opposition.

Do or die. Winners or losers. Binary.

But otherwise, he gives good face.

His colleagues are not aware that, before he joined the office squash league, he hired a coach, someone to train him twice a week before he ever suggested giving Jenkins a game. He also procured sessions with a tennis pro, golf instructor, and took private swimming lessons.

Have you got what it takes? Dick length, engine size, bank balance, trophy wife, points in the league table? Are you man enough? Or are you a gay boy?

He doesn't hear these comments any longer. No need. They're curled up nice and cosy inside, nestled next to Spazzy Pig-fuck.

He tells himself it's a whim. In fact, he is carrying his father's old address book, Miro's address in his father's faded writing, rescued from the binbag of Dudley's possessions thrown out by Jeanne more than three decades before.

The maisonette in Kemp Town is easy to find. Marc has not called ahead, half hoping, perhaps, that his father's *partner* has moved away, and he will be able to scuttle home telling himself he tried.

He rings the bell, which plays an ironic tinkly version of

'Pomp and Circumstance'. A man opens the door almost immediately.

A cat – Lilihip, the man calls it – scrawny, insistent, ingratiates itself around Marc's ankles as he steps inside. He wonders if the couple shared this animal. But no, that's patently ridiculous. Years have passed since his father died.

It's a cluttered space, with many photos of his dad smiling alongside a younger version of this tall slim man, Miroslav. Miro. Marc wonders who took them. How happy they look. His father's mouth wide with glee. The only time he's ever seen Jeanne laugh like that, with such abandon, was when Theresa May danced on to the stage at the Tory Party conference.

In the snug kitchen, cluttered with mismatched cups and saucers in bright colours and clashing patterns (Deborah would like those), Lilihip saunters across the table to lean heavily against Miro's rather bony chest as he pours from an old-fashioned teapot, presenting its bum to Marc before settling on the table and stretching out luxuriously and in Marc's view, unhygienically.

Miro, whip thin, cheekbones Jeanne aspires to, reaches around the cat to offer Marc a slice of homemade cake.

'He is becoming old,' he says fondly. 'He is no longer toyboy. But he still does the tricks for the Dreamies.'

Marc refuses the carrot cake. Miro helps himself to a slice, ensuring he cuts a wedge with a decent topping of frosting.

Marc pats the animal rather tentatively. He is not a cat person.

'We have predecessor. Cyril. Burmese rescue. Your father loves him very much.'

Marc feels a flash of something that might resemble jealousy. In a small voice he says, 'We had a dog.'

'Yes, I hear. *Vic-torr*,' says Miro. 'He always wants dog. We are not allowed. The lease.'

Marc wonders if the lease also stipulated *no children*.

He also wonders what Dudley's *lover* made of the will. Everything left to him, the son and heir. Instead, he enquires, in cautious terms, after his father's relationship with Jeanne, post-separation.

'She will not give divorce.'

'He asked?'

'Of course.'

The cat purrs ostentatiously.

'Did she know ... from the start?'

'Your mother? How does she not know?' says Miro.

After burning the roof of his mouth on another cup of tea, Marc manages to blurt out the question he has come to ask.

'Did he ever want to, perhaps, keep in contact?'

'To see you? Naturally.' Miro reaches across the small table for his cigarettes. 'Of course. Yes!'

'Then why—'

'She threatens. She says she make up cock and ball story that I touch you. She swears if you ever visit here, she has police on us. She does not allow him to visit. She wants to ruin his reputation.'

Marc wonders what sort of reputation you needed to run a coffee shop. But before his great escape to the sea, Dudley had worked in the Civil Service.

When he leaves, Miro startles him by lunging forward to hug him goodbye. The men are of a similar height, which means Marc has to take evasive action regarding eye contact. It is a warm embrace, despite the bird-like ribcage. Lilihip attempts to inveigle its way between their legs and Marc surreptitiously pushes the cat away with his foot.

He finds he needs to walk along the sea front for ten minutes or so before heading back to the station, reshuffling impressions.

On the train back to London, he leans his forehead against the window smeared with fingerprints. He wonders how many other lavender marriages there were in his father's day. As bad as old Hollywood.

The joke was that Dudley had only entered the service because he felt he couldn't hack the double life working in MI5. Jeanne swore his father had been approached, which Marc thought highly unlikely. The last person you'd confide in, spy or no spy, was Jeanne.

Whenever his mother mentioned Dudley, which wasn't often, her lips tensed and there was a slight retraction of her neck. Like a tortoise flinching away from a bad smell.

No, not a tortoise, thinks Marc. *A snake pulling back before striking.*

The night he returns from Brighton, he says nothing to Deborah. He goes upstairs and watches Patrick sleep.

Would anything tear him away from his boy? Wouldn't he fight harder?

It turns out not.

Five weeks later, he receives a card from Miro, inviting him back for another visit, sharing nonsense about the weather in small, neat handwriting and telling him that *Lilihip has passed away. He goes to sleep in my arms. It is pancreatitis.*

Marc wonders what his father died from. How he died.

Inside the card are a few photos of his dad. *These I find after you leave.*

One shows a young man swooping Marc up into the air on a sandy beach. Marc looks at this image for a long time. He has no memory of the day. Or the holiday. How old must he have been? About three, four? Perhaps the last holiday as a family.

He and Dudley are wearing shorts. They might share the knobbly knee gene. His hair is almost as fair as his father's in the sunlight. How it darkened, along with everything else, in the years to come.

There's a sting of sadness when he notices his ears. *Dumbo.* One he'd forgotten. One of the least hurtful names he was called at school, the least awful school, before his mother had them pinned back when he was six or seven. He has outgrown so many demeaning labels.

His own face is wide with laughter. His father's head is tilted back, grinning, beaming up at the child. He can read many things into that expression, good things like joy and pride and love.

It is proof, of a kind.

He considers what he might say to Jeanne. He can't think of what he could say without it all blowing up.

Instead, it rankles and festers.

The night before Christmas Eve. He means to confront his mother. Demand to know why she prevented his father from seeing him.

Why now?
Why not? He has nothing left to lose.
He merely wants to ask questions.
He is not looking for revenge.

86

6.21 a.m., 24 December

Defeated, Debs shuts the front door. She leans against the frame, braced for what might happen now. The security light clicks off. Sylvia is gone.

Only then does Marc steer Debs back to the kitchen. She complies.

'Stay here.'

She tries to say something to keep him beside her, away from the kids, but he's already turned, the knife held loosely by his side. She hears him walk up the stairs slowly, as if he's carrying something heavy.

She forces herself to stay upright. Shards of thoughts congeal. She just knows Sylvia hasn't got the message.

The tree lights are still flashing through their incessant cycle. World War Three in the house, yet Debs is still capable of being rankled by something so petty.

So pretty.

Debs has a vision of her car. Escape!

No. She needs to get something first. She needs her – what

is the word? – keys.

Hers should be in the kitchen drawer with the string and the Sellotape and the batteries and elastic bands. So much crap.

She can't see straight.

She knows the boy is just the other side of the door, near the tree. She also knows she's hallucinating.

She hates the kitchen. The appliances, the worktops, the central island; they expect too much of her. His insistence on brushed steel, charcoal-grey granite floor, clean lines, antiseptic surfaces, lifeless, soulless, like a morgue. Only the pink fridge, *Dolly's fridge*, gives it life.

Something trickles into her eye. She pulls off a sheet of kitchen towel and presses it to her temple. It comes away limp with blood.

She pauses, one hand in the drawer, rooting through the chaos, dizzy, trying to remember what the funny-shaped widget thing in her hand might be.

No. She needs the car keys. Where the hell are they? Marie Kondo is having the last laugh now, the bitch.

She has to get out of the house. But where could she go without her children?

He is upstairs with her children right now.

She cries out and Lulu's head shoots up.

She has no idea how to get the kids out of the house. But she has to stop him. Whatever it takes. Part of her has always been braced for this, divining the crack in his psyche. She knew it was coming. Some part of her sensed it. What if she wasn't hysterical? Catastrophising? What if she was just preparing for the worst?

What if the worst is here?

He means to harm her kids. He's not said it, but she just *knows*.

87

6.22 a.m., 24 December

Marc holds the knife so tightly his fingers cramp. He pants like a beast. He cannot control this animal part of himself.

In the night, in the shaky early hours, things come for him. They can smell fear. Vampires. Zombies, un-dead soldiers. The ghosts in his machine, in his games, crawl out into the darkness. His fears have shapes. Bodies.

He is haunted by the spirits of true heroes. Men who died out there. Real men who gave their blood and their flesh for the greater good.

Not men like him, cowards back at base.

He didn't see much action on the ground. Not for his country. Nor in the private sector. Other soldiers, better soldiers, they were the ones – blown to smithereens, ambushed, captured, tortured – as he sat safe in front of a computer screen back at base.

Guilt stabs at him. He did his tour. He did his bit, but ...

It wasn't nearly good enough.

He watches his son sleep. The child is still wired even when he's unconscious. He is dreaming hard, limbs twitching. Marc watches Patrick's shallow breaths and he cannot allow himself to think of what he must do.

What is his son dreaming of?

He should take the pillow and put an end to his boy's nightmares. Do it now—

He fears for his boy. What chance has he got? What sort of world will he inherit? How will he traverse the minefield of the #MeToo generation, where the wrong word or look, a genuine mistake, reading the signals badly, a misplaced hand or a clumsy comment, can end in carnage? A misunderstanding ruining a man's career, his life. Women ruining his boy's life out of spite and revenge.

He worries for both his children. He has failed to protect either of them. And now he can no longer provide for them. Of course, he worries about his daughter. But he is more afraid for his son. Patrick is infected by his lineage.

When his son was only a few months old, he was changing his nappy when the child's penis became engorged.

Panic and shame convulsed him. Had he caused this? What should he do? What sort of man is he? He felt a shiver of shame, the echo of his mother's 'Re-pug-nant!'

Of course, his wife walked in at that precise moment. And she laughed in her coarse cackling manner as if it was nothing, and said, 'Oh, for God's sake put that away Pat-Pat! Plenty of time for that when you're older.'

He was sickened to the pit of his stomach. Years of therapy ahead with a harpy like that for a mother.

A man like him for a father.

Jeanne's favourite words came to mind. 'Vile. Disgusting!'

Patrick does not say much.

Dolly claims her brother talks to her, and while some of those conversations might be her imagination, she does seem able to divine both what her brother wants *and* the perfect way to wind him up. She provokes him, then laughs at him when he loses his temper. She mocks his lack of control.

Is that normal? Isn't that bullying?

Is his son normal?

There's no one Marc could ask, even if he were the sort of man who asks for advice. For help.

There have been occasional breakthroughs. 'Look! Three ducks, Mummy!'

Sometimes he suspects his wife gives him good news to shut him up, to get him 'off her case'. But Marc was there that day in the park, when Patrick saw the ducks. He witnessed it for himself.

A whole sentence. An awareness of numbers. But he was almost three then. Surely his development is stunted?

Deborah says she's talked to the nursery workers. She claims they have no concerns about the boy. She says she's looked it up online. Boys often lag behind girls in communication skills. Apparently. Nothing to see here, please move along.

He wonders if Patrick can manage to get a word in edge-ways with Deborah and Dolly's incessant inane chatter. Yabber, yabber, yabber. Debs always on the phone to her sister. Sometimes lowering her voice.

They whisper together, plotting revenge and humiliations.

They disgust him.

Her washing takes over the spare room, sprawls over the radiators in the kitchen. Sports bras, brazen flags, wave on a line outside.

He asked her once why she couldn't use the dryer and it was explained to him, with a silent sigh and invisible eye rolling, that the expensive items from Sweaty Betty, Lululemon and Under Armour (kit he's indirectly paid for) were 'technical': sweat-wicking, anti-bacterial, compression garments to enhance performance. Drying them in the machine would ruin these magical properties.

And it's not enough that the children's bedrooms are chaotic – Dolly's clothes in a tangled pile, Pat-Pat's toys scattered to be trampled underfoot – their mess infiltrates the adult areas. He bought Deborah the Marie Kondo book, which languishes in an untidy pile of unread tomes on her bedside cabinet.

Her chaos infects him. He is fighting a losing battle against entropy. He desperately needs a clear mind. So much to do. So much work, so many plans to prepare for their future.

She makes it impossible.

Her endless words jabbing at him. A full blow-by-blow account of her dull days. A list of demands. On and on. So many things he will have to provide. Her voice shrill, blaming him for his failures.

He hates her. She repulses him.

She stopped tending to her pubic hair, whining, 'It itches when I shave, Marc!' He thought normal service would resume. But then she claimed it would give her a rash; it was uncomfortable in class; she didn't have time. So many excuses. It would catch him by surprise under the duvet, waiting like some *animal* down there.

He prefers clean territory. This does not make him a paedophile. Deborah's magnificent breasts would never fall into that category. He simply likes to see the action, as it were.

Liked.

He watches his son's fitful sleep.

He has failed him. How could he prepare him for this warped world? Everything stacked against young men now.

Mocked, tormented, redundant. Is it any wonder men want to do violence?

Beneath his son's delicate eyelids, flickering movements. Marc prays he dreams of football games and a dog, a proper dog, running across wide green fields. Prays Patrick's dreams are nothing like his.

How else can he protect his boy? To end it now would be a kindness.

88

11.22 p.m., 23 December

The weekend stopovers in Monaco, Paris, Munich. Captain Browning, so dishy. The giddy parties. How you danced!

Navy uniform hanging neatly on the back of the hotel door. Tan tights laid across the chair. Pale body arranged gracefully across the bed.

All the corny old promises: he'll leave his wife for you; he's never known anyone like you; he can really talk to you.

Did he ever talk much?

Of course, you weren't the only one to whom he'd spun those hoary old lines. But you only realised that after the crash landing.

Your body betraying you. Your eyes betraying you as you sobbed, your heart shattering as he shouted at you when you told him, pushing you away from him so abruptly that you stumbled.

'You stupid, stupid bitch!'

You couldn't fly pregnant, afflicted by constant morning sickness, but you still needed to pay the rent. And you could never go back home. Not to that mean little life in the provinces. London's your home. It's where you belong.

So ...

Your friend Dudley. Always kind. All the girls liked him. A close chum of one of the air traffic control boys. You got a little drunk on gin – another cliché – and spewed your secret along with your guts.

Charming, Dudley. Such a gentleman. He always smelled nice. Not the most handsome man in the world, but passable. At least he was tall. And he offered a solution. He made it clear; he didn't promise you anything he couldn't deliver. He offered you a nice home, financial security, a certain social standing as a senior civil servant's wife.

And still it didn't work. Your fault.

Because you really were, as Captain Browning pointed out, *a stupid cow, a stupid bitch.*

Your mistake was to hope for a future. A real marriage! You wanted more.

Such good fun, Dudley. A fabulous dancer. Always solicitous to your friends, picking up the bill, filling your glass. You actually fell for him. A little. One night – another gin night, was it? – you tried to seduce him. But he was appalled. Disgusted. He couldn't hide that from his face as he recoiled. God! Mortifying! You wanted to crawl away and die. After that, he couldn't even hug you.

And how scornful he'd looked when you suggested Marcus have a little brother or sister. Yet he would have been a wonderful father to another child.

Your mother, exasperated when you bleated to her a few

months after the hasty nuptials, 'Be thankful for what you've got.'

You whispered down the phone, 'But I'm so, so *lonely.*'

Your mother replied, her voice tired, her voice weary, 'Aren't we all.'

So, even though Dudley made a fine father for Marcus, loved the child as much as he would his own flesh and blood – you couldn't wish for much more on that front – your heart set against him.

And then he announced he couldn't bear it, this *fake marriage*. And he'd given up everything for that ridiculous Yugoslav waiter. Some *model type* in jeans! Endless legs. You saw a photo, found it in his wallet. Posing like James Dean with a cigarette, for God's sake! He rubbed it in your face, telling you he was, 'in love', whatever that means.

Your behaviour, far from exemplary, screeching, strident, 'Get out! Just get out!' And the shock was, he did. He left you.

So, naturally, you didn't let him see the child. You did not want Marcus around either of them in their sordid Brighton *love nest*. No place for an impressionable boy. But to rub salt in the wound, the child wailed for his daddy. He made such a drama about it.

When Marcus was tiny you would sleep with him in your bed. When he went away to school, it felt like an amputation. But needs must. You were determined he would have the very best start in life.

In the holidays you were so desperate to give him a cuddle, but he'd wriggle out of your arms and run off to play. There might have been a few times after that when you were a little tipsy and you crawled into his bed to hold him, but he pushed you away and once he shouted, 'Leave me alone, Mummy!' So, you did.

You had hoped, when Dudley died, that would be an end to it. Marcus could put it all behind him. A bright fresh start. You whisked him away to St Lucia for a restorative holiday. You held his hand as you walked along the beach. But as you told him about the Pitons – 'Like us, darling. Just the two of us!' – you felt his fingers pull away. And something cool grew and settled around you both. Some alien plant seemed to spread its spores, spawning a chill distemper in your home. An already tentative relationship fractured further.

Marcus turned out to be a daddy's boy through and through. With his sissy ways Marcus really was Dudley's spiritual son, if not his biological offspring. But, yes, you loved your boy – it's cruel to suggest otherwise – and of course you wanted your son to love you. But he eyed you coldly.

The grandchildren aren't exactly huggers either. A pity. But Marcus is a decent father. That wife of his, though!

Thinking of it, the only person who ever showed you true physical affection wasn't your mother or your husband or your son; it's your hairdresser.

But on nights when you've had too much to drink, or not nearly enough, you have to admit to yourself, you rather miss Dudley.

The banging on the door wakes Jeanne from a doze. She puts her gin on the coaster, her fourth of the evening, wraps her pashmina tightly around her shoulders and looks through the spy hole.

Marcus! He looks unkempt. Flushed. What on earth can he want, disturbing her at this hour the night before Christmas Eve?

89

12.02 a.m., 24 December

The rage is upon him. It has him in its grip; seeded within him, but now its own wild thing.

He will do her harm.

He phases in and out.

He can't see her face properly, just lips twisting into blame and curses and nastiness.

He cannot allow those words to continue. They poison everything. They seek to destroy him.

A weak man, a pathetic man. She's goading him.

He sees his hands around her windpipe, squeezing to stop the words. He sweats.

Fucking bitch.

The face contorts and the lips are snarling. The woman's face is an animal's face. She will rip out his heart.

This is the face of Agnieta, Hetty, the sneering woman on the Tube when he accidentally brushed by her in a crowded carriage. As if he would!

It's all of them. Vicious whores.

A man hisses and snarls, 'Just shut your fucking mouth! You fucking bitch! Shut up! Shut up! Shut up! Fucking *shut up!*'

He recognises that voice, but not the tone. Not those words. Hysteria has him.

He notices the gold wedding band on one of the fingers gripping the woman's neck. Harder now.

He will shut her up too.

She made a mockery of this wedding ring.

He never cheated. He had just cause. He had opportunity. But his word meant something. She made her word worthless. Dirty lying bitch!

He is aware he enjoys the feeling of strength. The woman's neck small, fragile underneath the hands. Powerful hands.

Gag Porn, Tiny Brunette Nailed and Strangled, Hot Slut Tamed, Blonde Destroyed, Slam That Bitch—

90

6.25 a.m., 24 December

He's on her before she even realises he's crept downstairs again. She has no idea where she's been for the last minutes. She was sitting against the wall in the hall. Her car keys are not in her hand.

His hands around her neck, dragging her on to the rug, now clamping his hand across her mouth and she wastes so much energy trying to bite it. Her knee-jerk response. Savage.

Cortisol, noradrenaline, all the good stuff courses through her bloodstream. She will not let him grab her throat again. He can fuck right off. She's had enough of all that malarkey.

She didn't mind the porn at the start. But some of the girls were really young. As soon as Dolly came along, she couldn't bear it any longer. She wanted to grab the blokes off the bodies and punch their lights out. She wanted to cover the girls in blankets and hug them.

*

He drags her back to the kitchen. His wife is kicking, but not screaming. She is, at least, considerate of the children. He has decided to deal with her first.

His son ... it was impossible.

But he won't make the mistake of thinking he can't go through with it.

He has form.

91

11.32 p.m., 23 December

He did not want a fight.

He asks her for money. Naturally, she requires he prostrate himself. She delights in toying with him, before the taunts begin.

He hates her with all his heart.

Jeanne seems drunker than usual. She trails through to her kitchen to pour another and when he suggests she pause, she slurs, 'But I'm celebrating Christmas, *chéri*! Silly sausage!' Her voice skims off the sibilance.

There's a disagreement, his courage, his belligerence stoked by substances, escalating, his voice higher, harsher, her prodding, poking. And it's the 'just like Dudley' that does it. How many times has he heard that, flung as a barb? But it takes a different turn.

Tonight, she snorts, 'He wasn't even your father!'

A barrage of words follows. Reeling, he tries to stop the curses. Incendiary words, 'Weak, pathetic—'

Language he's never heard before, 'Bastard! Fucking poof!' she cackles.

And suddenly he's free, like he's been uncorked; a giddy,

dangerous feeling, like he can do anything.

He experiences a power surging through his body, along what his acupuncturist describes as his meridians. An electrical energy that's dark and coppery.

The strength he feels!

He's so far inside the feeling it's a surprise when he notices that his hands are squeezing her throat.

The Christmas after his father died, she treated him to an expensive nouvelle cuisine lunch, which she picked at, sipping a cocktail. The food was arranged like a miniature artwork on the plate, providing little apart from visual nourishment. She handed him an envelope with a curt, 'Your present.' It contained a cheque from his father's estate.

He was nine.

He was subsequently allowed a small television and Nintendo Entertainment System in his room. He didn't watch much television at first. He preferred videogames. But in his teens he binged on anything that happened to be on. He was fascinated by the adverts. He had a crush on the Oxo mum, especially her smile and naughty twinkle. Those ordinary TV families held a weird glamour for Marc. He yearned for a dinner around a table with relatives and friends. He aspired to a jolly, rather than tasteful Christmas tree, with a pile of presents underneath it.

And hasn't he created that? He may not have married a wifely wife, but at least he has warmth in his home. He has a Christmas tree. He sees the lights now.

He's squeezing her throat.

92

6.26 a.m., 24 December

Once when Dolly was two or three, Debs caught her balancing unsteadily on a chair against the kitchen sink, poking about in the waste disposal with a knife. And she'd tried to shout 'NO!' but nothing would come out.

She can't speak now. She gags. She croaks. She can't even beg.

He has the handle of the knife clamped between his teeth like some insane pirate. His thumbs are round her windpipe.

The times she's felt herself slip away as he choked her, pumping into her again and again, bludgeoning her like she's a piece of meat to be tenderised.

She will not let him do that ever again.

The weight of him on her, the pressure on her chest, her larynx constricting. She's brought all this on herself.

Darkness descends...

Suddenly, she's free. The release confuses her.

He stops. His hands slacken.

She breathes and breathes. Her eyes re-focus.

He has slipped inside himself.

Sometime later, (seconds? minutes?) she catches her breath.

And somehow, despite her shaking muscles, she extricates herself from his grip and shuffles back across the kitchen floor, scrabbling like some fucked-up insect.

She can feel the floor, she can feel the cupboard door against her back, she can see Lulu trembling. But she's not wholly present. By the look of him, neither is he.

93

Two years ago

Debs assumed that Marc was suffering from some form of post-traumatic stress disorder. Why wouldn't she? He'd been deployed; he'd done his bastard duty.

Only it wasn't. Active. Not in that sense. A flaccid tour. Logistical support infrastructure. He was 'lucky'. His war was a piece of piss. Nothing bad happened. Not to him.

He doesn't feel lucky.

The day Terry came back in pieces. His friend. He'd not been there with him. Hearing what happened, imagining it – dreaming about it after – he feels that's almost worse.

And those dreams bring him such shame.

'Fucking splattered! All over the fucking shop!' That young chap, Smith, from Sutton Coldfield, the one with the jocular regional twang. 'Got his fucking gizzards all over me fucking shoes.' He would not shut the fuck up. Shaking uncontrollably as he listened, the horror juddering through him, otherwise Marc might have punched him. And carried on doing so.

Did they manage to scoop all of Terry into the body bag? Did they ship all of him home? This thought disturbs him.

But Marc does not suffer from PTSD. Not as such. Not from that time, at least. Perhaps what comes the closest to describing his particular brand of what his wife calls being 'well fucked up' is survivor's guilt.

No, in this lovely house, with the lovely acer tree in the front garden, in this lovely quiet residential road, with so many lovely shops just around the corner, home to their two lovely children, she's the one with fucking PTSD.

'No, Pat-Pat. Put that back!'

Pat-Pat's grabbing for the cold mug of coffee she's left within his reach, too tired for spatial awareness. She lunges for it a second before he can pull it over himself.

And he roars. If you deny him anything, her boy gives his all to this form of furious, outraged protest. He is, after all, a white middle-class male. The world is his by right.

Denied the coffee mug, he brings both his fists down on his plate, splattering himself, the chair, the table and the floor with a riot of tomato sauce. A predictable move with predictable results; a scenario she's christened Tarantino Teatime.

She wipes the mess off the kitchen floor.

She's not a fan of the kitchen, which is anything but cosy, but it's better eating in there than in the dining room. She has her tea with the kids – she doesn't like eating late; supper's his thing – and she shovels up their leftovers, which she shouldn't, because when she sits on the loo there's a little roll of squishiness on her belly.

They sit at the kitchen table, not the 'breakfast bar', which is too high. Eating with the kids reminds her of her mam's kitchenette at the Swan, where Kelly and Shirley and Debs would chow down on fish and chips out of newspaper on a Friday, before the long first night of the Wild West weekend kicked off downstairs.

Pat-Pat is so delighted with the effect he's created, looking down at his red-flecked arms, 'Pollock-esque', as Marc might say, flecks of tomatoes all over his squidgy fingers and the table-top, he grins his naughty smile – all cheeky charm and dimples and toothy-peg teeth – and she tries hard not to laugh, because he cannot be allowed to smash and destroy everything when he doesn't get his own way.

This is Muswell Hill, not Sparta.

She's surprised that it doesn't make her jump, this clattering, his wails, Lulu's enthusiastic joining-in barks or Dolly's shrieks because she's just noticed a few red spatters now decorate her pale pink top.

She's forced herself to become immune to some of these noises. She has learned to control her response. Deep breathing, mindfulness, being too tired to give much of a fuck.

But when Pat-Pat pitches forward, flinging his pudgy arms across the table, sweeping all before him, razing the surface like an angry demigod, Dolly's glass of milk hurtles up in a perfect parabola, a graceful arc, a millisecond's pause at the top – then – it crashes to the tiled floor. And when the glass shatters, oh, she jumps then.

Breaking glass is another matter.

She jolts right back into it. That time—

*

Kelly asked their mam to stop the lock-ins. They might bring in a bit of extra cash, but what with the mess and damage and aggro it was hardly worth it.

'Keith wants to carry on,' was their mam's answer every time. So that was that. No one questioned their lord and master.

Fat Keith was the licensee because he'd somehow avoided a record, yet possessed the requisite credentials for the area, basically a reputation as a hard bastard. If he'd been back at the pub that night, it would never have cracked off.

It had been a late one. But it might have happened in any case.

It started, as it often did, with the sound of something smashing. Debs was never stupid enough to go downstairs. Shocked awake, she looked over to her sister's bed, but Kelly was out. She was staying away most nights by then.

Debs curled up in her bed with the covers over her head for the longest time. She'd already had three double puffs on her inhaler when their mam started yowling.

She had to do something. But she didn't know what. Shirley yelped again.

Debs scuttled over to their mam's bedroom, and called Keith from the phone in there, whispering urgently as she left a message for him to 'Come quick!'

Another glass broke. Another wail.

Nothing else for it but to open the wardrobe and take Keith's gun from the shoebox hidden under his stack of *Razzle* mags, his beloved stash of 'vintage beaver'.

Fat Keith allowed her and Kelly to hold the gun once when he first showed it off to Shirley. Their mam warned them never to mention it. Keith warned them that if they ever touched it again, he'd break their fucking fingers.

He said he kept it for protection. Well, Debs needed to protect her mam from whatever was going on downstairs. She'd risk her fingers for that.

She crept downstairs and walked in slow motion through to the back of the bar.

Three guys she's never seen before are laughing at nothing. One has the till open, one's jerking about or dancing, she can't work out which, and the other has his arm round her mam's neck like he's giving her a hard hug, but the angle of her mam's head looks very wrong.

She takes a big breath, steps forward and says as loudly as she can, trying to copy Fat Keith's growl, 'Let. Her. Go.' She holds the gun out as straight as she can. It's shockingly heavy.

The one by the till pauses, then slowly backs away. But the way he puts his hands up is a piss-take, she can tell.

Her mam tries to say, 'Leave it, Debs,' but it comes out muffled on account of the bloke who's grappling her, squeezing tighter on her head, squashing her lips. The one dancing doesn't even look up.

Off their tits.

She points the gun at the guy next to her mam, and Till Bloke starts chanting, 'Shoot him! Shoot him!'

And the dancing bloke looks her way, eyes blazing with some

druggy shit and he grins like a maniac and joins in, 'Shoot him! Shoot him!'

And her mam looks proper terrified, gasping, 'No! No Debs!'

Then she doesn't know who to look at, but her arms start shaking, so they'll guess she won't do anything. And they laugh real nasty.

She makes a run for it, tries to get help, but she doesn't make it to the door before something hard catches her on the back of the head.

The gun's in her mouth. It makes her gag. There are no bullets in it, as far as she knows. But she's frightened what will happen next, although she has a pretty good idea.

Her mam is whimpering round the corner, begging them to stop and Dancing Man's kneeling on top of Debs, laughing. 'Open wide, darling.'

She tries to grab his hand, but he shouts, 'No!' and shoves the barrel in deeper, making her heave.

He doesn't have to tell her again. She struggles to breathe.

She feels his hard-on pushing into her belly. Something else is stabbing at her hip from his pocket. A handful of crisps are spilling out of a packet next to a chair leg. Salt and Vinegar.

The bloke by the till is picking up bottles, the empties her mam had started to collect, and he's letting them fall on the tiled floor by the bar. She jumps as each one explodes, some spurting out dregs. There's a starburst of glass and she has to turn her head and the one on top of her starts yanking down her pyjama bottoms.

He's hissing filth in her ear as Till Bloke shatters and splatters the glass bottles.

Smash. 'Dirty.' Smash. 'Bitch.' Smash. 'Fucking—'

Her stomach flips, and she thinks, *Here we go.*

From round the corner, she hears, 'Nez? Nez!' Insane giggling. 'How do you make a hormone?'

Dancing Man stops what he's doing and shouts back, 'What? How?'

She hears her mam scream.

'Kick her in the cunt!' and then there's a long, vile 'Yessss!' like he's scored a goal for Forest.

Till Bloke smashes another bottle and starts whooping. They're all laughing. Dancing Man is roaring, sobbing with laughter, rolling about, rolling off her.

And by the time he crawls back alongside her, and grabs her hair – 'Come on then, darling' – by then she has the knife from his pocket in her hand and she stabs it as hard as she can into his side, right up to its hilt.

He squeals, high and girly, a stuck fucking pig, and rears back.

And she rolls away and scrambles and trips and somehow gets to her feet, hoicking up her pyjama bottoms as she bolts for the ladies and into the end cubicle full of cock drawings and *Kelly is a slag* and she shoves the bolt across and she's up on the seat, wobbling as she reaches the grimy window, unlatching, hoisting herself, God knows how, and she squeezes through, twisting her ankle as she lands on the bin by the fence, but only a bit, thank Christ, and she's out and running and limping to Dev's twenty-four hour garage through the back way, startling the ginger cat, cutting her bare feet and banging her elbows on the brick walls and feeling nothing much apart from the cold and the fear.

When the police come, there's no sign of the men. Or the gun, which Dev shoves in a Tesco bag and takes away before he calls 999, and he keeps it in his safe until Shirley collects it on behalf of Keith when it's all blown over, which it does. Because things do.

No one mentions the gun to the police.

She doesn't mention the knife either. She doesn't even tell Kelly or their mam about the knife.

Dancing Man must have scarpered with the evidence inside him.

And she hates the hospital and the uniforms and all the faces that keep asking her questions.

The police never find the blokes. Keith puts the word out, but he doesn't find them either.

The roof of her mouth is covered in ulcers for the next few months.

Words find it difficult to pass them.

During that time, a weird time, truth be told – with Shirley grabbing her for hard hugs at every opportunity, when she doesn't want to be touched at all – she scans the local paper for headlines and feels sick every time *Midlands Today* comes on the telly, in case anyone was found bleeding to death in some alleyway, or has bled to death since, but there's nothing.

She's relieved. She's disappointed.

Not long after, their mam bins Fat Keith. She manages to make him think the split is his idea, so there's no blowback. He takes the gun with him.

Debs wants to forget it. Put it behind her. So, she does. She tells the Victim Support woman and Kelly and her mam to shut the fuck up about it. After a while they do.

Shirley buys her a new pair of pyjamas with strawberries on them like the ruined ones. She doesn't take them out the cellophane.

Her mam's strategy is gin-based. When she's had about three (but not four, which turns her from maudlin to rowdy) Shirley grabs her daughter's hand, so hard that it hurts, and tells her, 'Don't let the fuckers win, Debs. And don't you ever trust any bastard bloke, you hear me? Even the best is just a fucking animal underneath all the nicey-nicey shit. Don't you ever fucking forget that.'

In the circumstances, that's hardly likely.

Eventually Debs goes back to school. Sort of, part-time. Some days she doesn't bother. She especially doesn't bother on the days she's supposed to see the school counsellor.

She half-arses lessons, exams.

And Kelly and her mam leave off a bit. Although in the coming years when either of them call they always ask, 'You okay?' in a tone that suggests a bit more than the normal amount of concern.

'Yeah, I'm fine,' she tells them again and again.

She is. On the surface.

But every time she hears a car backfire, or someone shouts, or, when she's really jittery, next door but one's English setter barks, she jumps.

And every time a glass shatters, so does she, just a little.

And with all the tiny hairline cracks, one day she might jump too hard and implode.

94

6.28 a.m., 24 December

He's settled himself back against the fridge again. The dog watches him warily, but she seems too tired to raise her head from her paws.

Debs and Marc watch each other, too drained to move. A violent silence broods.

Just before half-six. But it won't be light for an hour. The darkest days, the longest nights right now.

She drifts.

They both seem to be beyond words.

A pressure builds.

'Silly Mummy.' Dolly.

Then, the other week, Pat-Pat— 'Tupid bit.' Bad enough.

She knows where that's come from. She meant to challenge Marc about it, but she was asleep before he came to bed. If he came to bed.

How long before her boy forms the other words. Hurtful,

heart-breaking words. Snarling, slicing, sawing words. The teeth of those words catch her skin, the fascia, slice through fat, muscle and gristle, tear down to the marrow.

Marc seems to disappear inside himself. The best part of him has checked out. All that's left is a blank zombie staring back at her.

Who is he? Who the fuck did she marry? Not this sad excuse for a man.

Perhaps her version of him, her Marc, never existed.

On the wall by the door is the faint outline of one of Dolly's scribbles from a few years ago, before her brother was born. Debs scrubbed it off, the wonky drawing of a little girl and a mummy and daddy. The ghost image of that perfect family remains.

Although Debs didn't aim for a perfect family, just a good enough one. Something better than she and Kelly had, at least.

He's ruined that dream. He's spoilt everything.

He makes an unintelligible sound.

'What? For fuck's sake, what, Marc?'

He's up and across the floor before she knows it. The blade slicing towards her. She dodges, grabs the small but heavy Le Creuset egg pan from the draining board and swings it round in the same move, whacking him hard in the solar plexus.

There's a deep 'whoomph'. He looks surprised. And in that half second of hesitation, she draws back, swings the pan again and catches him a glancing blow on the side of the head, swerves round him, and tries to bolt out the kitchen.

He roars and comes after her. She catches the vodka bottle with her arm as she dodges him. It falls off the worktop into Lulu's bed.

He grabs Debs from behind and pulls her down with him. The pan strikes the floor with a clang, but she manages to keep hold of it, her limbs splayed at weird angles.

He grapples her on to her back, kneels across her hips. She sees his face twitch in pain. A back spasm, she guesses. It distracts him for a beat, so he doesn't see the pan swing again.

It's not a big arc, yet she manages to bring it down on his fingers. The knife flies from his hand, skittering away across the granite floor.

They both go after it, Debs scrabbling on her elbows and knees, him diving across the cool slipperiness of the floor tiles on his belly.

He manages to get there first.

And before she's worked it out, he has her on her back with the knife at her throat and Lulu's at his side snapping at him, snarling, trying to bite him. He slashes the knife towards Lulu's head and Debs cries, 'Don't! *Please!*' Marc kicks out, knocking the dog's legs from under her. Lulu howls.

The bastard's hurt her dog.

She manages to twist and wrap her thighs around his waist and squeezes hard, trying to crush his ribs with her adductor muscles, as she claws at his face.

He grabs her hair and pushes her back down, rucking her dressing gown around her hips.

She hisses, 'No!'

Lulu whimpers.

They heave and roll around and Debs somehow gets on top of him, a wrestling move, using his own bulk against him. But he's still at her, pinning her legs under him so she can't get away.

She struggles, her knees hurting, her breathing more ragged. And she sees what he's reaching for and he's whispering, 'Bitch! Bitch! Bitch!' over and over like a mantra, and he's reaching for the bottle and she knows he means to impale her with it, ram it up her, gut her, and she suddenly empties her bladder on him. An involuntary response.

He looks disbelieving, and she smashes her fist downwards, clumsily connecting with his left cheek and lunges away from him.

And, as if that effort is all she's got left, she stays there, face down on the floor. Just for a moment. Long enough to draw a chalk outline round her.

He doesn't move either. He lies back in the mess they've both created.

The three creatures pant, each in their own way.

She listens to his breaths. They soften.

She hears the slow drip of water. She's not turned the tap off properly. She counts twenty-odd seconds between splashes. Her head's throbbing. She crawls further away from him in slow motion.

Turning, she sees defeat in his posture, curled around himself on the floor like a baby. Perhaps that was his last attack.

Part of her wants to go over and hold him – an old habit – but she doesn't move. She can't.

Lulu's panting quietens.

'What were you going to do?'

But she knows really. She knows what he intended to do.

'What?'

He closes his eyes, shutting out the question.

'Running away like your father?'

It's a low blow and she just doesn't care. She can risk it because she senses, like her, he's got nothing left.

95

6.35 a.m., 24 December

Time passes in a grim silent nothingness. They settle against opposite cupboards. Shattered. Two broken humans who still might do each other more harm. All she can do now is wait for the sky to brighten. Not long now. Surely. It will all seem better in daylight. Maybe.

The boy is standing next to him.

Marc's head is on his chest. He doesn't notice the pale child with the fair hair.

She feels sadness radiating off them both. A terrible emptiness. She wishes she could save them.

Marc lifts his head as if it's a great weight and stares across at her. The boy doesn't move from beside him.

They watch her with identical grey eyes.

Lulu growls quietly with her lips pulled back. If you didn't know animals, you might think she was smiling.

'I've done something terrible.' His voice, barely audible.

She feels sick. She tries to get up, struggling. 'What? The kids—?'

'No. I couldn't ever hurt ...'

He shakes his head, wipes his nose on the sleeve of his crumpled shirt. The childlike gesture clutches at her.

She slumps back down. She hasn't the energy to ask again. She can't bear to know.

All she wants is sleep, but she's afraid she'll never sleep again because of him. She will always have to stay on guard.

Marc never slagged off his mother. He put up with the old bitch, never complaining, not to Debs at least. But she guessed what it must have been like for him growing up. In the early days, when she had energy to spare, she felt so sorry for him.

The first night she slept over at his flat, she woke to find him pressed against her, curled around the curve of her back. When he realised she was awake he peeled himself away, and when she rolled over to look at him – the smile that made her soften, the dimples that made her melt – his eyes looked shy.

He would fall asleep almost instantly after sex, then, at some point in the night, a foot or a hand would reach across the bed to find her. She didn't mind waking up to find a clammy arm heavy across her, claiming her. He'd cling to her like she was his life raft.

When the kids were born, there were times she was so desperate for sleep she feared what she might do. Jolting awake as she sat nursing Dolly or Pat-Pat; tripping as she paced up and down the length of the house, bouncing her son in her aching arms; weeping, frantic, desperate to lie down, waiting for Marc, willing him to come home to relieve her of the never-ending duty. Only the love of a parent can get you through those long, fractured nights.

She could do that for her boy, her girl, but her energy fails when it comes to her husband. She is not his mother. Her children have first claim on her heart. There isn't room for him. There isn't enough of her to go around.

Who do you save from a fire?

The kids. The dog.

He's an adult. He should save himself.

Only he can't; he's not able to save himself, she knows that. But if she attempts to carry him on her back, she will break. They will all burn.

Out of nowhere he speaks.

'I'm sorry.'

Now she should say it back. Salvage something. But the words die in her mouth.

And she misses it – what he's apologising for – but she sees what he's done when the blood spurts down his hand.

A quiet clean cut across the wrist.

She gawps, for a second, amazed.

Compared to the lunging and punching, the terrible words, the move is almost graceful. He simply brings the edge of the blade across his wrist.

He hears himself say, 'I'm sorry,' from some distance away.

He hears her say, 'No!', the word seeming to coagulate in her throat.

A bright, sharp agony in his forearm, the first thing he's really felt for – how long? – and then the throbbing begins.

96

6.40 a.m., 24 December

She's on her feet, frantic to stop this new horror, half of her listening for a movement upstairs. She can't let the kids see him like this.

God!

Blood pumps out of him, dripping on to the floor. In the streetlight, she can't see the intensity of the red. Surreal.

Automatically she grabs the tea towel. He tries to bat her away with the hand that still, impossibly, holds the knife. She grapples for his injured wrist, which slips away from her, slicked with blood. She snatches for him again and feels a sting along her forearm, the knife catching it where the dressing gown has slid back, as he flails against her half-heartedly, like one of those wobbly inflatable-dancey-things outside American car dealerships in films, but she keeps at him and finally manages to grasp his hand and wrestle the cloth around the wound.

He starts a moaning sound, almost a lowing.

Lulu whines in reply.

'Shh.' She's not sure which one she's shushing.

She grips the material close to his skin, elevates it with both hands, like they showed her on the emergency first-aid course she had to do at the gym, although how many Pilates students bleed to death on their mats?

She holds tight. Her knuckles look ghostly, witch-like.

He tries to pull his arm away without conviction.

She whispers urgently, 'Marc! Stop that! Keep your arm up. I need to call an ambulance. Keep still.'

He lurches forward, almost head-butting her. She pulls back and says again, 'Stop that!'

He's waving the blade near her face, not seeing her. Lazy slashes that make her recoil, her knees suddenly weak.

She doesn't notice the blood trickling down her own arm until it drips from her elbow. She's so wired, there's surprisingly little pain.

Lulu crawls forward on her belly and squashes against Debs' hip, sniffing up at the new metal smell.

Debs wonders if she dares let his arm fall so she can find her phone, probably upstairs, plugged in on her side of the bed. Where's his phone? In his study? She could instruct him to prop his arm up while she goes to search, but she guesses that's not very likely. Her mind darts in different directions.

And then he starts to cry, which is worse than the blood.

His whimpering starts quietly. Lulu totters over and nuzzles his leg because the sound the man makes is like a puppy noise. But the volume builds, until he's bawling like Pat-Pat, jagged breaths turning into great wet heaving sobs. He gulps air and brings his hand to rub his eyes, to rub it all away.

Before she's thought about it, she pats his shoulder, saying,

'It's okay, it's okay,' like she does with the kids.

And he wails, 'Sorry. Sorry.' And – finally – he lets go of the knife to wipe his nose with the back of his hand.

She's never seen him cry like this. She holds his injured arm high with one hand and strokes his head, running her palm across his sweaty hair. She's angry with herself for feeling sorry for him.

But then, she always has.

The fridge stops humming. He stops his keening. There's a deep, disturbing quiet.

She blows air out slowly, trying to gather herself.

Could she persuade him to come with her if she knocked on Sylvia's door?

But...

She has to ask again, the question curdling up, demanding. She manages to keep the venom out of her voice, although she's not sure how. 'What were you going to do?'

But she knows – however she looks at it, hoping for a different answer – she knows.

In a dreamy voice, like he's a long way away, he says, 'I thought it would be better if we could all go to sleep and not wake up. They'd be better just going to sleep.'

She lets the words sink in, the weight of them confirming everything she feared.

'You were going to kill them.'

'I would never hurt them.' He doesn't look at her. 'They'd be asleep.'

He meant to kill her children. The bastard was going to kill her fucking kids. She can't forgive that. And she wonders where she was supposed to feature in this scenario. Was she supposed to sip drugged hot chocolate and go to sleep like a good little girl alongside Dolly and Pat-Pat?

And if he'd really meant it – this grand *gesture*, this cry for help – wouldn't he have cut up the artery, not across the wrist?

She watches herself as she slowly lets his arm fall to his side. She stops squeezing the tea towel, her fingers unclenching one by one.

Marc has no idea what he intended to do to Debs. He might have stabbed her. He might have left her to find him and the children in the morning.

He just wanted it to be over.

He wants it to be over.

97

6.50 a.m., 24 December

She might have forgiven him hurting her. She's wanted to stab him often enough. But he planned to murder her children. Some part of him has snapped clean away. She has no words left for her husband.

She grits her teeth and imagines screaming. She clamps down and swallows it back until her jaw hurts. Her chest constricts. She sees fireflies flicker at the side of her vision. She phases out for a second, a minute.

The boy stands across from the kitchen in the hall, indistinct against the Christmas tree glow. She feels the need radiating from him.

In her dreams, in her half-sleep, the boy doesn't move. He stands watching her. Now he takes one or two steps closer. The poor little sod's wearing shorts. In the middle of winter. She notices his sticky-out ears. She'd not seen that before.

She wants to hold him.

Mark is slumped, ashen. It seems her husband has left the building; what was left of him. He's breathing noisily through his mouth like a child, blood bubbling in his nostrils. A snot-nosed kid.

He murmurs. She can't make out what he's saying.

She watches the slow rhythmic spurt of blood from his arm, like a lazy orgasm.

Lulu starts licking the growing puddle. The motion brings Debs back from wherever she's been, and she gently pushes her away with her toe. The dog looks apologetic.

Marc's head is lolling on his chest. His eyes closed, like he's asleep. His shoulders protracted, defeated.

She shoos Lulu away, feeling dizzy.

The sky hasn't started lightening yet, but she senses it's over. And she sits.

Then she sits for a few minutes more, just to make sure.

Perhaps half an hour more. To be really, really sure.

She has to grab the handle on the cupboard to help herself up. One of her legs has gone to sleep. Despite the under-floor heating clicking on at some point, she's freezing.

Lulu looks at her with such hope. It might be food time at last!

Debs wobbles over to the kitchen door, the pins and needles making her limp, and opens it to let the dog trot into the desolate garden, glad for the slap of cold air, the glimpse of first light. She shuts it behind her.

She runs the tap and rinses blood off her hands, her arm, her face. Her blood. His blood. She wipes herself with kitchen towel. She roots in the drawer and finds her car keys. She's not sure if she's shivering or shaking.

He remains completely still.

98

7.25 a.m., 24 December

As the adrenaline disperses, she's suddenly perished. Exhausted. It hurts to move. Her arm's on fire where he slashed it.

She walks to the hall like she's drunk, and climbs the stairs on trembling legs. In the bathroom, she checks herself in the mirror and rubs smears of blood off her face, cleaning herself with wet wipes, wiping urine off her legs and feet, and then takes a drag from the Ventolin in the cabinet.

In the bedroom, she grabs her phone, then forces legs into tracksuit bottoms and shoves feet into her Uggs. She avoids looking over to his side of the bed.

Three calming breaths. She will not – cannot – cry. She has to keep this together.

She opens the door to her daughter's bedroom and whispers, 'Dolly! Get up, love. Get dressed.' She's not sure why she's whispering.

'Why?'

'We're going out for breakfast.'

'Why?'

She has no answer.

'Why, Mummy?'

'We can go to McDonald's if you like.'

Marc bans outings to fast food outlets. Used to. Past tense.

'Yes! Yes! Yes!' Then, suspicious, sleepy, confused, 'But isn't it Christmas?'

'Not yet. It's Christmas Eve, love. But ... hurry up, get ready, will you? And stay here. Wait for me. Don't go downstairs.'

'But why?'

'Because ... just don't.'

By the time she goes into his room, Pat-Pat's already awake, trampolining on his bed and making his favourite hooting noises.

'Has-he-been-has-he-been-has-he—?'

'Not yet. Tomorrow. Come on, buggerlugs.' She braces herself for a tantrum, but he simply allows himself to be lifted and doesn't even struggle much as she hurriedly dresses him.

She's not sure how they all troop downstairs.

She grabs Dolly quite roughly when Lulu barks outside and her daughter makes a move towards the kitchen, a door, the only thing shielding her kids from the carnage.

'No, love!'

'But, why—?'

Debs lunges for Pat-Pat who's pulling her towards the presents in the lounge.

'Look, I won't tell you again! Both of you. Come on.' Sharp.

Pat-Pat starts whining. Outside, Lulu joins in.

Automatic pilot, shoes, coats, hats. She hands the key fob to Pat-Pat, who loves the beeps that unlock car doors and make lights flash.

As the kids scramble towards her Beetle, she hesitates.

Just for a second, something catches her peripheral vision. She doesn't look, she doesn't have to; she knows the boy will be sitting near the Christmas tree.

She feels the grip of sadness drawing her back, but she wrenches herself away from it.

She shepherds them as quickly as she can, somehow getting them both in the car. Dolly pushes Pat-Pat when he grabs her hair.

'Stop that,' warns Debs.

'Sorry, not sorry,' trills Dolly.

She rushes back, grabs Lulu's harness, wrangles her into it and closes the front door behind them, leaves it unlocked.

As she fumbles the dog into the car, adjusting seats and thoughts, she considers what she'll tell them. What can she say? Perhaps 'Daddy was poorly' is the closest. The kindest.

He's their father.

She stalls the car. Tries again.

They will go and stay with Kelly. Her sister's got a tiny spare room, but she can kip on the sofa with the kids on the inflatable mattress in the living room. She needs to be near her kids. They'll make a nest out of cushions and pillows and pretend they're camping out for Christmas. She will not let them out of her sight.

She hopes Lulu gets on with Boz's dogs.

Her mind calculates as her body drives. She should call an ambulance, a token gesture. She has to call the police, tell them she needed to get the kids out the house, wasn't thinking straight.

The neighbour, what's her name, she'll tell them about the noises.

He pushed me downstairs. He knocked me out. I came to and he'd already ... gone.

He will always be their father.

I fell.

But the wound on her arm, the bruises—

I cut myself.

No.

I grappled for the knife. But I must have passed out.

No.

I cut myself earlier. He cut me by accident. He accidentally pushed me down the stairs.

The bruises round her neck...

'Mummy?'

Now she will have to face the questions.

'Yes, love?' She tenses. She'll ask where her daddy is. She'll demand to know why her mummy abandoned him. *Why did you let my daddy die?* She'll have to come up with something. She has no answers.

'Can we have McMuffins?'

A reprieve. 'Yes, love.'

Perhaps she won't ask about him, won't miss him much. Marc has never taken them out for breakfast.

The M1 is rammed.

She zones out for a few miles, Dolly singing along to 'Driving Home for Christmas' on the radio, Lulu panting.

She pulls into the car park at a motorway service station, checks her shocked face in the mirror.

She'll sell up, perhaps move back to Nottingham to be nearer Kelly. Cheaper up there. Go back to teaching Zumba and Pilates in the evenings while Kel watches the kids.

Her sister once told her she was jealous of her when they were little. After the gun thing that all changed, so something good came out of that, at least. Perhaps something good will come out of this shitstorm, although she can't see what, or how.

The only thing she's sure of right now is that she will never set foot inside the house again. Boz and Kelly can clear it out. Torch the place for all she cares. She and the kids can stay in a Travelodge or something for a week or so if needs be. Fuck the gym. Fuck the presents under the tree.

She'll live back up there. Safer.

'Mary's Boy Child' comes on the radio and the car park goes blurry and she has to blink hard.

99

8.05 a.m., 24 December

She's not sure how she got them there, but they're inside the service station McDonald's, Lulu in the car with the windows left open, and Dolly's asking, 'Really, Mummy?' like the treat might be a trick.

After they order, and she's settled them with their food, Dolly chirruping and Pat-Pat too busy with the apple slices to notice the wild look in his mother's eyes, she steps away from the table and perches on a seat across the aisle, where she's near enough to supervise them, but has a tiny bit of space to gather herself.

She wipes a small trickle of blood from her wrist along her leggings, takes her phone and calls the ambulance, quietly telling them where he is, where she is.

She calls Kelly, leaves a message. 'Phone me when you get this. Soon as you can. Something's happened. Something bad.'

She watches Pat-Pat shove fruit in his face as Dolly sings her version of 'My nana conga don't want none less you got buns, hun—'

No one takes any notice of the wrecked woman. Two other customers look at least as tired as she is.

She slides in back besides Pat-Pat and suggests, 'Would you like to go and see Aunty Kelly?'

Dolly squeals, 'Yes! Yes!'

She tries to find a smile. Fails.

Will the police let them go up there? What sort of Christmas can she give the kids now?

'Can my friend come?'

'What, chick?'

'Can my friend come with us?'

'I don't think Aunty Kelly has room for Tamara, love.'

'No,' Dolly squishes the sachet of tomato ketchup, splattering it over her egg like blood, 'my new friend.' She sucks sauce off her fingers. 'The boy.'

'What boy?' But as the words leave her lips, she knows.

'The little boy in my room. He's soooo sad, Mummy.'

Debs can't reply. She forces herself to breathe as she reaches for her coffee with both hands and tries to bring the bitter black liquid up to scald her lips without spilling it all over the lemon-fresh tabletop.

100

8.27 a.m., 24 December

In Chelsea, the blueing lips of a trim sixty-three-year-old widow are drawn back as if in a hiss, the tongue like a slug. Her usually moisturised skin is waxy and drawn in appearance, chill to the touch. Some hair has fallen out of its sleek, deftly arranged waves to form a messy net across her face.

A garland of grape-shaped purple bruises decorates her neck.

She will be discovered within the next forty-eight hours.

Her grandchildren are named in the will.

In a quiet residential street in Muswell Hill, lights on a Christmas tree flash red and blue and green and white, paling, along with the shadows, into the brightening daylight.

Flashing blue lights emerge to join them.

Acknowledgements

Thank you to everyone at my publishers, Viper Books, especially Momma Viper Miranda Jewess, chief bugle-blowers Anna-Marie Fitzgerald, Drew Jerrison and Flora Willis, head nest-fluffer Alia McKellar, Lord of Sound Nathan McKenzie, and Forensic Eyes Lottie Fyfe, Lucie Worboys and Emily Frisella, plus my agent and team at David Higham Associates, Jane Gregory, Stephanie Glencross, Mary Jones and Camille Burns, who made my dreams (a mere sixty-odd years in the making) come true. They all want you to buy this book as much as I do.

Big love to the (many) men and women who've grappled with me in past relationships — thanks for the wealth of material you've provided. Some exes have wanted to bludgeon me to death and the feeling was mutual. I've been married three times and engaged seven, so I'm a living example of hope over experience. Sales will fund further treatment for my obsessive compulsive confetti disorder.

Huge thanks to The Factory Fitness and Dance Centre. I've worked there as an instructor and personal trainer for fifteen years and love it. My fitness family keeps me sane (ish). None of them feature here – Ali from the gym is actually Ali Karim, who won his namecheck in our Viper Christmas competition. Anyone in my classes who refuses to buy my books is forced to do burpees.

Big hugs to my first reader, head cheerleader and really lovely husband, my Geoff, who provided one of my favourite lines – coming home after a hot day running his bar, he announced he felt a bit *desecrated*. I think we can all relate. Please buy this book to fund his dream of sitting on the sofa all day driving pretend cars round pretend racetracks.

And please, please buy this book so I can buy more Dreamies for Bertie the Emotional Support Kitten, Tiggy P, Pinky Snowdrop and Splodge Statham. (And rescue more cats, but don't tell Geoff.) I get most of my writing done when one has settled on my lap and I keep going so's not to disturb them. Fur families forever!

The recent pandemic prised open some deep faults in my wounded psyche and after fourteen months shielding, without the online community I think I'd have gone under. So, big love to everyone who's ever friended me, retweeted or liked my posts, my old schoolfriends on Facebook, bloggers and book-stagrammers on Insta and the writing community of Twitter. You kept me alive, literary and literally. (Please follow me @ tinabakerbooks.)

I've teetered on the brink several times in my life, most recently last year. Which is why ten per cent of the royalties from this book is going to the Samaritans. Whatever you're going through, any time, day or night, you can call the Samaritans from any phone for free at 116 123.

Have you bought it yet? If so, thank you and God bless. If not, give me ten press-ups in the bookshop right now!

About the Author

Tina Baker was brought up in a caravan after her mother, a fairground traveller, fell pregnant by a window cleaner. After leaving the bright lights of Coalville, she came to London and worked as a journalist and broadcaster for thirty years. She's probably best known as a television critic for the BBC and GMTV, and for winning *Celebrity Fit Club*. Her debut novel, *Call Me Mummy*, was published in 2021, and was a #1 Kindle bestseller, and featured on *Lorraine*. Her third novel, *Make Me Clean*, will be published by Viper in 2023.